EQUATION

E. F. Benson
THE FLINT KNIFE

J ACK ADRIAN has written comic-strip scripts, science fiction, and war, horror, and mystery stories under a variety of pseudonyms and is an authority on popular and genre fiction, especially of the inter-War years. He has edited a number of anthologies, including *The Best Short Stories of Sapper*, Edgar Wallace's *The Death Room: Strange and Startling Stories*, *Sexton Blake Wins*, and *Crime At Christmas*. He is presently writing a series of action-adventure novels for America, as well as delving into the archives for uncollected tales by that neglected master of the twentieth-century ghost story, A. M. Burrage.

Other ghost-story collections by E. F. Benson

The Room in the Tower (1912)
Visible And Invisible (1923)
Spook Stories (1928)
More Spook Stories (1934)

EQUATION CHILLERS

THE
FLINT KNIFE

Further Spook Stories by
E. F. Benson

Selected and Introduced by
JACK ADRIAN

EQUATION

This selection first published 1988

Stories © The Executors of the Estate of K. S. P. McDowell
Selection and editorial matter © Jack Adrian 1988

British Library Catologuing in Publication Data

Benson, E. F. (Edward Frederic), *1867-1940*
The Flint Knife: Further Spook Stories.
1. Short stories in English, 1837-1900—
Texts
I. Title
823'.8 F

ISBN 1-85336-029-5

Equation is part of the Thorsons Publishing Group Limited,
Wellingborough, Northamptonshire, NN8 2RQ, England

Printed in Great Britain by Richard Clay Limited, Bungay, Suffolk
Typeset by MJL Limited, Hitchin, Hertfordshire

1   3   5   7   9   10   8   6   4   2

CONTENTS

E. F. Benson. Photographed by Bassano, 1939 (National Portrait Gallery, London).

INTRODUCTION

EDWARD Frederic (Fred) Benson was born in 1867, the fifth child, of six, in what was by any standards a pretty rum family.

While at Cambridge, Edward White Benson, the patriarch, had a long-lasting, probably homosexual, liaison with the Bursar of Trinity; then, at the age of twenty-four, proposed to his second cousin Mary Sidgwick. At the time Mary was twelve. Benson was a master at Rugby, the first Headmaster of Wellington, and was prone to moods of profound despondency. A noted (and enthusiastic) flogger, he later became Archbishop of Canterbury, then 'one of the five most elevated persons in the most powerful single country in the world'. After he died, his wife (whom Gladstone once called the cleverest woman in Europe) formed a close lesbian attachment to Lucy Tait, daughter of the previous Archbishop.

Their eldest son, Martin, generally regarded as the brilliant one, was struck down by brain fever (meningitis) at seventeen. Arthur, the second son, went to Eton, then to Cambridge, then back to Eton, then back to Cambridge. His literary output was huge, encompassing novels, biographies, memoirs and poetry, as well as a private diary that runs to over four million words. But he was best known in his lifetime for his soothing ruminations in essay form which gave great comfort to an enormous number of people (particularly American ladies of a certain age), but which today are entirely forgotten; indeed, all that now remains of Arthur in print are the words to 'Land of Hope and Glory'. His sexual predilection was for clean-limbed, athletic young men, although he probably did nothing about it. He suffered, far more than his father did, from bouts of acute melancholia.

Eleanor (Nellie) seems to have had, more than the rest, a good deal of get-up-and-go about her, although she too at times endured bouts of the glooms. Still, she was diplomatic (which the others were not) and adaptable (which the others certainly were not), and she could well have turned out the most balanced of them all, had not diphtheria, the curse of the Victorians, carried her off at an early age.

Margaret (Maggie) was ferociously intelligent, ferociously neurotic, a bluestocking of the first water who yet, at the age of twenty-five had to write to her mother enquiring about the nature of the sexual act (almost certainly getting a very dusty answer in response). At forty-two, acute depression brought on delusions which rapidly gave way to homicidal mania; one night she turned on her mother with a carving knife. She died in an asylum ten years later.

Hugh was the youngest. He followed his father into the established church and was ordained in 1894. Less then ten years later he had rejected the faith of his fathers and turned aggressively Roman, much to the bafflement—indeed irritation—of his family. Worse, he became embroiled in the doings of that malevolent charlatan Frederick Rolfe (the self-styled Baron Corvo), even to the extent of aiding him in certain dubious magical experiments. Rolfe later turned against Hugh (par for the course for Rolfe: to make friends with him was akin to lashing oneself with scorpions) and savagely pilloried him in one of his absurd and cranky novels as 'the Reverend Bobugo Bonson'. Hugh wrote quantities of passionately propagandist novels exalting Catholicism, became secretary to Pius X, and died of pneumonia in 1914. He was rather keen on embroidery.

As for Fred...

Fred was practical, sporty, worldly-wise, more than a touch rackety (certainly by Bensonian standards). At Cambridge he landed a First in Classical Studies, became interested in archaeology (Gladstone, a family friend, showed him how to take impressions of Roman wall inscriptions on a dig in Chester), went off to Greece for three years to study at the British School of Archaeology, then did a short stint in Cairo for the Hellenic Society.

He liked the sun, the warm—though not intolerably warm—south, and was never happier than when meandering around the Mediterranean: Egypt, Algiers, Italy, Greece, the Hellenic Islands, Capri. But he also liked the snow, the high mountains; was a keen figure-skater (and Gold Medallist of the National Skating Association), climber, winter sportsman. During the long Edwardian summer his life was neatly compartmentalized: England in the spring; June to August in Italy; back to England and up to Norfolk for the golf; autumn in Scotland for more golf and a spot of fishing; winter—two months of it, at least—in the Alps. And always back to England in December for a family Christmas at his mother's house in Sussex.

On the face of it an agreeably idle existence: an eternal round of country-house parties as guest of Lord This or Lady That; listening to, and imparting, lightly malicious gossip in fashionable London drawing-rooms; sun-worshipping with congenial companions in faintly exotic places; cricket, golf, billiards, skating, climbing, even darts. What Jerome K. Jerome used to laud as 'loafing'. And not only on the face of it, for this is indeed what occupied most of Fred Benson's time for month after month, year after year, from the 1890s through to the First World War.

In short, Fred was the worldly one. Arthur might have pottered around in the Alps on the odd occasion (he was a keen walker and scrambler), but his world was essentially the world of academe. Hugh went off to America on lecture and bible-thumping tours, but his was the world of—if not exactly the cloister, at least, for the most part, the retreat. Nellie (when alive) and Maggie holidayed in Europe and the Near East, but for much of the time they were rarely far from their mother. Fred, in his prime, went everywhere and knew everyone.

But he also wrote. And, like the rest of the family, he wrote unstoppably.

In the literary sense (although in no other), the younger Bensons were uncontrollably prolific. Not only that, they all pushed the pen at such a furious pace.

Arthur could sit down of an evening with his writing-board across his knees, a supply of sharpened pencils to hand, and effortlessly toss off clean copy by the boxful. Hugh worked even faster, dashing off his hugely popular historical or fantasy novels at a headlong rate: 'My method', he once wrote to Rolfe, who was slow in coming up with the goods in a subsequently disastrous joint-writing venture they were engaged in, 'when once begun, is to work like lightning—I can't plod at all.' Maggie was an equally inveterate grafter who threw herself into all kinds of literary activities: cleaning up her father's unpublished papers, devilling for others on Egyptological treatises, co-writing, with her close friend Nettie Gourlay, a descriptive book on the temple of Mut at Karnak, as well as grinding out herself dauntingly-titled tomes such as *Capital, Labour, Trade and the Outlook* and the monumental *A Venture of Rational Belief* (which actually took several years to finish, but only because she scrapped it half-way through and started over). She also found time to teach logic at Croydon High School for Girls, write a book on cats, and at least one novel, *Subject to Vanity*. Even Nellie had a novel, *At Sundry Times and In Divers Manners,* posthumously published.

Yet Fred beat all. He got off to a flying start, scoring a sensational success with his first novel *Dodo* (1893). This frivolous and—due to the fact that a number of well-known people (including Margot Tennant and the composer Ethel Smythe) appear in it only thinly disguised—scandalous tale of a Bright Young Thing in High Society went into ten impressions in less than a year, and by the end of the decade had achieved no less than thirteen separate editions; its publisher, Methuen, was still cranking the reprint handle on it in the 1920s, and ten years later it gained a new lease of life as one of the very early Penguin paperbacks. It has come back into print yet again in the 1980s.

After *Dodo,* books poured out of Fred, despite all distractions. During his annual Grand Tour around friends' estates in England and Scotland there was always an hour or so to rack up the odd thousand words sometime in the day; when he left for foreign shores there was usually an unfinished novel somewhere amongst his bags and traps which, on his return to England, would just as usually be ready for the publisher. If he tended to play hard, he certainly worked hard.

In all he published well over 100 books of which 73 were works of fiction, the rest a miscellany of historical, literary, and contemporary biography, sport-oriented 'How To. . .' manuals, political overviews (mostly written during the First World War when he was involved in work for the Foreign Office), and family memoirs.

From the late 1890s, when he was into his stride, until the early 1930s, when he virtually abandoned novel-writing, it was a bad year when only one book by E. F. Benson was issued. Two was the norm, although there were years when readers were faced with an embarrassment of choices. In 1903 four novels appeared (three of them from the same publisher), as well as three books (for two other publishers) written in collaboration with an old friend from his school and university days, Eustace Miles. In 1918 he produced five books: two novels (including *David Blaize and the Blue Door,* a fantastic fairy tale which owes more than a little to Lewis Carroll's Alice books), as well as three lengthy glosses on the Central European political situation—and all this at the fag-end of a wearisome war and at a time, in any case, when first his elder sister Maggie (still in an asylum) and then his mother had only fairly recently died, and his brother Arthur had had a severe nervous breakdown (the effects of which were to last for over five years).

Yet nothing seemed to stop Fred. In the last decade of his life, in his late sixties, when most writers might have considered easing up, coasting along—especially if, like Fred, they were more than merely comfortably off—he turned out three hefty books on the Royal Family, an excellent biography of Charlotte Brontë, a couple of deeply researched descriptive commentaries on the period that led up to the Great War, and three highly entertaining volumes of family memoirs. He was also, during this final period, Mayor of Rye for three consecutive years.

Fred's best non-fiction, written in the twilight of his career, was much admired by contemporary critics—which is more than can be said for his fiction. Most of Fred's novels were of the light—the very light— variety. On the whole critics were sniffy, probably because he'd had such a roaring success at such an early age: he was just 26 when *Dodo* was published and instantly became the man of the moment amongst London's smart set. His second novel, *The Rubicon* (1894), was given a severe critical drubbing, and for most of his career Fred's fiction tended to be relegated to the 'short reports' section in the weekly papers, if it was reviewed at all.

Not that the reading public cared a jot; nor did Fred, until much later. The truth is, he was a dab hand at boiling the kind of pot beloved by subscribers to the circulating libraries run by the heirs of Messrs. Mudie, Smith, and Boot.

Arnold Bennett, who was a rather better writer but who certainly had his finger on the public pulse, once formularized the popular, as opposed to the literary, novel thus: 'Genuine quantities of wealth, luxury, feminine beauty, surprise, catastrophe, and genial incurable optimism'. As a prescription for success, this list of ingredients can hardly be bettered; yet Fred had already worked out the ground rules long before Bennett laid them down.

Here is a summary of the plot of *The Princess Sophia*, published in 1900: 'A fantasia, mixing comedy and sensation, after the manner of *The Prisoner of Zenda*. The Princess . . . is a born gamester [who] turns her domain into another Monte Carlo, but obtains as much congenial excitement from the intrigues of her husband and her diplomats as from the roulette table'. Not unnaturally, since it had all the right ingredients—money, intrigue, titled foreigners, luxury, 'congenial excitement'—*The Princess Sophia* was a runaway bestseller.

As Fred grew older he more or less put aside soft sensation and mild melodrama and concentrated on frothy social comedies, satires on the out-of-town arty set, novels of Apolloesque youths at university and after, and the absurd antics of grotesque female social climbers, of whom Miss Elizabeth Mapp and Mrs Emmeline Lucas ('Queen Lucia') are the best known, although by no means the only examples.

Novel after novel after novel. Really, the industry of the man is astonishing—and yet, one wonders, to what end? Indeed, if one considers the work of all three Benson brothers it is difficult to place it very high on the classic scale.

Hugh's doctrinaire views, his enthusiastic snow-jobs on some of the more terrible historical excesses of adherents to his own particular faith, make his novels—especially such blatant apologias as *Come Rack! Come Rope!* (1912), *By What Authority* (1904), and *The King's Achievement* (1905) —ludicrously unbalanced, and would surely now appeal to none but the most fanatical (in debate Hugh was equally unassailable: 'I belong to a Church that happens to *know*' was his invariable response to even the mildest argument or criticism).

As for Arthur, reading his work today is a distinctly lowering experience. His soothing, introspective prose meanders along, smooth as Irish cream, and ultimately just as sickly: you can, after all, have too much of a good thing. Oddly, as Fred once pointed out, Arthur— when he was not thrust down into an abyss of depression—was at times actually rather a jovial chap, a man's man, given to card-playing and guffawing over robust jokes. It might have been better if his work had reflected, not the character who wrote 'the usual twaddle' (as he often referred to his books to close friends) which was lapped up by an unthinking public, but the genial and at times sharply critical character who was more his real personality. But it didn't.

Fred has fared far better, but then he was by far the better writer. Over the past few years there has been a strong revival of interest in the best of his waspishly comic novels—most, if not all, of the Mapp and Lucia cycle is now back in print, to a good deal of critical acclaim, and at least one brand new sequel to the saga has been published, *Lucia In Wartime* (1985), a creditable pastiche of Fred's style by Tom Holt.

Even so, it is hard to imagine publishers falling over themselves to disinter his gruesomely sentimental portraits of beautiful and gifted youths in thrall to selfish, insincere, and over-emotional women, or simply struggling against the (decidedly mechanical) buffets of Fate. In *Robin Linnet* (1919), a pretty representative title, the hero is seen initially with his friends at university but his carefree existence is abruptly ended by the onset of war. His friends die around him in the trenches. At home, his parents' marriage is on the verge of cracking apart. He dies. His parents are reconciled. It is all neatly done and one can imagine the more emotionally inclined library subscriber having a good blub over it. But it is all quite forgettable.

Hard, too, to see publishers fighting over the rights to reissue, say, the unremitting high jinks of *The Babe, BA* (1897), or the gloomy pantheism of *The Angel of Pain* (1906), or the blazing, wild-eyed melodrama (wife, ten years older than husband, fights off marriage-breaking menace of a beautiful young girl) of *Mezzanine* (1926), or the decidedly odd *Colin* (1923) and *Colin II* (1925), in which the fate of a young man whose ancestor struck a deal with the Devil is followed in the kind of turgid prose that Lucia-lovers would baulk at in the first chapter.

Fred *was* a better writer than his brothers, but, like them, he was hasty and careless, and aimed mainly for the safe shots—the shots that would inevitably score—rather than the tricky ones, the in-offs, say, from the cush. The trouble was, it was so easy to write novel after novel after novel. His fertility, his industry, his speed of creation, like those of the rest of his family, was at once a wonder and a curse.

To give him credit, in the end Fred recognized this. In *Final Edition* (1940), his last, and in many ways most enjoyable, volume of memoirs, in a remarkably honest self-assessment, Fred looked back at his vast output and found little to cheer about. He recognized that although he despised sentimentality in the work of others, he ladled it out himself. He knew that the dialogue of his characters was sharp and witty and brilliant, yet the characters themselves 'lacked the red corpuscule'. He saw that he lacked insight.

This is tough stuff; all the more tough for being undeniably true. And in a brutal mental clear-out he consigned all but a handful of his fiction to oblivion. I think I would be a little more lenient. Some of his social comedies, which Fred himself probably despised—he certainly saw them as preposterous, with no 'serious' intent to them— happen to be classics of comic writing. There are a few of his novels which are certainly of interest today, although not perhaps for reasons Fred himself might care for. And there are his ghost stories.

All three Benson brothers wrote weird fiction. Perhaps it was in the blood. Their father, the Archbishop, had given Henry James (a family friend) the germ of the idea that was later to be transformed into *The Turn of the Screw*.

Arthur published two volumes of supernatural fiction in his lifetime: *The Hill of Trouble* (1903) and *The Isles of Sunset* (1904), as well as one or two tales in a mixed bag *Paul, the Minstrel* (1911). His ghost stories, like his essays, proceed at a leisurely pace, are ruminative rather than unnerving; there are few sudden shocks, few unpleasant jolts. After his death, Fred, his executor, found more stories in manuscript amongst his papers and published two of them, 'Basil Netherby' and 'The Uttermost Farthing', as the one-volume *Basil Netherby* (1927). These are superior (even though it's more than likely they were composed around the same period as the original tales, at least twenty years earlier), possibly because both are novelette-length and allow for a slow build-up of atmosphere and tension, a measured accumulation of horror. Even so, with Arthur's weird fiction one always gets the impression that his heart wasn't really in it.

Hugh's ghost stories—collected in *The Light Invisible* (1903) and *The Mirror of Shalott* (1907)—although inevitably coloured by his muscular religious convictions, are certainly a cut above Arthur's. Hugh was not a bad spinner of yarns: his narrative flow is fluid, his grasp of the mechanics of storytelling far more assured; and his proselytising streak, though in evidence throughout, is not over-obtrusive. As usual with Hugh, he wanted to put across a point of view but he also wanted to tell a good story, and succeeded more often than he failed. *The Mirror of Shalott* (tales told after supper around a presbytery drawing-room fire) in particular has some notable stories in it.

But Fred, in the writing of ghost stories as in so much else, outstripped both Arthur and Hugh put together. He published four volumes, *The Room in the Tower* (1912), *Visible And Invisible* (1923), *Spook Stories* (1928) and *More Spook Stories* (1934), as well as three other stories in *The Countess of Lowndes Square* (1920). In these five volumes appeared 57 ghost stories, many of them regarded, and rightly, as classics of the genre.

And yet Fred thought little enough of them. Certainly he did not see his work in the weird fiction field as being in any way profound, or significant to a proper critical assessment of himself as a writer, but regarded them rather as trivial stuff written to order—and like the good professional he was, when commissioned, he delivered. During the 1920s he wrote over forty of them, mainly for *Hutchinson's Magazine,* over half of which were published in the period 1922 to 1925. As payments can hardly have been the sweated-labour rates accorded to lesser scribes, he was, for a couple of years at least, actually making quite a decent living writing ghost stories alone.

His approach to the genre, though not unique, was quite unlike that of that other notable writer in the classic English ghost story tradition, his older friend M. R. James (who, in truth, didn't much care for Fred and had complained to Arthur, when *Dodo* was published, that he was 'a conceited bore'). Whereas James was notoriously reticent, there was more than a touch of 'raw and bloody bones' about Fred— or, more precisely perhaps, bloody necks, since a good many of his anguished or malevolent revenants had an unpleasant habit of shuffling themselves off, or being shuffled off, with a cut-throat razor.

Nor did he have much in common with the more literary toilers in the weird fiction field such as Algernon Blackwood, Walter de la Mare, Oliver Onions, and on occasion Hugh Walpole, whose approach, fine writers though they were, was often so oblique that one is at times not entirely certain that one is reading a ghost story at all.

With Fred no such problems or ambiguities arise. His ghost stories have ghosts in them that bite. In the main they are vengeful, horrid, predatory, utterly malignant. On the odd occasion a shouted appeal to God, a thrust with a handy crucifix, might scatter them to the four winds; but generally they are unstoppable in their thirst for destruction. Fred's ghosts are *excellent*.

And they are surely significant to a proper critical assessment—if not of him as a writer, then certainly as a human being—for they illuminate a side of his character, his sexual leanings, far more powerfully than any other kind of writing he indulged in.

Whether or not Fred was a thorough-paced homosexual he certainly swam in dangerous waters for the time, moving in the kinds of circles where men were more than merely (in the Victorian sense of the phrase) manly chums. He holidayed with Lord Alfred Douglas, had a long relationship with F. Yeats-Brown, shared a house (part-paid for by Willie Maugham) with the failed poet John Ellingham Brooks (who was unequivocally homosexual), and his favourite Mediterranean watering-hole was the island of Capri, where the fisher-boys, long before Norman Douglas arrived, had a reputation for being perfectly happy to accommodate the idiosyncratic tastes of rich male foreigners.

He certainly owned a copy of the privately-printed translation of the notorious and explicitly pederastic *Epigrams From Anthologia Palatina*

XII by 'Sydney Oswald' (S.F.M. Lomer) which, had the police ever stumbled across it, would have been more than enough to have had him hauled up before the Bow Street beak in short order.

The critic Michael Sadleir was perhaps being generous when he noted merely that Fred had 'a generalized dislike of women'. Frankly, however many women he might have known on a social basis, however many titled ladies he might have corresponded with, or hobnobbed with at dinner parties or during long weekends in country houses, the evidence is that, as a breed, he actively detested them. In the comedies they are, almost without exception, fools, fakers, brainless butterflies, useless appendages, social-climbing freaks; or, worse, active destroyers, in one way or another, of brilliant young men. It's significant that when you do come across a 'good' female character she exhibits many of the attributes society then deemed desirable in the perfect male. In effect, like many of the females in the novels of E. M. Forster, Fred's good heroines are men in drag.

In the ghost stories the position is even more clear-cut; indeed, stark: apart from the odd, and usually very shadowy, wife—thrown in, one suspects, to appease the largely female magazine-buying public—his women are thoroughly hateful.

If they are not simply shrews and harpies who drive good men to an early grave, or worse, then they are real vampires, soul-suckers, predators, witches, and, in one striking instance, the reincarnation of 'the worst being that ever lived', Judas Iscariot.

A. M. Burrage, that much-neglected ghost-story writer, had utilized the Judas theme two years before Fred in a story he wrote for *Lloyd's Magazine* called 'The Recurring Tragedy'. Here, his reincarnated Judas is a British Army general everyone loathes without knowing why. Fred's version (and there is no suggestion that he stole the idea), 'The Outcast', concerns a society woman who is charming and witty and good-looking (the epitome, in fact, of all Fred's society women), but from whom dogs turn tail and run and humans shrink in fear and disgust. When she dies, flowers wither on her coffin, the sea casts her up and, in an ugly finale, even the kindly earth rejects her. Only cremation can finish her off. Burrage's 'The Recurring Tragedy' is sensitively handled; Fred's story amounts to an act of revenge.

Other revenges on the female sex are to be found throughout his weird fiction. In 'How Fear Departed from the Long Gallery' (*The Room in the Tower*) the apparitions are two angelic-looking little toddlers who yet cause stark terror in, and hideous death to, all who see them. Fred relates what happened to three of their victims, two men and a woman. He dismisses the fate of the two men in a couple of brief paragraphs but spends two and a half pages describing in great, and almost gleeful, detail how the woman was struck down with a ghastly and decaying leprous growth across her face.

In 'Christopher Comes Back' (*More Spook Stories*) there is a dreadful inevitability about the eternal triangle of Old Husband, Young Wife, Other Man. The husband is dying of cancer; the wife gives him an overdose. In essence she is innocent: the husband is cruel, is in pain, cannot be saved; and she and the Other Man have not even kissed. It is all a happy release, and a release for her into happiness—which, naturally, does not happen. The husband returns; the Other Man rejects her; she commits suicide. In 'The Dance', which begins with a graphic description of a spider killing a fly, the tragedy is even more intense. Again there is a triangle, but this time the husband is not merely cruel but malevolence personified, the kind of man any sane being would shoot like a dog as soon as look at him. One feels, reading the story, that it is only right and just that he should be done in with the greatest despatch so that heroine and hero can at last enjoy the peace and happiness they so thoroughly deserve. Yet it's clear Fred took the greatest pleasure in denying them this, and in the most horrifying way.

There's no denying that he was overfond of the grisly, to the point where the reader's stomach has a tendency sometimes to lurch a bit. In 'And the Dead Spake. . .' (*Visible and Invisible*) an obsessive scientist, who has already created an artificial being—'with the brain of an ape and the heart of a bullock, and a sheep's thyroid, and so forth'—turns his hand to reanimating the still warm corpse of his female (of course) housekeeper with a battery, using a gramophone needle plunged into the open brain to force it to speak, with gruesome results. Fred, one does get the feeling, rather enjoyed constructing the little bits of descriptive matter he popped into this particular narrative, which is not for the squeamish. Even less is left to the imagination in 'The Horror Horn', in which the narrator is pursued across an Alpine glacier by a ravening Yeti-like creature, after having come across the beast dismembering a chamois: sucking its bloody haunch, crunching up an eyeball, and so on. Needless to say, the monster is female, with 'withered and pendulous breasts' and 'a fathomless bestiality' in her eyes.

Perhaps Fred's cruellest story is 'The Face' (*Spook Stories*), in which a young and beautiful woman, happily married (unusual, that) with two children, is pursued from beyond the grave for no reason at all. She is utterly blameless of even the remotest hint of a crime, either spiritual or moral, and yet in her dreams she is dogged inexorably by a malignant face, a greedy face, the face of an entirely unknown man who lusts after her soul. And in the end, in her waking life, in a dreadful denouement, she is carried off by him into the outer dark.

This story verges on the sadistic—yet it is a masterpiece of tension and terror, a masterpiece of *storytelling*. For despite a sense of moral unease one may feel when reading certain of Fred's ghost stories, there is no getting away from the fact that his talent for awakening not simply mental disquiet but downright dread, for being able to adminster to the reader a very nasty jolt when it is least expected, was enormous.

This, after all—the nasty jolt, the unnerving lurch, the uncomfortable few seconds when we are not entirely sure whether what we are experiencing on the printed page, and therefore in our imaginations, has not all at once taken on a dreadful existence in the shadows behind our chairs—is why we who elect to read ghost stories read them. It is not, of course, good to be frightened when we have no choice in the matter—when, on a lonely road, menacing figures advance towards us, or, in a lonely house, the noises-off are not wholly explicable. It is very good indeed when the option is ours alone; when we choose deliberately to try conclusions with a writer to see if he or she can excite us into a state of delicious alarm.

Did Fred believe in ghosts? He writes about them so well that the clear answer ought to be no.

Hannen Swaffer, who did believe in ghosts, wrote absurd ghost stories; Conan Doyle created one or two memorably weird tales, but before the First World War, before his son died, before he became obsessed with Spiritualism: afterwards, when he did believe, his talent seemed to desert him (his weird novel *The Land of Mist* is virtually unreadable). Fred's younger brother Hugh certainly believed—an article on haunted houses he wrote for the *Pall Mall Magazine* shows this quite plainly, although he wrapped it all up in a spiritual (as opposed to Spiritualist) haze, and in any case the trouble with Hugh was that he tended to believe, without question, everything that anyone he admired or respected told him. Not a good witness. One can imagine Arthur dismissing the notion, with a fruity laugh, as sheer bunkum.

In his stories Fred often came up with some powerful and very plausible arguments for all kinds of untoward happenings and experiences.

More than most ghost story writers, he had a knack of making his ghosts—or at least the reasons for their existence in the first place—perfectly credible. But then he was a professional writer (unlike, say, the graduates of the M. R. James school: E. G. Swain, Amyas North-cote, Dermot Chesson Spence, R. H. Malden, and so on), and his job, as he saw it, was not simply to terrify but to lay the solid foundations for terror, so that the terror, when it springs out at you, is all the more believable, all the more terrifying.

Significantly, in *Final Edition* he only refers to his ghost stories twice, and on each occasion it is to highlight their mechanical aspect. 'By a selection of disturbing details', he wrote, 'it is not very difficult to induce in the reader an uneasy frame of mind which, carefully worked up, paves the way for terror.' I like very much that 'carefully worked up'.

And yet Fred says that he once saw a ghost—a cloaked figure briefly glimpsed on a broiling hot day in mid-summer, and vouched for, it seems, by the local vicar. He subsequently turned this visitation into a story, then destroyed it because, he said, it was nowhere near to the reality of the experience itself. However, whether or not he did see some-thing that had no existence in the material world, it's hard to imagine Fred—the arch-pro—not being able to deliver the fictional goods. The (perhaps treacherous) thought does occur that he was gently pulling his readers' legs. The anecdote has just enough authentic detail, just enough touched-in atmosphere, to make it appear credible—just.

And what adds to one's suspicions is that the title-story of this present collection, 'The Flint-Knife', bears rather more than a passing resem-blance to that rejected and destroyed tale, as outlined in *Final Edition*.

No, surely Fred did not believe in ghosts. Apart from anything else, he didn't need to. In any case he was far too cynical, far too much the man of the world—far too *modern*, for he had little time for the antique, the Gothic, the dry-as-dust, and often snatched his plots from the world immediately around him, utilizing not only commonplace, everyday and essentially twentieth-century artefacts (a telephone, a haunted tube-train, the top deck of a bus, a malevolent motor-car), but also new concepts fresh off the printed page: 'Sir Roger de Coverley', again in this present collection, proves that, only a month or so after J. W. Dunne's celebrated *An Experiment With Time* (1927) was published, Fred was hard at it writing a story using one of Dunne's central ideas.

Edmund Gosse once sneered at him for being a spook-merchant, a believer in ghosts, but then Gosse had his waspish side just as Fred did. Again, Fred was far too *malicious* to be a believer. Some of his seance scenes, it is true, have a disturbing sense of reality about them, as though their creator had strong convictions in the matter. But then, as I've said, Fred was a pro, and equally often had great fun with table-turnings and spirit-rappings and the invariably large ladies that preside over the whole fantastic rigmarole. Too, he was never afraid of the deliberately farcical; indeed, he wrote some of the funniest ghost stories in the entire corpus of weird literature—yet even 'Spinach' (*Spook Stories*), 'The Psychical Mallards', and 'Thursday Evenings' (*More Spook Stories*), hilarious as they are, have their moments of unease.

Fred's excellent ghosts spring not from reality, not from some strongly believed-in and thriving spirit world existing side by side with ours, but from himself alone: his undeniably bizarre family background, his own peculiar tastes, his subsconsious fears and very conscious obsessions. And they almost invariably succeed in what Fred, the cunning teller of the tale, himself sets out to accomplish.

There's a splendid passage in *Final Edition* in which Fred is recalling his friendship with Lord Halifax, the noted (and decidedly prankish) collector of 'true' ghostly experiences who also delighted in the fictional variety, and particularly Fred's. Accordingly Fred wrote stories 'for his special discomfort' and, when staying with him, would read them aloud. The old man was getting rather deaf and would sit close, one hand cupped to his ear, urging on the reader, as each horrid climax neared, with cries of 'It's too frightful. Go on, go on. I can't bear it!'

If there is a more striking illustration of the pleasures to be gained from the ghost story—or, indeed, a stronger argument for its care, protection, and preservation—I don't know of it.

JA
November 1987

THE FLINT KNIFE

W E WERE philosophizing about gardens, Harry Pershore and I, as we sat one warm, serene June evening on the lawn outside his house, and the text of our observations was the scene in which we talked. The Pershore house, at which I had arrived that afternoon, was set in the very centre of a little country-town: its Georgian front looked out on to the main street, but at the back was this unsuspected acre of green lawn and flower beds, surrounded on all sides by high walls of mellow brick, over which peered the roofs and chimneys of the neighbouring houses. To me, weary of the heat and roar of London, it was indescribably delightful to sit, cool and at ease, in this green place, which to the inward sense seemed soaked in some peculiar tranquillity.

Just as old houses have their 'atmosphere' which has been distilled from the thoughts and the personalities of those who have inhabited them, so this garden seemed to me to have absorbed into the very soul of it the leisure of the generations whose retreat it had been. It was, I said, as if the spirit of that leisure had soaked into the darkling garden where we sat . . .

Harry was not encouraging about these mild sentimentalities.

'Very pretty indeed,' he said, 'but for myself I find your theory too fanciful.'

'Have it your own way,' I retorted. 'But I refuse to give up my theory that the inhabitants of houses create a special atmosphere in them. Walls and floors get soaked with them, and why not lawns and flower-beds?'

He rose from his seat and came to me.

'I don't believe a word of it,' he said, 'How can wood and stone receive qualities other than their own? But your remarks, though erroneous, are *à propos*, for we shall have an opportunity of testing their truth. There'll be a new atmosphere let into this garden tomorrow, and we shall see if it has any disturbing effect. Come across the lawn with me, and I'll show you what I mean to do.'

The lawn lay on a gentle slope, and to the west, where it declined down the side of a hill, there ran one of those tall brick walls which gave the garden so delightful a privacy. Harry set a ladder against this, and bade me mount it and look over.

'You won't be peering into the privacy of any neighbour of mine,' he said, so up I went and leaned my elbows on the top of the wall.

I found myself looking down into a small square plot, some eighty feet across, of wild uncultivated ground. It was thickly overgrown with weeds and wild flowers and rank seeding grasses, and though it lay on the slope of the hill, it instantly struck one that it must once have been levelled, for it was perfectly flat. All around its four sides ran high brick walls as tall as that over which I was now looking, with never a doorway or means of access in any of them: the square was completely sealed on every side. It had been grilled, of course, all day in the blaze of the sun, with not a breeze to stir the enclosed atmosphere, and now it was like leaning over a furnace, so heated was the air that met my face. Though the place lay naked to the sky, this warmth was not like that of the open; there was some indefinable taint about it, as of a room long shut up.

'But what is it?' I asked as I descended again. 'Why is it entirely closed?'

'Rather an odd affair,' he said. 'Only last week I was grubbing about in a box of old papers which I ought long ago to have sorted out, and I came across a diary of my mother's, written in faded ink and treating of faded topics. It began more than fifty years ago, soon after my birth. I did little more than glance at it, for it seemed to be occupied with the mere trivial chronicle of the days; how she walked one day, and hunted on another, and so forth.

'There were records of the arrival of visitors who came to stay with her and my father, and of their departure; and then I came across an entry which puzzled and interested me. She spoke of the building of a wall in the garden here, something to this effect: "I am sure it was only wise to have had it done," she wrote "and though it looks rather unsightly at present, it will soon get covered with creepers."

'That struck me as odd: I couldn't understand to what wall she referred.'

We had strolled back to the house as he spoke, and had entered his sitting-room. A shabby calf-bound volume lay on the table, and he pointed to it.

'There's the book,' he said. 'You might like to look at it, as it is most atmospheric. But I must finish my story: By one of those odd coincidences which mean nothing, on the very day on which I found and glanced at that diary, there was one of those summer gales which detached a big shoot of a climbing rose from the wall over which you have just been looking. My gardener had already gone home when I noticed it, and so I got a ladder and secured it again.

'Naturally,' he went on, 'one doesn't climb up walls and peer into one's neighbour's garden and I had always supposed that the garden of the next house to mine lay behind that section. But since I was already at the top of the wall, I looked over, and there saw what you have just seen—a little square overgrown plot with high walls and no access whatever to it from any side. At that, what I had read in my mother's diary about the building of a wall occurred to me, and later I found in the same box in which I had found the book, an old plan of this house and garden. This made it quite clear that the square plot had once been part of the garden, for there was no indication on the plan of the wall that now separates it.

'So next I called in my builder to examine that section of the wall. He told me that it was certainly much later than the rest and had probably been built fifty or sixty years ago, for he found at either end of it the straight perpendicular line where it joined the older walls. The date therefore is correct, and no doubt that is the wall mentioned in my mother's diary. Finally I consulted my good friend, the Town Surveyor, and he agreed that the square plot is quite certainly part of my estate.'

'So you're going to throw it in again?' I asked. 'Is that the new influence you spoke of as entering your garden?'

'Yes, that's it,' he said, 'though I shan't demolish the wall altogether, but only cut an arched doorway through it. I shall make a little secret garden of the place; it is absolutely sheltered, tall walls on every side, and it must be a wonderful sun trap. I shall have a little grass lawn in the middle of it, and a path of crazy pavement running round that, and deep flower beds against the walls. It will be a perfect gem of a place, and the builder is to begin cutting the doorway tomorrow.'

I took up to bed that night the diary of Harry's mother, and feeling disinclined for sleep I read in it for a considerable time. A very pleasant impression emerged of this lady who, in the early days of the seventies, had found life so absorbingly filled with small interests.

She was just eighteen when Harry, her only child was born, and his remarkable precocity soon became an almost daily entry. But then I began to pick out certain scattered sentences which somehow seemed to be connected with each other: 'A lovely morning, but something rather uncomfortable about the garden'. . . 'Baby cried dreadfully in the garden this morning, but he was as good as gold when Nannie took him out in his perambulator into the street'. . . 'I sat on the square little lawn in the sun, but wasn't very happy. The flies were horrible. They buzzed continually round me, and yet I couldn't see them'. . . 'Something drove me in from the garden this evening, such an odd feeling, as if there was something looking at me from the little square lawn, and yet there was nobody there. Dick says it is all nonsense, but it isn't quite. . .'

Then after some interval was recorded the building of the wall, and following that came the entry which Harry had told me of, saying that she was sure it was wise. After that there was no more mention of the new wall, or of trouble in the garden. By this time I was drowsy with the deciphering of those faded lines, and I put out my light and went to sleep.

Now dreams are, of course, only a nonsensical medley of impressions lately received, or of those which in some stirring of the subconscious mind break like bubbles on the surface of the sleeping senses, so it was no wonder that I had vague and disquieting adventures in the garden, after I had fallen asleep. I seemed to be out there alone in some cloudy twilight; the wall over which I had peered that evening was gone, and in the center of the small lawn that lay beyond was standing a tall upright figure toward which my steps were drawn.

In this veiled dimness I could not make out whether it was a man or some columnar block of stone. But the terror that began to stir in me was mingled with a great curiosity, and very stealthily I advanced toward it. I stood absolutely still, and, whether stone or flesh and blood, it seemed to be waiting.

There was the sound of innumerable flies buzzing in the air close about me, and suddenly a cloud of them descended on me, settling on my eyes and ears and nostrils—foul to the smell and loathsomely unclean to the touch. The horror of them overpowered my caution, and in a frenzy I beat them off, still keeping my eye on that silent figure. But my movements disclosed its nature: it was no stone column that stood there, for it slowly raised an arm, and made passes and beckonings to me.

A stricture of impotence was closing in on me, but the panic of sheer nightmare broke in on my dreams, and suddenly I was sitting up in bed, panting and wet with terror. The room was peaceful and silent; the open window looking out on the garden let in an oblong of moonlight, and there by my bedside was the closed volume which no doubt had induced this unease.

Next day the work of cutting a door in the garden wall began, and by the afternoon we could squeeze in through the slit of aperture and examine more closely the aspect of the new plot. Thick grew the crop of weeds and grasses over it, but underneath the northerly and easterly walls there was mingled with the wild growth many degenerated descendants of cultivated plants, showing that one time (even as the diary had indicated) there had been flower beds there. But otherwise the wild growth was rank and triumphant, and a deep digging over the soil would be necessary before the plot could be reclaimed.

Sun trap indeed it was: the place was a stew of heat, and though on the outer lawn close by it had been pleasant enough to sit out in the unshaded blaze of the day, thanks to the steady north-easterly breeze, here no faintest stir of moving air freshened the sultriness. Coming from that ventilated warmth outside, there was something deadly and oppressive about this hot torpor; the air was stagnant as the heart of some jungle, and there hung about it a faint odour of decay like that which broods in deep woodlands. I thought, too, that I heard the murmur of large flies, but that perhaps was an imagination born of the pages which I had read last night, and which had already worked themselves up into a most vivid and unpleasant dream.

I had not mentioned that to Harry, nor, in returning the diary to him, had I alluded to those curious entries I had found there. I had my own reason for this, for it was clear that his mother had felt there was something queer and uncanny about the spot where we now stood, and I did not want any suggestion of that from outside to enter Harry's mind.

Evidently there was nothing further from his thoughts at present, for he was charmed with this derelict little plot.

'Marvelously sheltered,' he said. 'No east wind can get near it; it will pass right over it. One could grow anything here. And so perfectly private; not a roof or a chimney looks over the walls—nothing but sky. I love a secret place like this! I shall have a door fitted with a bolt inside, and no one can disturb me. As for the rest, it is all in my head, ready to be realized. Beds, deep flower beds where the old ones have been, a square of grass, and a round bed in the centre. I can see it; it will turn out precisely as I want it.'

Next morning, while the bricklayers were finishing the doorway, Harry got in a couple of men in addition to his gardener, and all day barrowfuls of weeds and grasses were carted away for burning. The position of the flower beds was staked out, and that of the path, but all had to be deeply dug in order to get rid of the burrowing roots of the old vegetation, before the crazy pavement and the turfs of the lawn could be laid down. That afternoon as I lazed in the hot sun, Harry came out from his labours, hot and grimed, and beckoned to me.

'Come here!' he called, 'We've hit upon an odd thing, and I don't know what it is. Bring your archeological knowledge to bear.'

It was indeed rather an odd thing: a square column of black granite, some four feet high and about eighteen inches across. In shape it some-what resembled one of those altars which are not uncommonly seen in collections of Roman remains. But this was certainly not Roman; it was of far ruder workmanship, and looked far more like some Druidi-cal piece. Then suddenly I remembered having seen, in some Museum of early British remains, something exactly like it: it was described as an altar of sacrifice from an ancient British temple. Indeed there could be no reasonable doubt that this stone was of the same nature.

Harry was delighted with this find.

'Just what I want for the centre of my flower bed in the middle of the lawn,' he said. 'I've got the place marked; let's haul it into posi-tion at once. I'll have a sundial on the top of it, I think.'

I was strolling that evening in the garden waiting for Harry to come out. The sun had just set behind a bank of stormy red clouds in the west, and as I came opposite the yet doorless archway into the new plot, it looked exactly as if it was lit by some illumination of its own. The tall black altar now in place glowed like a lump of red-hot iron, and as I stood there in the doorway, wondering at this lurid bright-ness, I felt something brush by me, just touching my shoulder and left side in its passage.

This was startling, but there was nothing visible, and immediately I heard—this time without any doubt whatever—the sonorous hum of many flies. That certainly came from the new garden, and yet in the air there was no sign of them.

And simultaneously with both these invisible impressions, there came to me a sudden shrinking and shuddering of the spirit, as if I were in the presence of some evil and malignant power. That came and went: it lasted no longer than the soft touch of the invisible thing that had pushed by me in the doorway, or that drone of hovering flies.

Then Harry appeared, coming out of the house and calling me to our usual diversion of piquet which we both enjoyed playing.

The laying of the lawn and the replanting of the old beds went on with great expedition: strips of turf from the downland were plastered onto the fresh-turned soil and rolled and watered, while against the walls for autumnal flowering Harry planted sunflowers, dahlias and Michaelmas daisies, and in the bed around the black column a company of well-grown young salvias.

A couple of days sufficed for this, and one evening we strolled down there in the dusk, marvelling at how well the turf was taking, and how vigorous and upstanding were the young plants.

There were heavy showers that night; blinks of lightning glared through my panes; distant thunder reverberated, and later, in the hot hours of darkness, I had to get up to close the window, for the rain was spattering on the carpet within. Having shut it, I stood there for a few moments looking out on the shrouded dimness and listening to the hiss of the thick shower on the shrubs outside. And then I saw something that curiously disquieted me.

The door into the new garden had been fitted that day, but it had been left open. The archway was thus visible from my windows, and now it stood out in the darkness as if there was light within. Then a very vivid flash zig-zagged across the sky, and I saw that in the doorway there was standing a black-draped figure.

It seemed hardly credible that a human being had got into the garden: why should a cloaked and living man be standing out there in the storm? If he was a burglar why should he be waiting out there, for the house had long been wrapped in quiet? And yet, supposing that in the morning it was found that someone had broken into the house, I should cut a very foolish figure if, having seen him before any damage was done, I went tranquilly back to bed again without investigation.

But I know that I did not really believe this was a man at all. What then was to be done? I decided that I would not wake Harry until I

had carried my investigations a little further by myself, and I started
to go downstairs. But as I passed Harry's door, I saw a chink of light
underneath it, then a loose board creaked under my foot, and next
moment he came out.

'What is it?' he asked. 'Did you see it too? Someone coming acros
the lawn from the new garden? Look here: I'll go out by the back door
into the garden and you go through the dining room. Then he'll be
between us. Take a poker or a big stick with you.'

I waited till he had time to get around to the back, and then, pulling
aside the curtain in the dining-room, I unlocked the door that led into
the garden. The rain had ceased and now through the thunder-laden
canopy over-head there shone the faint light of a cloud-beleaguered
moon. There in the centre of the lawn stood the figure I had seen in
the archway, and on the moment I heard the click of the lock of the
back-door.

Was it after all only a living man who now stood within ten yards
of me? Had he heard the unlocking of the two doors? At any rate he
moved—and that swiftly—across the lawn toward the archway where
I had first seen him. Then I heard Harry's voice:

'Quick; we've got him now!' he cried, and while he took the path,
I ran across the lawn toward the doorway through which the figure
had disappeared. There was light enough to see, when we got there,
that it stood in the centre of the garden; it was as if the altar was one
with it. Then a near and vivid flash of lightning burst from the pall
overhead, and showed every corner of the high-walled plot. It was
absolutely empty, but the stillness was now broken by the buzzing of
innumerable flies. Then the rain begin, first a few large hot drops.
then the sluices of heaven were opened, and before we could regain
the house we were drenched.

Of all the men I have ever known, Harry Pershore has the pro-
foundest disbelief in 'the unseen and the aware', and in the few minutes
of his talk before we turned in again, and at breakfast next morning
he was still absolutely convinced that what we had both seen was real
and material, not ghostly.

'It must have been a man,' he said, 'because there's nothing else
for it to be; and after all, the walls are not unscaleable for an active
fellow. Certainly we both thought we saw him in the centre of the
garden. But the light was dim and confusing, and I haven't the slightest
doubt that we were both staring at the altar while he was shinning
it up the wall. Come down and look.'

We went out. The garden was still dripping with the rain of the night, but the vigorous salvias planted yesterday in the bed around the altar were scorched, as if a flame had passed over them. Withered, too, though not so sorely burned, was the new-laid grass, and the sunflowers and Michaelmas daisies were drooping and yellow of leaf. It was as if some tropic day, instead of a warm night with copious showers of rain, had passed over them; or rather as if from the altar had emanated some withering ray, completely scorching all that lay nearest to it. But all this only stiffened Harry into an angry stubbornness when I asked him what explanation he offered.

'Good Lord, I can't tell you,' he said, 'but you've got to find the connection between a man who popped over the wall and my poor withered plants. I'll tell you what I'll do. I'll bring out a ground-sheet and a rug and sleep here tonight, and we'll see if anyone comes round with a warming-pan again. No, don't be alarmed; I'm not going to ask you to keep me company. That would spoil it all, for you might somehow infect me with your nonsense. I prefer a revolver. You think there's something occult and frightful at work. So let's have it; bring it out. What's your explanation?'

'I can't explain it any more than you,' I said. 'But I believe there is something here in this garden, some power connected, I imagine, with that altar you found. Your mother also believed there was some-thing queer, and had the place walled-up. You've opened it again, and set the thing free, and I expect it's vastly intensified by your having disinterred that which lay buried.'

He laughed.

'I see,' he said. 'An instance of your theory that material objects can absorb and give out force they have derived from living folk—'

'Or years ago, from the dead,' said I.

He laughed again.

'I really think we won't talk about it,' he said. 'I can't argue about such monstrous nonsense. It isn't worth that much to me.'

During the day I made several efforts to dissuade him from his scheme, but it was perfectly fruitless. Indeed I began myself to wonder whether I was not the prey of ridiculous imaginings; whether my mind was not reverting to the bygone beliefs and superstitions of primitive man.

A lump of stone like that altar was just a lump of stone. How could it possess properties and powers such as those which I was disposed to attribute to it. Certainly that figure which we had both seen was difficult of rational explanation; so, too, was that withering and scorching flame that had passed over the garden. But it was a flight of conjecture, wholly unsupported, to suppose that a rough-hewn block of granite had any connection with them.

My fears and forebodings receded and dwindled till they lay back in my mind, cloaked with the darkness that common sense spread round them, and became no more than a tiny spark smouldering there. And so it came about that when, about eleven that night, Harry went forth from the house with his pillows and blanket and ground-sheet, revolver in hand, to spend the night on the new-laid lawn, I soon went up to bed.

The door from the dining-room into the garden Harry had left unlocked, for again the night was thickly over-clouded, threatening rain, and he laughingly said that though he would gaily face the fires of the powers of darkness, a downpour of common rain would certainly rout him and send him running for shelter. Throwing open my window, I leaned out into the night, and in the stillness heard Harry shut and bolt the door into the little garden.

I went to sleep at once, and from dreamlessness awoke suddenly to a consciousness of terror and imminent peril. Without waiting to put on a coat or slippers I ran downstairs and across the lawn towards the door in the wall.

I stopped outside it, listening and wondering why I had rushed out like that, for all was perfectly still. Then, while I stood there, I heard a voice—not Harry's—from within. I could not distinguish any words at all, and the tones of it were level, as if it were chanting some prayer, and as I listened I saw above the wall a dim red glow gradually brightening.

All of this happened in a moment, and with some swift onrush of panic I called aloud to Harry, and wrestled with the handle of the door. But he had bolted it from within. Once more I rattled at it and shouted —and still only that chanting voice answered. Then, exerting my full strength and weight, I hurled myself against the door: it creaked, the bolt snapped and it gave way, falling inward. There met me a buffet of hot air tainted with some rank smell, and round me was the roar of hosts of flies.

Harry, stripped to the waist, was kneeling in front of the altar. By his side stood a figure robed in black; one of its hands grasped his hair, bending his head back, the other, stretched out, brandished aloft some implement. Before the stroke fell, I found my voice.

'By the power of God Almighty!' I yelled, and in the air I traced the sign of the Cross.

I heard the chink of something falling on the altar; the red light faded into the dusk of earliest dawn, and Harry and I were alone. He swayed and fell sideways on the grass, and without more ado I picked him up and carried him out past the shattered door and through the archway, not knowing yet if he was alive or dead. But he breathed still, he sighed and stirred like one coming out of deep trance, and then he saw me.

'You!' he said. 'But what's been happening? Why am I here? I went to sleep, and I dreamed something terrible. A priest, a sacrifice... What was it?'

I never told him what had happened beyond that I had felt uneasy about him, had come out and called him, and getting no answer had burst in the door and found him lying on the grass. He knew no more than that; but for some reason he took a dislike to the altar which had pleased him so much. Somewhere in the dim recesses of his subconsciousness, I imagine, he connected it with the very terrible 'dream' which he could only vaguely recall, and he said he would have it buried again: it was an ugly thing. As we looked at it next morning, talking of this, he took up from it something that lay on the top of it.

'How on earth did that get here?' he said. 'It's one of those early flint knives, isn't it?'

THE CHIPPENDALE MIRROR

No CRIME, perhaps, of recent years aroused more interest, or stimulated to so high a degree the acumen of the amateur detective, as that known as the Wimbledon Mystery, whereby Mrs Yeats met the death that so long went unavenged.

For nearly six months, it may be remembered, the police, even with the aid of the suggestions so liberally supplied them by their unprofessional colleagues, failed to lay hands on the murderer, who certainly exhibited the most consummate control of himself and did not, as is generally the case, commit any of those acts of carelessness, born of regained confidence, whereby crime is commonly brought home to the criminal.

Whether he would have escaped altogether, indeed, is doubtful, for though he had not, when the guilt was fastened upon him, incurred danger by reaping the fruits of his crime, he had not made up his mind to part with the evidence of it. His detection, however, was due to no blunder of his own, but to circumstances against which he could not possibly have guarded himself.

It will be well to recall in outline the main facts of his crime. Mrs Yeats had lived for a number of years with her husband in one of the pleasant detached residences that face Wimbledon Common. The marriage, chiefly owing to her intemperate habits, had long been an unhappy one, and a week or so before her death husband and wife had determined to live apart. She was Italian by birth, and proposed to go back again to her southern skies, and, with the very handsome allowance that he was prepared to give her, to make her home there.

The day before she left, he had supplied her with money to the extent of a hundred and fifty pounds as travelling expenses for herself and her maid, and to enable her to have control of ready cash until she had established her banking account in Rome. This sum was now in her possession, chiefly in the form of five-pound notes, with a certain amount of English gold.

That afternoon her husband was summoned to London on some urgent business affairs, and in the evening telephoned to her that, since he would be detained over them till after midnight, he would sleep in town, and meet her next morning at Victoria Station. She would drive up there in the motor-car which had taken him to town that afternoon, and would now return without him.

Next morning, at seven o'clock, her maid went into her room to call her, and found her lying on the floor by the bed with her throat cut. Her head was smothered in one of her pillows, which was tied round it, and the bed and the floor and the furniture of the room were thickly dabbed with her blood.

The murderer, it seemed, had worn gloves, for no finger-prints were found, and, indeed, the charred remains of a pair belonging to her husband were discovered among the ashes in the grate. The fact that they were burnt seemed to indicate that the crime had taken place early in the night, for otherwise the fire in her room would have gone out. The motive for it was clear enough, for her money was missing. Servants sleeping in the house had not heard anything.

For nearly six months no clues of any kind were obtained. It was ascertained beyond doubt that her husband was not implicated, for he was occupied at his office till after midnight, and shortly before one o'clock the night porter of the hotel where he stayed let him in, and took him up in the lift to his room, while for the rest of the night no one entered or left the hotel.

The strictest interrogatories were held of the servants in the house, and search made for the missing money, but no light of any sort was cast on this black and baffling crime. It seemed certain, however, that the murder was committed by someone who had entered the house for that purpose for the flower-beds below the drawing-room windows, which were open, were marked with footprints which appeared to have been erased by the murderer, for they were blurred and without value as a clue.

Among the bank notes there were certain new ones, of which the numbers were known, but no attempt was made to cash these. The four men-servants—butler, chauffeur, and two footmen—were narrowly

watched, but none showed signs of being in unexplained affluence. The
murderer had gone out again into the night as silent and as unobserved
as he had entered.

Mr Yeats, finally, never lived in the house again, the lease was put
up for auction, and a certain part of the furniture—that of his wife's
bedroom—was sold, for he could not bear to look on the things that
had beheld so grim a tragedy.

It was some five months after these events that I went in, on my way
back from dinner, to see my friend Hugh Grainger, who had not long
ago settled in town. A sudden inheritance had come to him, and he
had lashed out into a new and wonderful motor, a gem of a chauffeur,
a fur coat, and a house in Bedford Square, at present rather sparsely
furnished, for he had moved into it from narrower quarters.

With a wisdom that refused to be hurried, he did not instantly fill
up his ungarnished spaces with random purchases, but, by dint of keeping his eyes and pockets well open, was gradually acquiring pieces that
admirably suited the tall Adam-decorated rooms, and now a sideboard,
now a rout-chair, now a Sheraton cabinet would contribute to the
embellishment.

Tonight I found him in a state of high content over a Chippendale
mirror, which he had found in some incredible place in Putney, and
had purchased for an incredibly low price. It had only just arrived,
and at present stood on the floor of a sitting-room, till fixed in the
divinely-appointed place over the chimney-piece.

Certainly it was a charming acquisiton, and gloatingly he pointed
out to me the fineness of its inlay, the graceful curves of its framework,
its original gilding, and, in particular, its original glass.

'And the price, too,' he said. 'Why, a modern copy would cost more.
Putney! I didn't know such a good thing could come out of Putney.'

A faint but imperious mewing was heard at the door, and Hugh has-
tened to obey the orders of Cyrus the Great, his Persian cat, who came
very slowly into the room in order to give the maximum amount of
trouble to the person holding the door open for his impressive entry.

He took no notice, of course, either of the man ironically known
as his master, or of myself, and was just preparing to spring on his
usual chair when he turned quickly and ran tail erect towards the mirror. Something about it pleased him enormously (the mirror might
have been cold grouse), and, with loud purrings, he proceeded to patrol

in front of it, rubbing himself against it. He trod high and delicately, protruding and sheathing his claws at each step, with flashing eyes and switching tail. He went round behind it, positively roaring in his throat with satisfction, and finally sat down close in front of it, his nose almost touching the glass, and looking rapturously into it. But he was not, as you may sometimes see a cat do, regarding his own reflected image; his eyes travelled over the whole surface of it, with quick turnings of his head.

'Cyrus is as pleased as you,' I remarked. Hugh did not answer; he was watching the cat curiously. If there is one subject that interests him more than beautiful things, it is queer things—things connected with the invisible psychical world, which exists round us as surely as the material world, and of which we occasionally catch glimpses. Together we have had numerous strange experiences in *séances* and haunted houses, and it just occurred to me to wonder whether Cyrus' behaviour was being of psychical interest to him. For myself, as far as I am aware, at that moment this rapturous preoccupation of the cat with the mirror gave me no further sentiment than interest in the mysterious perceptions of animals.

'I would give the mirror itself to know what Cyrus sees in it,' said Hugh at length. 'I know—' He stopped suddenly, and pointed at the reflecting surface.

'What *is* that?' he said. 'There is something happening in the mirror.'

At that moment—it may have been merely the suggestion on his part—I felt that sensation which is so well known to those who have experienced psychical phenomena. It is exactly as if some summons had come to you, not from outside at all, but from inside the brain, which commands your attention. Simultaneously with that mysterious signal I felt a sudden movement of air stir in the room—a faint, but quite perceptible, cold current. At the same moment Cyrus, who had been sitting quite still, got up in a sort of ecstasy of content, and looking fixedly into the mirror, clawed at the carpet.

I followed Hugh's pointing finger, and looked, too. The surface of the glass, in spite of the bright light in which it stood, had grown dark, so that I no longer saw the reflection of the cat, of Hugh standing behind him, of the candles that burnt on the table near it. It was dim and dusk in the mirror, and in the dimness something—I could not see what—moved across it. Immediately afterwards I saw the normal reflections resume themselves, and Cyrus, suddenly losing interest in it, turned away, and marched across the carpet to his usual chair.

Hugh spoke.

'It's gone,' he said. 'But I thought... no, tell me if you thought anything?'

I own to having been considerably startled; this sudden vanishing of the reflections, above all the sense that there had been something *below* that darkness, was peculiarly uncomfortable.

'It went dark,' I said, 'and something moved in the darkness.'

He laughed.

'It's a cheaper bargain than I imagined,' he said; 'I saw exactly the same thing. I suppose the Psychical Society would call it a case of collective hallucination. But that doesn't seem to explain much.'

'Let's call it the haunted mirror, then,' said I, 'though, perhaps, that explains even less!'

'But one knows what it means,' said he.

It was some two days afterwards that I was in the house again. In the interval the mirror had been put in its appointed place, and looked admirable there, but it had not shown any further signs of behaving in the way mirrors are not expected to behave, and losing its reflecting powers.

Here, now it was more on a level with my eyes, I could examine it easily and admire the excellence of the work. The glass, as I have said, was original, and, as is usually the case with such things, there were a quantity of dark spots on it, where the glaze of mercury behind it had crumbled and fallen off.

But in this more detailed examination I saw that certain of these spots were not under the glass, but on it. There were not more than some half-dozen of them, but at the lower edge of the glass, where it was set into its wooden frame, there was in the crack a little brown deposit, similar to the minute specks on the glass itself, as if some liquid had run into it and dried there rustily, forming just such a stain as you will get below a nail driven into the wall of a fruit-garden. But I noticed this so incuriously that when Hugh joined me, I did not even speak of it. He was inclined to be querulous about the normal behaviour of the mirror.

'I looked at it half the morning,' he said, 'and could see nothing but my own face. And I held Cyrus up to it, to his great disgust. He didn't take the smallest interest in it, and merely wriggled. But did you ever see a mirror so clearly made for that particular place?'

'But no more hallucinations?' I asked.

'Not one—not the ghost of one, I may say. All the same, Cyrus saw something the other night, and he enjoyed it immensely. Cats have tremendous perceptions, I believe, and they love horrors; they love the dead, you know. By the way, I want you to dine here tomorrow night. Two marvellously tiresome cousins have asked themselves, and, as I always help you out on similar occasions, I expect reciprocal advantages. Free trade, isn't it?'

The marvellously tiresome cousins lived up to their character, and we spent a dismal evening. They did not play cards, the lady objected to the smell of cigarettes, they neither of them appeared to possess any ideas on any subject, and, worst of all, they would not go away.

Already it was close on midnight; Hugh with eyes of despair, was talking the most dreary nonsense on the subject of foreign politics, when suddenly there came to my brain that secret signal I have spoken of, and a little cold draught crept round my head.

At that moment Cyrus, who had been sleeping peacefully in his red chair, awoke in a state of purring excitement. He stretched and waved his tail, and then, suddenly catching sight of the mirror, made one superb bound and landed on the chimney-piece.

Hugh's voice ceased from its stream of foreign politics, and he took two steps across to the fireplace, and looked in the mirror.

'What a beautiful cat!' said the lady who did not like the smell of tobacco, 'and how beautifully it jumps! How lucky there was nothing on the chimney-piece for it to break! Poor pussy!'

I had stood up, too, and her voice came to me as in a dream, for all that was real was comprised in the bright glass which had again grown suddenly dark. I leant over Hugh's shoulder, hearing his breath coming quick and short as he looked, and in the darkness that hung on the wall of the bright room I saw certain things.

I was looking into a dark room that was lit only by a faint gleam that came through a window-blind opposite, and by a lantern that was being carried across that room. A bed glimmered whitely there, and in the bed was a figure that suddenly sat upright as the moving lantern came close to it. The lantern was carried by a man, and for one second I caught a glimpse of his face.

How long this vision lasted in the actual world of time and space I cannot say; it seemed to last for just as long as it would take a man to cross a room. And then I became aware that Hugh and I were looking into a perfectly normal mirror, and that Cyrus jumped down on the hearthrug with a soft thud.

But in that minute I had descended into some horror of great darkness; I was entangled in a terror that was only bearable because it was mingled with the intensest curiosity. I knew that what I had seen, that which had dimmed the polished surface of the glass for those few seconds, was something hellish and awful intruding into the quiet boredom of this room in a solid house in a commonplace square.

Some silent witness of a tragedy had come to trouble the house; it was not just a photograph of some mysterious, fiendish deed that had been presented, it was the very deed itself. And, as yet, I knew not nor guessed what the deed was. Simply, at some time or another, a man with lean, clean-shaven face, which, somehow, I thought I had seen in actual life, had come with a lantern into a bedroom. But I did not doubt that it was of something terrible that I had had a glimpse.

All this flashed through my consciousness as I turned back into the room again. The two guests were already on their feet, preparing at last to go. Cyrus was curled up in his chair, and Hugh was saying in a rather odd voice, 'What, already? Surely it is very early?'

We confabulated together, when he returned from his work of speeding the departing, with occasional glances at the mirror till late into the early hours. We had seen, it appeared, very much the same thing, but whereas I had noticed the face of the man who carried the lantern, he had seen that of the woman who had sat up in bed. To me that part of the room had been blurred; I had not seen whether it was woman or man who lay there. To him, also, the lantern light had gleamed on something the man carried. It was then that I remembered the brown deposit in the crack between the mirror and its frame.

Now this vision had appeared on two occasions about midnight, and our theory, fantastic and terrible, began to take shape. Had some tragedy, such as we had seen the opening of, taken place, somewhen, somewhere, at that hour? Had the mirror retained, as on a photographic plate, some image, which was ready, if the conditions for its psychical transmission were favourable, to be reproduced again, made visible to mortal eye? By strange coincidence the mirror had come into my friend's possession, and he and I, both sensitive to psychical phenomena, had seen a fragment of the deed that had been enacted in front of it. It seemed, too, as if the power that made this visible was on the increase; the message was getting through more clearly. On the first occasion we had seen little more than darkness, on the second we had seen something of that which took place below it.

We had agreed to meet again the next night, and I arrived at the house about eleven, only to find a note from Hugh that he had been unavoidably called away, but expected to be back before midnight. 'Look at the woman's face,' he had underlined, 'an idea has occurred to me. . .'

It was with a certain faltering of courage that I settled to go upstairs and wait for him. As I went up, a great flounce of movement from behind the curtain on the stairs startled me, and Cyrus pounced out, preceding me to the room where the mirror hung. He ran in eagerly when I opened the door, and, turning on the electric light, I found him erect and superb and pleased in the centre of the carpet.

For some while I occupied myself with the evening papers, which contained news of merit. Cyrus was coiled up on his chair, footsteps, which had sounded muffled as they passed up the back staircase, grew quiet, and the hush of night settled down on the house. Outside, where the air was foggy, the square was noiseless, save for an occasional hoot of a motor passing into the streets. By degrees I found the light growing rather dim, as if the fog had penetrated into the room, and soon it became impossible to read the paper. Yet the air seemed clear enough, and the mirror above the chimney-piece sharply reflected, from where I sat, the ceiling and cornice of the room, on which the light from the hearth played and flickered.

I had no watch with me, and thus no accurate idea of the speed with which time passed, but I was conscious of an increasing anxiety that Hugh should return. Then, quite suddenly, Cyrus awoke, and stood up on his chair with eyes flashing and eager. With one bound he perched himself on the chimney-piece, and, following his movement, I saw that the brightness of the reflections in the mirror was growing dim and blurred. Simultaneously came the strong inward call to attend, and I felt my hair just raised by a draught of cold breeze that came from nowhere. It, whatever it was, was coming.

At that, sheer unreasoning terror seized me. It had been bad enough the night before, when Hugh was here, and when his two guests gave the comforting sense of companionship. Now, when it had caught me alone, the terror was ten times magnified. Yet, in spite of it, I did not, simply because I could not, merely leave the room. The flesh and blood of me cried out to go, but some force, as overmastering as brute, physical compulsion, made me get up and walk across the room to where the mirror hung, already a black oblong on the wall.

It was dark in the mirror, but very soon I saw that it was dark because I was actually standing in the dim room which it disclosed. A little light came filtering through the blind of the window opposite me, and in the dimness I began to see the objects that the room contained. Everything appeared life-size, as if I was actually standing there.

Opposite, then, was the window through which this little light came; on the left of it was a dressing-table, where silver faintly gleamed, and also I could just see a glass and a decanter. To the left of that was another window, over which curtains were drawn. On the left-hand wall a bed projected into the room, and on the pillow was a woman's head. I appeared to stand close to the foot of this bed. On the right-hand wall beside the window was a closed door, and near it a fireplace. Over the fireplace hung a mirror, and I saw that in form and curve and size it was the mirror into which I was now looking.

Suddenly this door opened, and a man carrying a lantern came in. He flashed it quickly round the room, and then came across towards the bed, where the woman lay. She sprang up to a sitting position, and the light fell on her face, so that for one second I saw it quite clearly. Next moment he had seized her pillow and bent it round her head, appearing to tie it there, and wildly groping, she wrestled with him. He made one dreadful slicing movement with his hand across her throat, and I saw the blood stream on to her night-dress. She still clutched him, and across the room they struggled together, while the blood flowed from her.

Then, as the life ebbed, her struggles ceased, and presently she sank in a heap on the floor. But I had seen her face, before it was smothered in the pillow, and I knew I had seen it or its presentment before.

Gradually the light came back into the mirror, and I found myself looking no longer at these horrors, but at my own white reflection. There was a soft thud on the ground beside me, and Cyrus had jumped down again.

At that moment I heard a motor stop at the street door, and went downstairs. Hugh had just let himself in, and behind him, carrying a rug, stood his chauffeur. And instantly I knew who was the man who had come into a bedroom one night and done to death the woman who slept there.

A hunt through picture-papers next day confirmed the identity of the woman, and after making certain arrangements, Hugh rang his bell that night at a little before twelve, which was the summons for his chauffeur. He talked to him for some minutes, while I watched the mirror, and when again it began to grow dark, I nodded to Hugh, who got up from his chair.

'Look in that mirror, Atkinson,' he said, and as he spoke the curtain behind me twitched. For myself, I merely watched Atkinson's face, and presently there passed over it a change so appalling that the mask of horror I looked on seemed scarcely human. A hideous pallor spread over the man's face, the sweat poured from him, his mouth opened and panted for breath, and his eyes, glued to the glass that showed him his own crime, seemed to bulge and protrude from his head.

Then, with a yell that still sounds in my ears, he fell in a heap on the hearthrug, and from behind the curtain there stepped out the two men whom Scotland Yard had sent down.

There remains but little to be told. In the wretched man's bedroom, hidden behind a chest of drawers, were found certain bank-notes of which the numbers were known. Subsequently I went down to Wimbledon, and there in the bedroom where Mrs Yeats' body was discovered in the morning by her maid, was an oblong of unfaded paper above the chimney piece commensurate with the shape of the Chippendale mirror.

THE WITCH-BALL

IT WAS quite impossible to determine which of us had seen it first, where it gleamed, blue and resplendent, in spite of the coating of grime which covered it, behind the dingy panes of that obscure little shop. It reposed on a rusty steel fender, in the middle of frayed rugs, Britannia-metal teapots, wine-glasses, cracked plates, billiard balls, stamp-albums, glass beads, pewter mugs, odd volumes of obsolete fiction and history primers at twopence each, false teeth with coral-coloured gums, all the depressing miscellany of an unprosperous curiosity shop. Simultaneously and without a word we stepped off the pavement and hurried across the street.

'But is it to be yours or mine?' I said to Margery. 'Who saw it first?' Margery's good sense is always admirable.

'Oh, what does that matter at present?' she said. 'The only important thing just now is that it should be ours. We'll settle the other point when we've got it.'

She opened the door of the shop, setting a bell attached to the back of it querulously jangling, and, after an anxious pause made hideous to us both by the frightful thought that, before we had secured it, somebody else might come in on the same quest, a slow step creaked down the stairs within, and the proprietor, eyeing us suspiciously, entered and waited for us to speak.

'I should like to look at that glass ball in your window,' said Margery quite calmly. 'How much is it?'

Ten shillings was all that he asked for it, and though Margery dearly loves a little genteel chaffering, she made no attempt to get it cheapened or to examine too closely for cracks or other blemishes, for it must be securely ours without delay; so a minute later we emerged again with the witch-ball wrapped in a greasy leaf of antique newspaper. Though our intention had been to go for a stroll through the streets of Tillingham till lunch-time on this hot May morning, there was no thought of that now, and we went straight back to my house, a few hundred yards distant, with our treasure.

'I shall go and wash it at once,' she said, 'and then we'll settle who's it is.'

She hurried upstairs while I went on into the book-room where, but a few minutes before, we had left her husband Hugh Kingwood.

'Back again?' he asked. 'I expected you would be. Far too hot to walk on such a morning.'

'Oh, that's not why we're back,' said I. 'We found something in a shop which we had to buy and bring straight home. A witch-ball, the most wonderful ever seen; Margery's washing it. And then we've got to settle who's it is, for we saw it absolutely at the same moment.'

Presently she came downstairs with it. Even when it had been covered with dust and dirt it had gleamed like blue fire veiled beneath a scum of ashes, and now she had washed it, it burned with a far intenser splendour. It was of uncommon size, more than a foot in diameter, and of soft brilliant sapphire blue and it reflected, gorgeously steeped in its own colour, the rounded image of the room. Fireplace and bookcases, ceiling and floor, sofa and piano all appeared there with that magical distortion which convex reflection gives, and all was dyed deep in that superb hue. The window was there with curved sashes, and where at the top of it was a blink of sky, that was of some luminous turquoise tint such as shines in dreams or in fairyland. And yet, though these pictures were only a matter of reflecting surface, it was like looking into fathomless depths of blue; the vision seemed to sink into that shining globe and dive further and further into gulfs of azure. Witch-balls have always had for me some mysterious charm, born perhaps of the memories of twinkling Christmas-trees in childhood, but here there was something more; something of intrinsic lure, that would enchant anyone without the spell of recollection to abet it.

Then arose the agonizing question of ownership; Margery, as a matter of fact, had actually paid for it, but, being one of the few women I know who is a thorough gentleman, she spurned so feminine an argument, merely calling attention to her nobility.

'I can't think what's to be done,' she said. 'I shall go into a decline unless I have it, but then no doubt you will too. And as far as I can judge, we saw it on the same tick of time. Hughie, what's the fair thing?'

Hugh did not answer, and I saw he was looking steadfastly into the witch-ball with some sort of rapt detachment. Then, as if with an effort, he shook himself free of it.

'What a marvellous piece,' he said. 'But I don't like it, Margery; there's something uncanny about it. It may be enchanting, but it is enchanted as well. Let Dick have it.'

'If that's all you've got to suggest,' she remarked severely, 'you might as well not have said anything.'

She turned from him with scorn.

'I can only see one way of settling it,' she said to me, 'and that's by the foolish device of tossing up. If I believed that you saw it a fraction of a second before me, I promise you that I should let you have it. But by chance we saw it absolutely together; so let's go to chance again.'

I could think of nothing better, so I spun a shilling, and Margery called 'Heads.' I opened my hand, and the witch-ball was hers.

'Rapture!' she said. 'Oh, Dick, how I sympathize with you!'

'I don't.' said Hugh. 'I congratulate you. There's something queer about it.'

The two of them, Margery, a first cousin of mine, and Hugh, one of my oldest friends, were staying with me in this small Sussex town for a week or ten days. The South of England was basking in a spell of blazing weather, and though golf had been an intended diversion, it was really impossible to play in this smiting and windless heat. The sky was as brass above and the ground as brass beneath, and instead we often motored down to the shore for a bathe in the afternoon, with some subsequent expedition vaguely in view, such as a visit to Bodiam or Dungeness, or merely drove about the lanes and by-ways of the Romney Marsh and the wooded country further inland, but did not very much care whether we got anywhere in particular, for the hedgerows were brimming with pink rose-blossoms and the woods still milky-green with the foliage of the spring. We lighted on adorable little villages nestling in folds of the downs, on hammer-ponds fringed with cotton-rush, from the edge of which mallards got up with a clangour of wings, or on the wide levels of the marsh we came to antique and solitary farm-houses of timber and rough-cast with glowing gardens set in red brick walls, and Margery would declare that life was but a tinkling cymbal unless lived in such a place within sound of the sea and within sight of Rye.

It was the pearl of them all that we passed that afternoon on our ramble; a plot of garden rather wild and overgrown fronted the road, and on the tall iron gate in the wall was affixed a board to announce that it was to be sold or let unfurnished. Margery, of course, insisted on our stopping, the gate ground on rusty hinges, as it grudgingly admitted us, and we went up the paved garden-walk to the house. But the door was locked and no knockings or ringings produced any response, and we had to get an idea of the interior by peering through the unblinded windows. The rooms were absolutely empty, but the paint and papering looked fairly fresh and it was clear that the house had not been untenanted for long. The flower-garden, through which we had passed and the kitchen-garden at the back, afforded similar evidence, for neither had been neglected for long; vegetables, for instance, peas and beans, had been sown in the spring, though not staked. The kitchen-garden was unwalled, and had only a wooden paling between it and the meadows of the marsh, and up the longer side of it ran one of the drainage dykes that intersect the marsh. Along the raised edge of it had been planted, evidently not more than a year or two ago, a row of young willows; these had prospered, and now formed a screen for the garden against the prevailing south-westerly winds. At one end of them was a tool-shed, the roof of which was beginning to sag, at the other a couple of derelict beehives. It certainly was an entrancing retreat for any who cared to live the solitary life, and it was sad to see a house and garden full of such charm and tranquillity beginning to suffer from want of care.

'Oh, how I long for it,' said Margery. 'Hughie, how happy we should be here! You would start very early every morning to go up to Town, driving into Rye—not more than four miles, I should think—and then a mere two hours and a half in the train. What's five hours every day in the train with such a nice drive at each end?'

'Delicious!' said Hugh. 'Especially on a winter evening with a south-westerly gale blowing. And I don't like the feel of this place. There's something sinister.'

'Darling, you're rather hard to please,' said Margery. 'You didn't like my witch-ball, and now you don't like my adorable house. How blissful I should be living here with my witch-ball.'

He shook his head.

'No, you wouldn't,' he said. 'There's something here—you would feel it before long.'

'Don't be spooky,' said Margery.

She could not tear herself away without another look through the ground-floor windows of the house and, meantime, Hugh and I strolled down to the gate where we had left the car. In spite of his almost savagely practical mind in matters of business, he has always had some queer clairvoyant power of perception, which every now and then pushes its way to the surface of his mind. He sees odd scenes which prove to be actual, if he looks in a crystal, whenever he will content to try the experiment, but his conscious mind fights shy of this gift, and he will not often attempt to exercise it. Another queer thing is that if I look into the crystal at which he is gazing, I see there what he sees, thought I might crystal-gaze day and night by myself without seeing any tremor or shadow appear there. But we have tested this odd joint phenomenon many times, and always successfully, so that it seems proved that he can establish some telepathic communication with me, though I have no independent power myself, and that this conjunction of my mind with his helps his own power. It occurred to me now, when he said that there was 'something here,' that some blink of this psychic perception had come to him. I asked him whether it was so.

'Yes, there is something here,' he said, 'which I don't like a bit. There's a wicked, unquiet atmosphere in the kitchen garden particularly; it's steeped in horror of some sort. And the queer thing is that Margery's witch-ball gives me the same feeling; no, I don't mean a similar feeling, but the same. I think you and I will have to gaze and see if we can get at anything.'

It so happened that Margery went early to bed that night, and as soon as she had gone Hugh and I moved in from the garden, where we had been sitting after dinner for the sake of coolness, into the library, where stood the witch-ball. His idea was to make it his crystal, and see if, by gazing into it, any manifestation appeared. We turned out all the lights but one, so that the reflections should not be distracting, and now in the dimmer illumination the witch-ball lost its sapphire-hue, precisely as the stone itself does by artificial light, and seemed black. Just one point of radiance reflected from the solitary light gleamed in the middle of this pool of clear-deep darkness.

We must have sat there long before anything came through to Hugh's vision, for the house had grown quiet and the church clock had twice chimed a quarter-hour before he spoke.

'Look; something is coming,' he said in that dreamy monotonous voice, which always means that he is in that state of half-trance which precedes vision. 'Tell me what you see.'

There was something seething far down in the dark pool of the ball: it was as if clear black water were beginning to boil from below and break into bubbles. These bubbles bursting on the surface were slightly luminous, and, as they multiplied, the darkness in the ball cleared as if with the approach of dawn or night.It grew rapidly brighter, not with its native blue but with a greyish twilight.

'There's a line of house-roofs against the sky,' I said, 'and in front of the house there's a garden. There's a row of trees on the left, young trees, and they're blowing about in a wind. And there's the figure of a woman—I can't make it out: she seems to be lying under the trees, among their roots, I mean, not on the ground beside them. And there's a tool-shed close by —'

Suddenly, with a gasp of my breath, I recognized the scene. It was the kitchen-garden of the house in the marsh which we had visited that afternoon. In the shock which came with this recognition my attention was jerked from its quiet scrutiny, and on the instant the vision had vanished. I was staring into a black witch-ball with one point of light in it.

Hugh was still gazing into it with wide eyes.

'Yes, yes,' he said, 'I see all that. But she's moving now: she's standing upright; and now she's coming straight towards me out of the witch-ball—Ah, the whole thing has vanished. Yes, of course, it was that place we went to today. But who was the woman? We didn't see her this afternoon. Why did she seem to be lying among the roots of the trees? And where has she gone?'

He raised his head and peered out, as if trying to focus something, through the open door into the garden, and, though, following his eyes, I saw nothing but the deep dusk there, I knew that there was some presence which had come out of the witch-ball and was hovering there watching us.

'Hugh, what are you looking at?' I said sharply.

With an effort he detached his gaze, and looked back into the room.

'I don't know,' he said, 'but there was someone there, though I saw nothing. We won't try it again tonight, because I've got the jumps, but tomorrow we must sit again. Don't tell Margery anything about it.'

I came down next morning after an uneasy night, during which again and again, in drowsy half-wakenings I thought I heard some movement in the house, to find that Margery had already breakfasted and gone out. Presently, she came back in a state of excitement.

'I have been clever,' she said, 'I've found out all about the adorable house. A certain Mr Woolaby is the owner of it, and two years ago his wife disappeared and was never traced. He lived on there alone till this spring, when he made up his mind to sell the house and had an auction of all its contents.'

'Where did you learn all this?' I asked.

'From the house-agent whose name and address was on the board there. He lives just down the street. And the name of the house is Beetles. Just Beetles! Did you ever hear of anything so attractive?'

'Beetles would smell as sweet—' I began.

'No, they wouldn't. And then I was cleverer still, and you'll never guess where I went next. It was an inspiration.'

'Do you want me to have an inspiration, too?' I asked, 'or say that I've no idea?'

'No; have an inspiration if you can,' said Margery.

'You went to the shop where we bought the witch-ball yesterday, and found that it came from the sale at Beetles.'

'Heavens! We're both inspired,' she said. 'Quite right. But how did you think of that?'

'Well, you mentioned an auction.'

'Very brilliant,' she said. 'And now, as I know you hate talking at breakfast, I shall go away and look at my witch-ball. Isn't it odd that I said I should be so happy living at Beetles with it, and that now I find that it came from there?'

Though I was late this morning, Hugh was later, and it was not for some minutes after Margery had gone that he appeared. He helped himself to food, and propped up a daily paper in front of his place, but after staring at it in silence, whisked it away again.

'There are odd things happening,' he said. 'Something or somebody came out of the witch-ball last night—at least, that's how I felt—and stood at the open door of the book-room. I saw nothing any more than you did, but it was there. And it's been here ever since, it was moving about this house all last night, and it wants something of us.'

'I felt it was here, too,' I said.

'Well, we've got to give it a chance,' he said. 'We must sit again, and now that it has established some sort of communication it will pro-bably manifest itself more clearly. I believe that the figure we first saw lying underneath the trees is what is wanting us. Let's have a gaze at the ball this morning when Margery's occupied elsewhere. I fancy there's something horrible behind it all, and I don't want her to know about it.'

That was easily arranged, for Margery soon announced her intention of sketching in one of the old streets of the town; and, as soon as she had gone, we went into the library again. There, on a table near the door into the garden, stood the witch-ball, a huge, blazing sapphire, and once more we prepared to gaze. There were disturbing cross-lights, and we drew the curtains over all the windows, so that the illumination came only from the open garden-door. But, though it was daylight now, we had hardly begun to concentrate when the colour faded from the ball, and presently I was gazing into thick, clear darkness, depth upon depth, in which, as last night, there seethed the luminous bubbles, and there emerged again the house we had seen, and the kitchen-garden, and the row of willows stirring in the wind. But now there was no figure of a woman lying there beneath them, and, remembering how Hugh had seen her last night coming out of the scene of vision, I told him what I was seeing, and he nodded, without speaking.

And then, with some cold shuddering and sinking of the spirit, I knew that once more there was someone else here besides us, but now more palpably, more perceptibly. Then a dimming of the light which came in from the garden-door made me look up. Just outside, in the hot, bright sunshine, there stood the figure of a woman. She was dressed in some sort of cloak, mould-stained and rent and decaying, and snails and fibres of root clung to it. One hand was wrapped in it, holding it to her; but the other, with the arm up to the elbow, was visible. Here and there the bone showed; here and there lumps of rotting flesh dangled from it. Above, thick, rust-coloured hair dropped on each side of what had been a face. But now the lips had perished away from the mouth, exposing the rows of discoloured teeth; the nose was a riddled earth-stained stump of cartilage, and the eye-sockets were empty. The horror of it all was vivid in the sunlight.

And then the spectre advanced to the open door, as if it were about to step into the room. It did not walk; it came nearer as if blown towards us by a breeze. At that my panic-stricken nerves broke through their paralysis of terror, and I screamed out. And, behold, there was nothing there but the wash of hot summer sun over the garden and the wind gently stirring in the myrtle bush.

The inspector of police at Tillingham is a friend of mine, and ten minutes later we were closeted with him.

'There are a couple of questions my friend and I wanted to ask you. I fancy that, about two years ago, Mrs Woolaby disappeared from her house down in the marsh.'

'That's correct,' he said. 'And her husband continued living there till the spring of this year, when he had an auction of his furniture and put the house up for sale.'

'And has anything ever been heard of Mrs Woolaby?' I asked.

'Never a word. Not a trace has been seen of her since she disappeared. Most mysterious thing. Have either of you gentlemen anything to tell me about her?'

'Was search made for her round about the house?' asked Hugh.

'Certainly, sir. The dykes were dragged in case she had fallen into one, for there was a spell of foggy weather at the time of her disappearance, and she might have slipped in and been drowned; but we found no trace of her in the dykes, and there wasn't much else to search, for it's a bare bit of land.'

'We were there yesterday,' I said. 'There's a kitchen-garden adjoining the house, and on one side of it a row of young willows, planted evidently not very long ago. My friend and I both believe that if you dig under them at the end which adjoins the toolhouse, you may learn something about Mrs Woolaby's disappearance.'

The inspector stared at us a moment in silence.

'Can you give me any reason for your believing that?' he asked.

'Nothing that would carry any weight with you,' said Hugh. 'But we're both perfectly serious about it.'

The inspector got up.

'I should like to know more,' he said. 'But if you don't mean to tell me, there it is. I'm bound to look into any information given me. I expect what you gentlemen mean is that her body will be found there, though I can't tell why you think so. I'll let you know at once if anything is discovered.'

A few hours later I was called to the telephone. The inspector wished to tell me that the body of a woman had been found at the place indicated. Later at the inquest her identity was established.

For several days after that, Hugh and I gazed into the witch-ball. But never again did we see that black boiling-up to something within it which presently disclosed the row of willows and what had lain beneath, nor did any apparition again manifest itself. It hangs still, a blue and radiant splendour, in Margery's sitting-room, and sometimes she almost makes up her mind to give it to me, but has never

yet quite scaled those heights of altruism. And the sequel to the discovery of the body of Mrs Woolaby I am sure is familiar to all those
who take an interest in murder trials.

THE APE

Hugh Marsham had spent the day, as a good tourist should, in visiting the temples and the tombs of kings across the river, and the magic of the hour of sunset flamed over earth and heaven as he crossed the Nile again to Luxor in his felucca. It seemed as if the whole world had been suddenly transferred into the heart of an opal, and burned with a myriad fiery colours. The river itself was of the green that beech trees are clad in at spring-time; the columns of the temple that stood close to its banks glowed as if lit from within by the flame of some perpetual evening sacrifice; the cloudless sky was dusky blue in the east, the blue of turquoise overhead, and melted into aquamarine above the line of desert where the sun had just sunk. All along the bank which he was fast approaching under the press of the cool wind from the north were crowds of Arabs, padding softly home in the dust from their work, and chattering as sparrows chatter among the bushes in the long English twilights. Even the dust that hovered and hung and was dispersed again by the wind was rainbowed; it caught the hues from the river and the sky, and the orange-flaming temple, and those who walked in it were clad in brightness.

Here in the South no long English twilight lingered, and as he walked up the dusky fragrant tunnel of mimosa that led to the hotel, night thickened, and in the sky a million stars leaped into being, while the soft gathering darkness sponged out the glories of the flaming hour. On the hotel steps the vendors of carpets and Arabian hangings, of incense and filigree work, of suspicious turquoises and more than suspicious scarabs were already packing up their wares, and probably recounting to each other in their shrill incomprehensible gabble the iniquitous bargains they had made with the gullible Americans and English, who so innocently purchased the wares of Manchester. Only in his accustomed corner old Abdul Hamid still squatted, for he was of a class above the ordinary vendors, a substantial dealer in antiques, who had a shop in the village, where archaeologists resorted, and bought, *sub rosa*, pieces that eventually found their way into European museums. He was in his shop all day, but evening found him, when serious business hours were over, on the steps of the hotel, where he sold undoubted antiquities to tourists who wanted something genuine.

The day had been very hot, and Hugh felt himself disposed to linger outside the hotel in this cool dusk, and turn over the tray of scarabs which Abdul Hamid presented to his notice. He was a wrinkled, dried-up husk of a man, loquacious and ingratiating in manner, and welcomed Hugh as an old customer.

'See, sir,' he said, 'here are two more scroll-scarabs like those you bought from me before the week. You should have these; they are very fine and very cheap, because I do no business this year. Mr Rankin, you know him?, of the British Museum, he give me two pounds each last year for scroll-scarabs not so fine, and today I sell them at a pound and a half each. Take them; they are yours. Scroll-scarabs of the twelfth dynasty; if Mr Rankin was here he pay me two pounds each, and be sorry I not ask more.'

Hugh laughed.

'You may sell them to Mr Rankin then,' he said. 'He comes here tomorrow.'

The old man, utterly unabashed, grinned and shook his head.

'No; I promised you them for pound and a half,' he said. 'I am not cheat-dealer. They are yours—pound and a half. Take them, take them.'

Hugh resisted this unparalleled offer, and, turning over the contents of the tray, picked out of it and examined carefully a broken fragment of blue glaze, about an inch in height. This represented the head and shoulders of an ape, and the fracture had occurred half-way down the back, so that the lower part of the trunk, the forearms which apparently hung by its side, and the hind legs were missing. On the back there was an inscription in hieroglyphics, also broken. Presumably the missing piece contained the remainder of the letters. It was modelled with extreme care and minuteness, and the face wore an expression of grotesque malevolence.

'What's this broken bit of a monkey?' asked Hugh carelessly.

Abdul Hamid, looking much like a monkey himself, put his eyes close to it.

'Ah, that's the rarest thing in Egypt,' he said, 'so Mr Rankin he tell me, if only the monkey not broken. See the back? There it says: 'He of whom this is, let him call on me thrice'—and then some son of a dog broke it. If the rest was here, I would no take a hundred pounds for it; but now ten years have I kept half-monkey, and never comes half-monkey to it. It is yours, sir, for a pound it is yours. Half-monkey nothing to me; it is fool-monkey only being half-monkey. I let it go—I give it you, and you give me pound.'

Hugh Marsham felt in one pocket, then in another, with no appearance of hurry or eagerness.

'There's your pound,' he said casually.

Abdul Hamid peered at him in the dusk. It was very odd that Hugh did not offer him half what he asked, instead of paying up without bargaining. He regretted extremely that he had not asked more. But the little blue fragment was now in Hugh's pocket, and the sovereign glistened very pleasantly in his own palm.

'And what was the rest of the hieroglyphic, do you think?' Hugh asked.

'Eh, Allah only knows the wickedness and the power of the monkeys,' said Abdul Hamid. 'Once there were such in Egypt, and in the temple of Mut in Karnak, which the English dug up, you shall see a chamber with just such monkeys sitting round it, four of them, all carved in sandstone. But on them there is no writing; I have looked at them behind and before, they not master-monkeys. Perhaps the monkey promised that whoso called on him thrice, if he were owner of the blue image of which gentleman has the half, would be his master, and that monkey would do his bidding. Who knows? It is of the old wickedness of the world, the old Egyptian blackness.'

Hugh got up. He had been out in the sun all day, and felt at this moment a little intimate shiver, which warned him that it was wiser to go indoors till the chill of sunset had passed.

'I expect you've tried it on with the half-monkey, haven't you?' he said.

Abdul Hamid burst out into a toothless cackle of laughter.

'Yes, effendi,' he said. 'I have tried it a hundred times, and nothing happens. Else I would no have sold it you. Half-monkey is no monkey at all. I have tried to make boy with the ink-mirror see something about monkeys, but nothing comes, except the clouds and the man who sweeps. No monkey.'

Hugh nodded to him.

'Goodnight, you old sorcerer,' he said pleasantly.

As he walked up the broad flagged passage to his room, carrying the half-monkey in his hand, Hugh felt with a disengaged thumb in his waistcoat pocket for something he had picked up that day in the valley of the tombs of the kings. He had eaten his lunch there, after an inspection of the carved and reeking corridors, and, as he sat idly smoking had reached out a lazy hand to where the thing had glittered among the pebbles. Now, entering his room, he turned up the electric light, and, standing under it with his back to the window, that opened, door fashion, on to the three steps that led into the hotel garden, he fitted the fragment he had found to the fragment he had just purchased. They joined on to each other with the most absolute accuracy, not a chip was missing. There was the complete ape, and down its back ran the complete legend.

The window was open, and at this moment he heard a sudden noise as of some scampering beast in the garden outside. His light streamed out in an oblong on to the sandy path, and, laying the two pieces of the image on the table, he looked out. But there was nothing irregular to be seen; the palm trees waved and clashed in the wind, and the rose bushes stirred and scattered their fragrance. Only right down in the middle of the sandy path that ran between the beds, the ground was curiously disturbed, as by some animal, heavily frolicking, scooping and spurning the light soil as it ran.

The evening train from Cairo next day brought Mr Rankin, the eminent Egyptologist and student of occult law, a huge red man with a complete mastery of colloquial Arabic. He had but a day to spend in Luxor, for he was *en route* for Merawi, where lately some important finds had been made, but Hugh took occasion to show him the figure of the ape as they sat over their coffee in the garden just outside his bedroom after lunch.

'I found the lower half yesterday, outside one of the tombs of the kings,' he said, 'and the top half by the utmost luck among old Abdul Hamid's things. He told me you said that if it was complete it would be of the greatest rarity. He lied, I suppose?'

Rankin gave one gasp of amazed surprise as he looked at it and read the inscription on the back. Marsham thought that his great red face suddenly paled.

'Good Lord!' he said. 'Here, take it!' And he held out the two pieces to him.

Hugh laughed.

'Why in such a hurry?' he said.

'Because there comes a breaking-point to every man's honesty, and I might keep it, and swear that I had given it back to you. My dear fellow, do you know what you've got?'

'Indeed I don't. I want to be told,' said Hugh.

'And to think that it was you who only a couple of months ago asked me what a scarab was! Well, you've got there what all Egyptologists, and even more keenly than Egyptologists all students of folklore and magic black and white—especially black—would give their eyes to have found. Good Lord! what's that?'

Hugh was sitting by his side in a deck-chair, idly fitting together the two halves of the broken image. He too heard what had startled Rankin, for it was the same noise as had startled him last night, namely, the scampering of some great frolicsome animal, somewhere close to them. As he jumped up, severing his hands, the noise ceased.

'Funny,' he said, 'I heard that last night. There's nothing; it's some stray dog in the bushes. Do tell me what it is that I've got.'

Rankin, who had surged to his feet also, stood listening a moment. But there was nothing to be heard but the buzzing of bees in the bushes and the chiding of the remote kites overhead. He sat down again.

'Well, give me two minutes,' he said, 'and I can tell you all I know. Once upon a time, when this wonderful and secret land was alive and not dead—oh, we have killed it with our board schools and our steamers and our religion—there was a whole hierarchy of gods—Isis, Osiris, and the rest, of whom we know a good deal. But below them there was a company of semi-divinities, demons if you will, of whom we know precisely nothing. The cat was one, certain dwarfish creatures were others, but most potent of all were the Cynocephali, the dog-faced apes. They were not divine, rather they were demons, of hideous power, *but*'—and he pointed a great hand at Hugh—'they could be controlled. Men could control them—men could turn them into terrific servants—much as the genii in the "Arabian Nights" were controlled. But to do that you had to know the secret name of the demon, and had yourself to make an image of him, with the secret name inscribed therein, and by that you could summon him and all the incarnate creatures of his species. So much we know from certain very guarded allusions in the Book of the Dead and other sources, for it was one of the great mysteries never openly spoken of. Here and there a priest

in Karnak, or Abydos, or in Hieropolis, had had handed down to him
one of these secret names, but in nine cases out of ten the knowledge
died with him, for there was something dangerous and terrible about
it all. Old Abdul Hamid here, for instance, believes that Moses had
the secret names of frogs and lice, and made images of them with the
secret name inscribed on them, and by those produced the plagues
of Egypt. Think what you could do, think what he did, if infinite power
over frog-nature were given you, so that the King's chamber swarmed
with frogs at your word. Usually, as I said, the secret name was but
sparingly passed on, but occasionally some very bold advanced spirit,
such as Moses, made his image, and controlled—'

He paused a moment, and Hugh wondered if he was in some
delirious dream. Here they were, taking coffee and cigarettes underneath the shadow of a modern hotel in the year AD 1912, and this great
savant was talking to him about the spell that controlled the whole frog-
nature in the universe. The gist, the moral of his discourse, was already
perfectly clear.

'That's a good joke,' Hugh said. 'You told your story with extraordinary gravity. And what you mean is that those two blue bits I hold
in my hand control the whole ape-nature of the world? Bravo, Rankin! For a moment, you and your impressiveness almost made me take
it all seriously. Lord! You do tell a story well! And what's the secret
name of the ape?'

Rankin turned to him with the shake of an impressive forefinger.

'My dear boy,' he said, 'you should never be disrespectful towards
the things you know nothing of. Never say a thing is moonshine till
you know what you are talking about. I know, at this moment, exactly
as much as you do about your ape-image, except that I can translate
its inscription, which I will do for you. On the top-half is written, "He,
of whom this is, let him call on me thrice—" '

Hugh interrupted.

'That's what Abdul Hamid read to me,' he said.

'Of course. Abdul Hamid knows hieroglyphics. But on the lower
half is what nobody but you and I know. "Let him call on me thrice,"
says the top-half, and then there speaks what you picked up in the valley
of the tombs, "and I, Tahu-met, obey the order of the Master." '

'Tahu-met?' asked Hugh.

'Yes. Now in ten minutes I must be off to catch my train. What I
have told you is all that is known about this particular affair by those
who have studied folklore and magic, and Egyptology. If anything—if

anything happens, do be kind enough to let me know. If you were not
so abominably rich I would offer you what you liked for that little
broken statue. But there's the way of the world!'

'Oh, it's not for sale,' said Hugh gaily. 'It's too interesting to sell.
But what am I to do next with it? Tahu-met. Shall I say Tahu-met
three times?'

Rankin leaned forward very hurriedly, and laid his fat hand on the
young man's knee.

'No, for Heaven's sake! Just keep it by you,' he said. 'Be patient
with it. See what happens. You might mend it, perhaps. Put a drop
of gum arabic on the break and make it whole. By the way, if it interests
you at all, my niece Julia Draycott arrives this evening, and will wait
for me here till my return from Merawi. You met her in Cairo, I think.'

Certainly this piece of news interested Hugh more than all the possibilities of apes and super-apes. He thrust the two pieces of Tahu-met
carelessly into his pocket.

'By Jove, is she really?' he said. 'That's splendid. She told me she
might be coming up, but didn't feel at all sure. Must you really be
off? I shall come down to the station with you.'

While Rankin went to gather up such small luggage as he had
brought with him, Hugh wandered into the hotel bureau to ask for
letters, and seeing there a gum-bottle, dabbed with gum the fractured
edges of Tahu-met. The two pieces joined with absolute exactitude,
and wrapping a piece of paper round them to keep the edges together,
he went out through the garden with Rankin. At the hotel gate was
the usual crowd of donkey-boys and beggars, and presently they were
ambling down the village street on bored white donkeys. It was almost
deserted at this hottest hour of the afternoon, but along it there moved
an Arab leading a large grey ape, that tramped surlily in the dust.
But just before they overtook it, the beast looked round, saw Hugh,
and with chatterings of delight strained at his leash. Its owner cursed
and pulled it away, for Hugh nearly rode over it, but it paid no attention to him, and fairly towed him along the road after the donkeys.

Rankin looked at his companion.

'That's odd,' he said. 'That's one of your servants. I've still a couple
of minutes to spare. Do you mind stopping a moment?'

He shouted something in the vernacular to the Arab, who ran after
them, with the beast still towing him on. When they came close the
ape stopped and bent his head to the ground in front of Hugh.

'And that's odd,' said Rankin.

Hugh suddenly felt rather uncomfortable.

'Nonsense!' he said. 'That's just one of his tricks. He's been taught it to get baksheesh for his master. Look, there's your train coming in. We must get on.'

He threw a couple of piastres to the man, and they rode on. But when they got to the station, glancing down the road, he saw that the ape was still looking after them.

Julia Draycott's arrival that evening speedily put such antique imaginings as the lordship of apes out of Hugh's head. He chucked Tahumet into the box where he kept his scarabs and ushapti figures, and devoted himself to this heartless and exquisite girl, whose mission in life appeared to be to make as miserable as possible the largest possible number of young men. Hugh had already been selected by her in Cairo as a decent victim, and now she proceeded to torture him. She had no intention whatever of marrying him, for poor Hugh was certainly ugly, with his broad, heavy face, and though rich, he was not nearly rich enough. But he had a couple of delightful Arab horses, and so, since there was no one else on hand to experiment with, she let him buy her a side-saddle, and be, with his horses, always at her disposal. She did not propose to use him for very long, for she expected young Lord Paterson (whom she did intend to marry) to follow her from Cairo within a week. She had beat a Parthian retreat from him, being convinced that he would soon find Cairo intolerable without her; and in the meantime Hugh was excellent practice. Besides, she adored riding.

They sat together one afternoon on the edge of the river opposite Karnak. She had treated him like a brute beast all morning, and had watched his capability of wretchedness with the purring egoism that distinguished her; and now, as a change, she was seeing how happy she could make him.

'You are such a dear,' she said. 'I don't know how I could have endured Luxor without you; and, thanks to you, it has been the loveliest week.'

She looked at him from below her long lashes, through which there gleamed the divinest violet, smiling like a child at her friend. 'The loveliest week,' she said. 'And tonight? You made some delicious plan for tonight.'

'Yes; it's full moon tonight,' said he. 'We are going to ride out to Karnak after dinner.'

'That will be heavenly. And, Mr Marsham, do let us go alone. There's sure to be a mob from the hotel, so let's start late, when they've all cleared out. Karnak in the moonlight, just with you.'

That completely made Hugh's mind up. For the last three days he had been on the look out for a moment that would furnish the great occasion; and now (all unconsciously, of course) she indicated it to him. This evening, then. And his heart leaped.

'Yes, yes,' he said. 'But why have I become Mr Marsham again?'

Again she looked at him, now with a penitent mouth.

'Oh, I was such a beast to you this morning,' she said. 'That was why. I didn't deserve that you should be Hugh. But will you be Hugh again? Do you forgive me?'

In spite of Hugh's fixing the great occasion for this evening, it might have come then, so bewitching was her penitence, had not the rest of their party on donkeys, whom they had outpaced, come streaming along the river bank at this moment.

'Ah, those tiresome people,' she said. 'Hughie, what a bore everybody else is except you and me.'

They got back to the hotel about sunset, and as they passed into the hall the porter handed Julia a telegram which had been waiting some couple of hours. She gave a little exclamation of pleasure and surprise, and turned to Hugh.

'Come and have a turn in the garden, Hughie,' she said, 'and then I must go down for the arrival of the boat. When does it come in?'

'I should think it would be here immediately,' he said. 'Let's go down to the river.'

Even as he spoke the whistle of the approaching steamer was heard. The girl hesitated for a moment.

'It's a shame to take up all your time in the way I'm doing,' she said. 'You told me you had letters to write. Write them now, then— then you'll be free after dinner.'

'Tomorrow will do,' he said. 'I'll come down with you to the boat.'

'No, you dear. I absolutely forbid it,' she said. 'Oh, do be good; run indoors and write your letters. I ask you to.'

Rathe puzzled and vaguely uncomfortable, Hugh went into the hotel. It was true that he had told her he had letters that should have been written a week ago, but something at the back of his mind insisted that this was not the girl's real reason for wanting him to do his task now. She wanted to go and meet the boat alone, and on the moment an unfounded jealousy stirred like a coiled snake in him. He told himself that it might be some inconvenient aunt whom she was going to meet, but such a suggestion did not in the least satisfy him when he remembered the obvious pleasure with which she had read the telegram that no doubt announced this arrival. But he nailed himself to his writing-table till a couple of very tepid letters were finished, and then, with growing restlessness, went out through the hall into the warm, still night. Most of the hotel had gone indoors to dress for dinner, but sitting on the veranda with her back to him was Julia. A chair was drawn in front of her, and facing her was a young man, on whose face the light shone. He was looking eagerly at her, and his hand rested on her knee. Hugh turned abruptly and went back into the hotel.

He and Julia for these last three days had, with two other friends, made a very pleasant party of four at lunch and dinner. Tonight, when he entered the dining-room, he found that places were laid here for three only, and that at a far-distant table in the window were sitting Julia and the young man whom he had seen with her on the veranda. His identity was casually disclosed as dinner went on; one of his companions had seen Lord Paterson in Cairo. Hugh had only a wandering ear for table-talk, but a quick glancing eye, ever growing more sombre, for those in the window, and his heavy face, as he noted the tokens and signs of their intimacy, grew sullen and savage. Then, before dinner was over, they rose and passed out into the garden.

Jealousy can no more bear to lose sight of those to whom it owes its miseries than love can bear to be parted from its adoration, and presently Hugh and his two friends went and sat, as was usual with them, on the veranda outside. Here and there about the garden were wandering couples, and in the light of the full moon, which was to be their lamp at Karnak tonight when the 'tiresome people' had gone, he soon identified Julia and Lord Paterson. They passed and repassed down a rose-embowered alley, hidden sometimes behind bushes and then appearing again for a few paces, and each sight of them, each vanishing of them again served but to confirm that which already needed no confirmation. And as his jealousy grew every moment more bitter, so every moment Hugh grew more and more dangerously enraged. Apparently Lord Paterson was not one of the 'tiresome people' whom Julia longed to get away from.

Presently his two companions left him, for they were starting now to ride out to Karnak, and Hugh sat on, smoking, and throwing away half-consumed, an endless series of cigarettes. He had ordered that his two horses, one with side-saddle, should be ready at ten, and at

ten he meant to go to the girl and remind her of her engagement. Till
then he would wait here, wait and watch. If the veranda had been on
fire he felt he could not have left it to seek safety in some place where
he was unable to see the bushy path where the two strolled. Then they
emerged from that on to the broader walk that led straight to where
he was sitting, and after a few whispered words, Lord Paterson left
her there, and came quickly towards the hotel. He passed close by
Hugh, gave him (so Hugh thought) a glance of amused derision, and
went into the hotel.

Julia came quickly towards him when Lord Paterson had gone.

'Oh, Hughie,' she said. 'Will you be a tremendous angel? Lord Paterson—yes, he's just gone in, such a dear, you would delight in him—
Lord Paterson's only here for one night, and he's dying to see Karnak
by moonlight. So will you lend us your horses? He absolutely insists
I should go out there with him.'

The amazing effrontery of this took Hugh's breath away, and in that
moment's pause his rage flamed within him.

'I thought you were going out with me?' he said.

'I was. But, well, you see—'

She made the penitent mouth again, which had seemed so enchanting to him this afternoon.

'Oh, Hughie, don't you understand?' she said.

Hugh got up, feeling himself to be one shaking black jelly of wounded
anger.

'I'm not sure if I do,' he said. 'But no doubt I soon shall. Anyhow,
I want to ask you something. I want you to promise to marry me.'

She opened her great childlike eyes to their widest. Then they closed
into mere slits again as she broke out into a laugh.

'Marry you?' she said. 'You silly, darling fellow! That is a good joke.'

Suddenly from the garden there sounded the jubilant scamper of
running feet, and next moment a great grey ape sprang on to the
veranda beside them, and looked eagerly, with keen dog's eyes, at
Hugh, as if intent on obeying some yet unspoken command. Julia gave
a little shriek of fright and clung to him.

'Oh, that horrible animal!' she cried. 'Hughie, take care of me!'

Some sudden ray of illumination came to Hugh. All the extraordinary fantastic things that Rankin had said to him became sober
and real. And simultaneously the girl's clinging fingers on his arm
became like the touch of some poisonous, preying thing, snake-coil,
or suckers of an octopus, or hooked wings of a vampire shook and

trembled like a quicksand, but his conscious mind was quite clear and collected.

'Go away,' he said to the ape, and pointed into the garden, and it scampered off still gleefully spurning and kicking the soft sandy path. Then he quietly turned to the girl.

'There, it's gone,' he said. 'It was just some tame thing escaped. I saw it, or one like it, the other day on the end of a string. As for the horses, I shall be delighted to let you and Lord Paterson have them.' It is ten now; they will be round.'

The girl had quite recovered from her fright.

'Ah, Hughie, you are a dear,' she said. 'And you do understand?'

'Yes, perfectly,' he said.

Julia went to dress herself for riding, and presently Hugh saw them off from the gate, with courteous wishes for a pleasant ride. Then he went back to his bedroom and opened the little box where he kept his scarabs.

An hour later he was walking out alone on the road to Karnak, and in his pocket was the image of Tahu-met. He had formed no clear idea of what he was going to do; the immediate reason for his expedition was that once again he could not bear to lose sight of Julia and her companion. The moon was high, the feathery outline of palm-groves was clearly and delicately etched on the dark velvet of the heavens, and stars sat among their branches like specks of golden fruit. The caressing scent of bean-flowers was weighted over the road, and often he had to stand aside to let pass a troop of noisy tourists mounted on white donkeys, coming riotously home from the show-piece of Karnak by moonlight. Then, striking off the road, he passed beside the horse-shoe lake, in the depths of whose black waters the stars burned unwaveringly, and came by the entrance of the ruined temple of Mut. And then, with a stab of jealousy that screamed for its revenge, he saw, tied up to a pillar just within, his own horses. So *they* were here.

He gave the beasts a wide berth, lest, recognizing him, they should whinny and perhaps betray his presence, and, creeping in the shadow of the walls behind the row of great cat-headed statues, he stole into the inner court of the temple. Here for the first time he caught sight of the two at the far end of the enclosure, and as they turned, white-faced in the moonlight, he saw Paterson kiss the girl, and they stood there with neck and arms interlaced. Then they began walking towards him again, and he stepped into a dark chamber on his right to avoid meeting them.

It had that strange stale animal odour about it that hangs in Egyptian temples, and with a thrill of glee he saw, by a ray of moonlight that streamed in through the door, that by chance he had stepped into the shrine round which sit the dog-faced apes, whose secret name he knew, and whose controlling spell lay in his breast-pocket. Often he had felt the underworld horror that dwelt here, as a thing petrified and corpse-like; tonight it was petrified no longer, for the images seemed tense and quivering with the life that at any moment he could put into them. Their faces leered and hated and lusted, and all that demonic power, which seemed to be flowing into him from them, was his to use as he wished. Rankin's fantastic tales were bursting with reality; he knew with the certainty with which the night-watcher waits for the day, that the lordship of the spirit of apes, incarnate and discarnate, would descend on him as on some anointed king the moment he thrice pronounced the secret name. He was going to do it too; he knew that also, all he hesitated for now was to determine what orders the lord should give. It seemed that the image in his breast-pocket was aware, for it throbbed and vibrated against his chest like a boiling kettle.

He could not make up his mind what to do; but fed as with fuel by jealousy, and love, and hate, and revenge, suddenly his sense of the magical control he wielded could be resisted no longer, but boiled over, and he drew from his pocket the image where was engraven the secret name.

'Tahu-met, Tahu-met, Tahu-met,' he shouted aloud.

There was a moment's absolute stillness; then came a wild scream of fright from his horses, and he heard them gallop off madly into the night. Slowly, like a lamp turned down and then finally turned out, the blaze of the moon faded into utter darkness, and in that darkness, which whispered with a gradually increasing noise of scratchings and scamperings, he felt that the walls of the narrow chamber where he stood were, as in a dream, going farther and farther away from him, until, though still the darkness was impenetrable, he knew that he was standing in some immense space. One wall, he fancied, was still near him, close behind him, but the space which was full of he knew not what unseen presences, extended away and away to both sides of him and in front of him. Then he was aware that he was not standing, but sitting, for beneath his hands he could feel the arms as of some throne, of which the seat's edge pressed him just below his knees. The animal odour he had noticed before increased enormously in pungency, and he sniffed it in ecstatically, as if it had been the scent of beanfields, and mixed with it was the sweetness of incense and the savour as of roast meat. And at that the withdrawn light began to glow once more, only now it was not the whiteness of the moon, but a redder glow as of flames that aspired and sank again.

He saw where he was now. He was seated on a chair of pink granite, and a little in front of him was a huge altar, on which limbs smoked. Overhead was a low roof supported at intervals by painted pillars, and the whole of the vast floor was full of great grey apes, squatting in dense rows. Sometimes they all bowed their heads to the ground, sometimes, as by a signal, they raised them again, and myriads of obscene expectant eyes faced him. They glowed from within, as cat's eyes glow in the dusk, but with an infinity of hellish power. All that power was his to command, and he gloried in it.

'Bring them in,' he said, and no more. Indeed, he was not sure if he said it; it was just his thought.

But as if he spoke the soundless language of animals they understood, and they clambered and leaped over each other to do his bidding. Then a huddled wave of them surged up in front of where he sat, and as it broke in a foam of evil eyes and paws and switching tails, it disclosed the two whom he had ordered to be brought before him.

'And what shall I do with them?' he asked himself, cudgelling his monkey-brain for some infamous invention.

'Kiss each other,' he said at length, in order to inflame the brutality of his jealousy further, and he laughed chatteringly, as their white trembling lips met. He felt that all remnants of humanity were draining from him; there was but a little in his whole nature that could be deemed to belong to a man. A hundred awful schemes ran about through his brain, as sparks of fire run through the charred ashes of burnt paper.

And then Julia turned her face towards him. In the hideous entry that she had made in that wave of apes her hair had fallen down and streamed over her shoulders. And at that, the sight of a woman's hair unbound, the remnant of his manhood, all that was not submerged in the foulness of his supreme apehood, made one tremendous appeal to him, like some final convulsion of the dying, and at the bidding of that impulse his hands came together and snapped the image in two.

Something screamed; the whole temple yelled with it, and mixed with it was a roaring in his ears as of great waters or hurricane winds. He stamped on the broken image, grinding it to powder below his heel, and felt the ground and the temple walls rocking round him.

Then he heard someone not far off speaking in human voice again, and no music could be so sweet.

'Let's get out of the place, darling,' it said. 'That was an earthquake, and the horses have bolted.'

He heard running steps outside, which gradually grew fainter. The moon shone whitely into the little chamber with the grotesque stone apes, and at his feet was the powdered blue glaze and baked white clay of the image he had ground to dust.

SIR ROGER DE COVERLEY

CONSIDERING that it was Christmas Eve, the weather was almost portentous: not only were 'the oldest inhabitants' (whose memory had quite gone) unable to remember anything like it at this time of the year, but even the young and the middle-aged, with faculties unimpaired, could recollect nothing of the sort. All the way down in the train I had looked on to fields sparkling with snow under a gay sun: I had passed frozen water populated with skaters, and now stepping out at the small station there was a sunset red and frosty, and holly bushes by the roadside covered with berries. In the village I saw a poulterer's shop full of fat turkeys, and as I passed the church the bells broke out into a merry peal... I muttered to myself, 'It is all the fault of Charles Dickens. Seventy years ago he invented an English Christmas like this, and now it has come true. Nature would never have thought of it by herself.'

The house to which I was bound lay a mile on the further side of the little Sussex town. My brother-in-law with whom I was to spend the festivity had bought it six months ago, but I had never yet seen it, and all I knew of it was that it had once been a coaching-inn, and that the photographs of it which my sister Margery had sent me showed a big square Georgian front, and within large panelled rooms. 'We're settling in now,' she had said in the letter which accompanied these, 'and you must come down for Christmas. Everything will be ready by then, central-heating, electric light, and bathrooms. Tony is absolutely in love with it, and swears he will never go away any more till he leaves it in his coffin. He has a lovely room for his work, and all his apparatus is installed. Rumours of a ghost, and stories of lights

seen in the big parlour, but we fear there is no truth in them. . .' There
had followed another note a few days ago to say that I was to travel
from London by the 3.15 on December 24th, and this I had done.

The motor gave a hoot, skidded and slewed, and drew up with
its back to the front door. The hoot had been heard, and before I
could ring the bell Tony had come out. I stepped into a big hall—
bigger, oddly enough, than it had appeared in the photograph—and
there was Margery sitting on the floor making wreaths out of evergreens.

'I must get up cautiously,' she said, 'because there's a mine-field
of holly all round me. I am glad to see you.'

Charles Dickens had evidently penetrated indoors.

'But why holly?' I asked. 'Why evergreens? Pure Charles Dickens.'

'I know. It's Tony's idea. I'll tell you all about it, and you must be
pleasant. . . Let's go and have tea at once in the parlour.'

She got up and took my arm. From the time she was a child, she
has always taken my arm when she wanted me to do something for
her, or acquiesce in something she had done.

'Tell me what you want, then?' I asked. 'I don't promise to do it.'

'Want? I want nothing except that you should enjoy yourself,' said
she, 'and enter into what we've planned for tomorrow. Dickens, you
know. We're going to have a Dickens-Christmas. Church in the
morning, and far too much to eat at lunch. Then we're going to skate
till it's dark, and have a Christmas tree for the school-children. Then
games. Then too much to eat again at dinner, and mistletoe: you shall
kiss me. And—and Tony's found out what wassail is, and we shall have
a bowl of it afterwards.'

'But why? What for? What's the point?' I asked. 'It will only make
us extremely cross and tired, and liverish.'

'Oh, but it musn't. It would spoil it all if it did. There's a purpose
in our revels. But come and have tea anyhow, and you shall see the
big parlour.' She opened the door and clicked on the lights. 'Isn't it
divine?' she said. 'I adore a big room. In the days when the gentry
used to stop at home and live in their nice houses in the country, in-
steady of going up to London and stuffing themselves into pill-boxes,
it used to be the ballroom of the neighbourhood. All the folk living
round used to give dances here. It's seventy feet long, and we're going
to keep it almost empty. Just this little encampment round the fire,
and the dark polished floor stretching away for ever, and thick red curtains over the windows. So nice for the old folk if they look in again.

They always had a dance here on Christmas night, and those who lived far away stayed till morning.'

A sentence in Margery's letter came into my mind.

'Margery, this is the room where the lights are seen,' I said.

'It ought to be, but I'm sorry to say they are not seen,' she said, 'unless we turn them on. But, perhaps if—'

I interrupted.

'I begin to see,' I said. 'You want to martyrize us all with an old-fashioned Christmas, and games and gluttony to make an atmosphere. Don't deny it. You've got the snow and the frost outside, and you think that if you complete it within you'll have the stage set. I never heard such nonsense in my life. And how a materialistic scientist like you, Tony, can lend yourself to such foolery, I can't imagine.'

Tony had established himself in the chair opposite me, and was gazing in his far-away manner at the fire.

'It's just because I'm so materialistic,' he said. 'Yes, just that.'

'Oh, do explain yourself,' I said.

He sat up.

'Obvious,' he said. 'I am quite convinced that there's nothing in this world which has ever been heard or seen or felt that would not be capable of a materialistic explanation if we only knew enough. I'll give you an illustration of what I mean. Let us suppose that you and Margery are living a hundred years ago, and that I am living now, with all the inventions and discoveries of today. I turn on my wireless, and you hear the bells of Malines. Or I point up to the sky, and you see people flying. Or I ring up the poulterer's shop in the village and say to the little black trumpet of my telephone that a turkey is to be sent round at once, and round it comes. What would you make of that, you two people of 1827? You would say it was magical, supernatural. But you would be quite wrong: it is purely scientific—a phenomenon perfectly in accordance with the appliance of certain natural laws, which had not been discovered in your day. Do you grant that?'

'Of course. But what then?'

'This. What is the greatest discovery of all during the last century? One far bigger than aviation or X-rays—namely, the discovery that time is a dimension. Just as in a box, or a room, or a teacup there is length, breadth, and height, so there is also time. And just as that wireless will make audible in this room a noise that is going on many miles off, so it will not be long before we have a machine that will bring to us what happened many years before in time, or what will happen years hence. Don't get hold of the notion that we shall travel through time, for that's a great mistake; we shall remain here in time, and the machine will bring us what in time is far off, just as the wireless brings us what in space is far off. We don't go to Malines to hear the carillon; the carillon comes to us. Perhaps, more accurately, I should say that the carillon is here all the time, but we materialize it to our senses. So, too, is the past here all the time.'

He paused a moment, and, quite involuntarily, I peered into the dim light of the room, conscious that my eye had caught sight of something moving there. But there was nothing: the light gleaming on the polished boards no doubt had given me the impression. Tony's quiet, persuasive voice continued:

'It is quite simple really, when once you grasp the idea,' he said. 'For instance, there is a whole class of phenomena which imaginative people call psychical, but which are really as materialistic as mutton. Things like ghosts and premonitions: they are far too well attested for any but the most wooden-headed scientists to deny them, but just because they can't explain them, they lose their tempers and refer them to imagination or lobster-cutlets or coincidence. But when once you grasp the idea of time as a dimension, you will understand that if you see a ghost, some faded image of what has been, faint and transparent, has come along the etheric time-waves, just as a sound comes to you on the wireless from a distance on the etheric space waves. The latter comes to you from a distance in space, the other from a distance in time. Or, supposing you see in a dream something which actually hapens some days later, its image has come to you out of time, but out of future instead of past time. But to say that ghosts or spirits, or that premonitions are supernatural is almost certainly to make the same mistake as the man a hundred years ago would have made, if he had called the telephone a supernatural thing. We know now that it's nothing of the sort.'

Tony, as always, was admirably lucid in his statement of theory. But an objection to his application of it, at any rate, occurred to me.

'But I understand we are to eat too much tomorrow,' I said, 'and get prickled by pieces of holly falling from Margery's wreath in order to produce an atmosphere. If the time-waves are there, and something out of the past can travel to us along them, how does it help if I get indigestion?'

Tony laughed.

'It doesn't,' he said, 'but it's possible that if we reproduce as well

as we can the conditions in which the people round here came and
danced in this room on Christmas night, we may make the atmos-
pherics, as we call them in wireless, favourable to transmission.'

'And is this what you are working at?' I asked.

'Rather. Getting along famously, too. As far as Margery and I are
concerned, we've had no results at all. But things are happening: my
chauffeur distinctly heard something out of the past the other day, when
the machine was working.'

'What was that?' I asked.

He considered a moment.

'I think I won't tell you,' he said, 'because I'll show you the machine
presently, and you'll see if you can perceive anything. It might set your
imagination to work if I told you what happened to my chauffeur.'

'But surely if things are coming through from the past,' I said,
'they're perceptible to everybody.'

'Not necessarily. The personal human element comes in there. Some
people can hear a bat squeak, but others can't. So also some people
can see ghosts, which they call the spirits, but most people can't. Just
as some sound-waves reach a few people, but not most, so the time-
waves reach a few people, and they see or hear something out of the
past. When we get better machines, no doubt they will be perceptible
to everybody.'

I must confess that all this sounded very fanciful, and it was with
no expectations at all that presently I followed Tony into his work-room.
A big machine, all wires and wheels and cylinders and batteries stood
in the middle of the room, and he turned a handle here, and adjusted
a screw there, and finally tugged a lever over. There came a crackling
noise like that emitted by X-rays, and below it a soft, continuous hum.

'It's working,' said Tony. 'Now, listen carefully.'

We sat there in silence for perhaps a couple of minutes. And then
I quite distinctly heard Tony's voice say, 'Listen very carefully.'

For the moment I had no doubt in my mind that it was he who had
repeated this injunction, in a voice lower and softer than that in which
he had said it first.

'Yes, I am listening,' I said.

He jumped to his feet.

'Ha! Did you hear something, then?' he asked.

'You said for the second time, "Listen very carefully." '

'No; I only said it once. That's interesting, extremely interesting.
Now, I'll tell you about my chauffeur. He came in here the other day

when the machine was working, and, out of the blue said to me, 'I did, sir, last Monday.' I asked him what he meant, and he looked astonished. He thought I had told him, as I had done a week before, to order some new tyres.'

'But it's mad stuff,' said I. 'He heard what you had said a week ago, and I heard what you had said two minutes ago. And you heard nothing on either occasion?'

'Not a whisper. But it is not mad. We're just feeling our way, and of course the machine is a rough, ramshackle affair, ill-regulated and ill-adjusted. But we're on the right track.'

'Explain to me something about it,' I cried.

He laughed.

'Before I had said two sentences, you wouldn't have the smallest idea what I was talking about,' he said. 'Now, let's have another try.'

For half an hour more we sat there; the machine crackled and hummed, but no result of any sort arrived. It was time then to dress for dinner, and we went upstairs.

The evening passed tranquilly, and I woke next morning after a long, sound sleep with the conviction that I had been dreaming very vividly, but not one incident or scene of these nocturnal adventures could I remember. I only knew that there had been gaiety and movement and laughter, and even this impression was speedily swallowed up in the knowledge that it was Christmas Day, and that an intolerable round of gaiety and movement was ordained for me. This gloomy outlook was amply justified: active and uproarious diversions succeeded each other with bewildering rapidity. We fell about on the ice, we decked a Christmas tree, we sang carols and played games with a regiment of highly-polished children from the village, and it was not till seven o'clock that night that the continuous festal vortex subsided. The children slid and snowballed their way back to their homes. Margery went up to her bedroom to lie down, Tony slinked off to his machine, and I was left to sprawl in a chair in the big parlour till dinner-time.

Suddenly something, white and in motion, caught my eye at the far end of the dusky room. Before I could look directly at it, it was gone; it fluttered away like a butterfly, vanishing into shadow. Simultaneously, I smelt the fragrance of lavender, and even while I wondered why there should be the smell of lavender here, that was gone too. Then came very faintly to my ear a musical note as of a thrummed string of a violin . . . All these were faint impressions, echoes of impressions, one might call them, and then Tony entered.

With his entrance all the odd little stirrings that had moved about in my solitude were dispersed, and no faintest hint of them returned during the rest of the evening. We dined; we listened to some throaty waits singing 'Good King Wenceslas,' and we looked with dismay on Tony's wassail. Small red apples bobbed about in it, and he ladled it out into thick glasses. Margery took one sip of it.

'My dear, if that's wassail, I would sooner die of thirst,' she said.

'Nonsense; it's delicious,' said Tony, tasting it. 'Dear me, I wonder if they really drank much of it...'

Margery yawned, I yawned, we all yawned, and the debilitated procession went sadly to bed. But, after all, it only came once a year.

I went to sleep instantly, stupefied with fatigue, and woke, knowing that some noise had roused me. Someone had tapped on my door, and my thoughts instantly went back to the wassail which I had been prudent enough not to taste, and I wondered if either of the others had been taken ill. No entry came in answer to my response bidding the knocker to come in, and then the noise came again, just that sharp tapping which had awakened me. But now I perceived that it was not a knocking on my door, but the footstep of someone passing down the polished oak-boards of the corridor. It died away, and then was suddenly renewed.

I sat up in bed, and tried to puzzle this out. Three people had walked past my door, and who on earth could they be? The passage must be lit, for the steps were brisk and firm, as of folk moving confidently, and the brilliant idea struck me to open my door and see. I turned on the light in my bedroom and looked out. But the passage was absolutely dark. Even as I stood there another step came. It started from some distance off; it grew louder as it approached, and it crossed the oblong of bright light thrown across the passage from my open door. There accompanied it, quite audibly, the rustle of a dress, but my eyes looked in vain to see who it was that had passed within a foot or two of me.

I was far too much interested to be frightened, and indeed it definitely occurred to me that these invisible folk who stepped so lightly on some unconjecturable errand, were full of gaiety and good-will.

I put on a dressing-gown and a pair of slippers, and went to the head of the stairs. There was a switch there somewhere, but I could not find it, and indeed I perceived that I did not need more light, for there now came from below a soft radiance as of candles. As I turned the corner of the stairs I saw what caused this illumination, for the embers of the wood-fire still glowed in the open hearth. But the hall was quite empty, though the air was now full of those distant voices. Then suddenly they were overscored by the sound of violins: the rhythm caught my ear first, and then the tune, and the tune was 'Sir Roger de Coverley.' It came from the big parlour, the door of which was shut.

I crept across the hall and feeling for the handle of the door, threw it open. A blaze of light poured out, and with it the louder sound of music. Up the centre of the room, from the door to the far distant end, stretched two lines of people, men on one side, women on the other. . . And then I became aware that I was looking into darkness. There had been just that flash of perceptive sound and sight together, and now it had gone.

I found my way back to my room, but with difficulty, for the light which I felt sure I had left burning was out. I supposed some wire had fused, for the switch was still on.

I was very late for breakfast next morning. Tony had finished and had gone to his beloved machine, but Margery had stayed behind to give me her companionship.

'Such an odd thing happened last night,' she said. 'When the house-maid went into the big parlour to light the fire, she found that all the furniture had been moved to the sides of the room, as if to clear it for a dance. And both Tony and I woke in the night and thought we heard dance-music going on. I wanted him to get up and explore, and he wanted me to. So we both went to sleep again.'

'Wassail,' said I.

'Yes; but no amount of wassail would move tables and chairs about. Did you hear anything?'

Tony came in.

'Ha! down at last!' he said. 'Do you know, I must have done a most absurd thing yesterday evening. I left the machine working, instead of turning it off. It must have run till the current was exhausted. It uses up the deuce of a lot.'

'And would it stop quite suddenly?' I asked.

'Yes: and any electric light there was on in the house would have gone out. Probably it ran till about three in the morning.'

'Sit down, Tony,' said I, 'and listen to my story. About a quarter to three last night. . .'

THE CHINA BOWL

I HAD long been on the look-out for one of the small houses at the south end of that delectable oblong called Barrett's Square, but for many months there was never revealed to me that which I so much desired to see—namely, a notice-board advertising that one of these charming little abodes was to be let.

At length, however, in the autumn of the current year, in one of my constant passages through the square, I saw what my eye had so long starved for, and within ten minutes I was in the office of the agent in whose hands the disposal of No. 29 had been placed.

A communicative clerk informed me that the present lessee, Sir Arthur Bassenthwaite, was anxious to get rid of the remainder of his lease as soon as possible, for the house had painful associations for him, owing to the death of his wife, which had taken place there not long before. He was a wealthy man, so I was informed, Lady Bassenthwaite having been a considerable heiress, and was willing to take what is professionally known as a ridiculously low price, in order to get the house off his hand without delay. An order 'to view' was thereupon given me, and a single visit next morning was sufficient to show that this was precisely what I had been looking for.

Why Sir Arthur should be so suddenly anxious to get rid of it, at a price which certainly was extremely moderate, was no concern of mine, provided the drains were in good order, and within a week the necessary business connected with the transference of the lease was arranged. The house was in excellent repair, and less than a month from the time I had first seen the notice-board up, I was ecstatically established there.

I had not been in the house more than a week or two when, one afternoon, I was told that Sir Arthur had called, and would like to see me if I was disengaged. He was shown up, and I found myself in the presence of one of the most charming men I have ever had the good fortune to meet.

The motive of his call, it appeared, was of the politest nature, for he wished to be assured that I found the house comfortable and that it suited me. He intimated that it would be a pleasure to him to see round, and together we went over the whole house, with the exception of one room. This was the front bedroom on the third floor, the largest of the two spare rooms, and at the door, as I grasped the handle, he stopped me.

'You will excuse me,' he said, 'for not coming in here. The room, I may tell you, has the most painful associations for me.'

This was sufficiently explicit; I made no doubt that it was in this room that his wife had died.

It was a lovely October afternoon, and, having made the tour of the house, we went out into the little garden with its tiled walk that lay at the back, and was one of the most attractive features of the place. Low brick walls enclosed it, separating it on each side from my neighbours, and at the bottom from the pedestrian thoroughfare that ran past the back of the row of houses.

Sir Arthur lingered here some little while, lost, I suppose, in regretful memories of the days when perhaps he and his companion planned and executed the decoration of the little plot. Indeed, he hinted as much when, shortly after, he took his leave.

'There is so much here,' he said, 'that is very intimately bound up with me. I thank you a thousand times for letting me see the little garden again.'

And once more, as he turned to go into the house, his eyes looked steadfastly and wistfully down the bright borders.

The regulations about the lighting of houses in London had some little while previously demanded a more drastic dusk, and a night or two later, as I returned home after dinner through the impenetrable obscurity of the streets, I was horrified to find a bright light streaming cheerfully from the upper windows in my house, with no blinds to obscure it.

It came from the front bedroom on the third floor, and, letting myself in, I proceeded hurriedly upstairs to quench this forbidden glow. But when I entered, I found the room in darkness, and, on turning up

the lights myself, I saw that the blinds were drawn down, so that even
if it had been lit, I could not have seen from outside the illumination
which had made me hasten upstairs.

An explanation easily occurred to me: no doubt the light I had seen
did not come from my house, but from windows of a house adjoining.
I had only given one glance at it, and with this demonstration that
I had been mistaken, I gave no further conscious thought to the matter.
But subconsciously I felt that I knew that I had made no mistake: I
had not in that hurried glance confused the windows of the house next
door with my own; it was this room that had been lit.

I had moved into the house, as I have said, with extraordinary expedition, and for the next day or two I was somewhat busily engaged, after
my day's work was over, in sorting out and largely destroying accumula-
tions of old books and papers, which I had not had time to go through
before my move. Among them I came across an illustrated magazine
which I had kept for some forgotten reason, and turning over the pages
to try to ascertain why I had preserved it, I suddenly came across a
picture of my own back-garden. The title at the top of the page showed
me that the article in question was an interview with Lady Bassenthwaite, and her portrait and that of her husband made a frontispiece
to it.

The coincidence was a curious one, for here I read about the house
which I now occupied, and saw what it had been like in the reign of
its late owners. But I did not spend long over it, and added the magazine to the pile of papers destined for destruction. This grew steadily,
and when I had finished turning out the cupboard which I had resolved
to empty before going to bed, I found it was already an hour or more
past midnight.

I had been so engrossed in my work that I had let the fire go out,
and myself get hungry, and went into the dining-room, which opened
into the little back-garden, to see if the fire still smouldered there, and
a biscuit could be found in the cupboard. In both respects I was in
luck, and whilst eating and warming myself, I suddenly thought I heard
a step on the tiled walk in the garden outside.

I quickly went to the window and drew aside the thick curtain, letting all the light in the room pour out into the garden, and there,
beyond doubt, was a man bending over one of the beds. Startled by
this illumination, he rose, and without looking round, ran to the end
of the little yard and, with surprising agility, vaulted on to the top of
the wall and disappeared.

But at the last second, as he sat silhouetted there, I saw his face in the shaded light of a gas-lamp outside, and, to my indescribable astonishment, I recognized Sir Arthur Bassenthwaite. The glimpse was instantaneous, but I was sure I was not mistaken, any more than I had been mistaken about the light which came from the bedroom that looked out on to the square.

But whatever tender associations Sir Arthur had with the garden that had once been his, it was not seemly that he should adopt such means of indulging them. Moreover, where Sir Arthur might so easily come, there, too, might others whose intentions were less concerned with sentiment than with burglary.

In any case, I did not choose that my garden should have such easy access from outside, and next morning I ordered a pretty stiff barrier of iron spikes to be erected along the outer wall. If Sir Arthur wished to muse in the garden, I should be delighted to give him permission, as, indeed, he must have known from the cordiality which I was sure I showed him when he called, but this method of his seemed to me irregular. And I observed next evening, without any regret at all, that my order had been promptly executed. At the same time I felt an invincible curiosity to know for certain if it was merely for the sake of a solitary midnight vigil that he had come.

I was expecting the arrival of my friend Hugh Grainger the next week, to stay a night or two with me, and since the front spare room, which I proposed to give him, had not at present been slept in, I gave orders that a bed should be made up there the next night for me, so that I could test with my own vile body whether a guest would be comfortable there.

This can only be proved by personal experience. Though there may be a table apparently convenient to the head of the bed, though the dressing-table may apparently be properly disposed, though it seem as if the lighting was rightly placed for reading in bed, and for the quenching of it afterwards without disturbance, yet practice and not theory is the only method of settling such questions, and next night accordingly I both dressed for dinner in this front spare room, and went to bed there.

Everything seemed to work smoothly; the room itself had a pleasant and restful air about it, and the bed exceedingly comfortable, I fell asleep almost as soon as I had put out the electric light, which I had found adequate for reading small print. To the best of my knowledge, neither the thought of the last occupant of the room nor of the light that I believed I had seen burning there one night entered my head at all.

I fell asleep, as I say, at once, but instantly that theatre of the brain, on the boards of which dreams are transacted, was brightly illuminated for me, and the curtain went up on one of those appalling nightmare-pieces which we can only vaguely remember afterwards.

There was the sense of flight—clogged, impotent flight from before some hideous spiritual force—the sense of powerlessness to keep away from the terror that gained on me, the strangling desire to scream, and soon the blessed dawning consciousness that it was but with a dream that I wrestled.

I began to know that I was lying in bed, and that my terrors were imaginary, but the trouble was not over yet, for with all my efforts I could not raise my head from the pillow nor open my eyes.

Then, as I drew nearer to the boundaries of waking, I became aware that even when the spell of my dream was altogether broken I should not be free. For through my eyelids, which I knew had closed in a darkened room, there now streamed in a vivid light, and remembering for the first time what I had seen from the square outside, I knew that when I opened them they would look out on to a lit room, peopled with who knew what phantoms of the dead or living.

I lay there for a few moments after I had recovered complete consciousness, with eyes still closed, and felt the trickle of sweat on my forehead. That horror I knew was not wholly due to the self-coined nightmare of my brain; it was the horror of expectancy more than of retrospect. And then curiosity, sheer stark curiosity, to know what was happening on the other side of the curtain of my eyelids prevailed, and I sat and looked.

In the armchair just opposite the foot of my bed sat Lady Bassenthwaite, whose picture I had seen in the illustrated magazine. It simply was she; there could be no doubt whatever about it. She was dressed in a bedgown, and in her hand was a small fluted china bowl with a cover and a saucer. As I looked she took the cover off, and began to feed herself with a spoon. She took some half-dozen mouthfuls, and then replaced the cover again. As she did this she turned full face towards where I lay, looking straight at me, and already the shadow of death was fallen on her. Then she rose feebly, wearily, and took a step towards the bed. As she did this, the light in the room, from whatever source it came, suddenly faded, and I found myself looking out into impenetrable darkness.

My curiosity for the present was more than satisfied, and in a couple of minutes I had transferred myself to the room below.

Hugh Grainger, the ruling passion of whose life is crime and ghosts, arrived next day, and I poured into an eager ear the whole history of the events here narrated.

'Of course, I'll sleep in the room,' he said at the conclusion. 'Put another bed in it, can't you, and sleep there, too. A couple of simultaneous witnesses of the same phenomena are ten times more valuable than one. Or do you funk?' he added as a kind afterthought.

'I funk, but I will,' I said.

'And are you sure it wasn't all part of your dream?' he asked.

'Absolutely positive.'

Hugh's eye glowed with pleasure.

'I funk, too,' he said. 'I funk horribly. But that's part of the allurement. It's so difficult to get frightened nowadays. All but a few things are explained and accounted for. What one fears is the unknown. No one knows yet what ghosts are, or why they appear, or to whom.'

He took a turn up and down the room.

'And what do you make of Sir Arthur creeping into your garden at night?' he asked. 'Is there any possible connection?'

'Not as far as I can see. What connection could there be?'

'It isn't very obvious certainly. I really don't know why I asked. And you liked him?'

'Immensely. But not enough to let him get over my garden wall at midnight,' said I.

Hugh laughed.

'That would certainly imply a considerable degree of confidence and affection,' he said.

I had caused another bed to be moved into Hugh's room, and that night, after he had put out the light, we talked awhile and then relapsed into silence. It was cold, and I watched the fire on the hearth die down from flame into glowing coal, and from glow into clinkering ash, while nothing disturbed the peaceful atmosphere of the quiet room. Then it seemed to me as if something broke in, and instead of lying tranquilly awake, I found a certain horror of expectancy, some note of nightmare begin to hum through my waking consciousness. I heard Hugh toss and turn and turn again, and at length he spoke.

'I say, I'm feeling fairly beastly,' he said, 'and yet there's nothing to see or hear.'

'Same with me,' said I.

'Do you mind if I turn up the light a minute, and have a look round?' he asked.

'Not a bit.'

He fumbled at the switch, the room leapt into light, and he sat up in bed frowning. Everything was quite as usual, the bookcase, the chairs, on one of which he had thrown his clothes; there was nothing that differentiated this room from hundreds of others where the occupants lay quietly sleeping.

'It's queer,' he said, and switched off the light again.

There is nothing harder than to measure time in the dark, but I do not think it was long that I lay there with the sense of nightmare growing momentarily on me before he spoke again in an odd, cracked voice.

'It's coming,' he said.

Almost as soon as he spoke I saw that the thick darkness of the room was sensibly thinning. The blackness was less complete, though I could hardly say that light began to enter. Then by degrees I saw the shape of chairs, the lines of the fireplace, the end of Hugh's bed begin to outline themselves, and as I watched the darkness vanished altogether, as if a lamp had been turned up. And in the chair at the foot of Hugh's bed sat Lady Bassenthwaite, and again putting aside the cover of her dish, she sipped the contents of the bowl, and at the end rose feebly, wearily, as in mortal sickness. She looked at Hugh, and turning, she looked at me, and through the shadow of death that lay over her face, I thought that in her eyes was a demand, or at least a statement of her case. They were not angry, they did not cry for justice, but the calm inexorable gaze of justice that must be done was there. . . Then the light faded and died out.

I heard a rustle from the other bed and the springs creaked.

'Good Lord,' said Hugh, 'where's the light?'

His fingers fumbled and found it, and I saw that he was already out of bed, with streaming forehead and chattering teeth.

'I know now,' he said. 'I half guessed before. Come downstairs.'

Downstairs we went, and he turned up all the passage lights as we passed. He led the way into the dining room, picking up the poker and the shovel as he went by the fireplace, and he threw open the door into the garden. I switched up the light, which threw a bright square of illumination over the garden.

'Where did you see Sir Arthur?' he said. 'Where? Exactly where?'

Still not guessing what he sought, I pointed out to him the spot, and loosening the earth with the poker, he dug into the bed. Once again he plunged the poker down, and as he removed the earth I heard the shovel grate on something hard. And then I guessed.

Already Hugh was at work with his fingers in the earth, and slowly and carefully he drew out fragments of a broken china cover. Then, delving again, he raised from the hole a fluted china bowl. And I knew I had seen it before, once and twice.

We carried this indoors and cleaned the earth from it. All over the bottom of the bowl was a layer of some thick porridge-like substance, and a portion of this I sent next day to a chemist, asking him for his analysis of it. The basis of it proved to be oatmeal, and in it was mixed a considerable quantity of arsenic.

Hugh and I were together in my little sitting room close to the front door, where on the table stood the china bowl with the fragments of its cover and saucer, when this report was brought to us, and we read it together. The afternoon was very dark and we stood close to the window to decipher the minute handwriting, when there passed the figure of Sir Arthur Bassenthwaite. He saw me, waved his hand, and a moment afterwards the front door bell rang.

'Let him come in,' said Hugh. 'Let him see that on the table.'

Next moment my servant entered, and asked if the caller might see me.

'Let him see it,' repeated Hugh. 'The chances are that we shall know if he sees it unexpectedly.'

There was a moment's pause while in the hall, I suppose, Sir Arthur was taking off his coat. Outside, some few doors off, a traction engine, which had passed a minute before, stopped, and began slowly coming backwards again, crunching the newly-laid stones. Sir Arthur entered.

'I ventured to call,' he began, and then his glance fell on the bowl. In one second the very aspect of humanity was stripped from his face. His mouth drooped open, his eyes grew monstrous and protruding, and what had been the pleasant, neat-featured face of a man was a mask of terror, a gargoyle, a nightmare countenance. Even before the door that had been open to admit him was closed, he had turned and gone with a crouching, stumbling run from the room, and I heard him at the latch of the front door.

Whether what followed was design or accident, I shall never know, for from the window I saw him fall forward, almost as if he threw him-

self there, straight in front of the broad crunching wheels of the traction engine, and before the driver could stop, or even think of stopping, the iron roller had gone over his head.

THE PASSENGER

On a certain Tuesday night during last October I was going home down war-darkened Piccadilly on the top of a westering bus. It still wanted a few minutes to eleven o'clock, the theatres had not yet disgorged their audiences, and I was quite alone up aloft, though inside the vehicle was full to repletion. But the chilliness of the evening and a certain bitter quality in the south-east wind accounted for this, and also led me to sit on the hindmost of the seats, close to the stairs, where my back was defended from the bite of the draught by the protective knife-board.

I had barely taken my seat when an incident that for the moment just a little startled me occurred, for I thought I felt something (or somebody) push by me, brushing lightly against my right arm and leg. This impression was vivid enough to make me look round, expecting a fellow-passenger or perhaps the conductor. We were just passing underneath a shaded lamp in the middle of the street when this happened, and I perceived, without any doubt whatever, that my nerves or a sudden draught must have deceived my senses into imagining this, for there was nobody there. But, though I did not give two further thoughts to this impression, I knew that at that moment my pleasurable anticipations from this dark and keen-aired progression had vanished, and, with rather bewildering suddenness, a mood uneasy and ominous had taken possession of me.

I did not, as far as I am aware, make in the smallest degree any mental connection between this sense of being brushed against by something unseen and the vanishing of the contented mood. I put the one down to imagination, the other to the desolate twilight of the streets and the inclemency of the night. A falling barometer portended storm, there had been disquieting news from the Western battleline that afternoon, and those causes seemed sufficient (or nearly sufficient) to account for the sudden dejection that had taken hold of me. And yet, even as I told myself that these were causes enough, I knew that there was another symptom in my disquietude for which they did not account.

This was the sense that I had suddenly been brought into touch with something that lay outside the existing world as I had known it two minutes before. There was something more in my surroundings than could be accounted for by eye and ear. I heard the boom and rattle of the bus as we roared down the decline of Piccadilly, I saw the shaded lamps, the infrequent pedestrians, the tall houses with blinds drawn down according to regulations, for fear of enemy aircraft, and soon across the sky were visible the long luminous pencils cast on to the mottled floor of clouds overhead by the searchlights at Hyde Park Corner; but I knew that none of these, these wars and rumours of wars, entirely accounted for my sudden and fearful alacrity of soul. There was something else; it was as if in a darkened room I had been awakened by the tingling noise of a telephone bell, had been torn from sleep by it, as if some message was even now coming through from unseen and discarnate realms. And on the moment I saw that I was not alone on the top of the bus.

There was someone with his back to me on the seat right in front. For a second or two he was sharply silhouetted against the lamps of a motor coming down the hill towards us, and I could see that he sat with heat bent forward and coat-collar turned up. And at that instant I knew that it was this figure unaccountably appearing there that caused the telephone-tingle in my brain. It was not merely that it had appeared there when I was certain that I was the sole passenger up on the top; had the roof been crowded in every seat I should have known that one of those heads, that belonging to the man who sat leaning forward, was not of this world as represented by the tall houses, the searchlight beams, the other passengers. Then, mixed up with this horror of the spirit, there came to me also a feeling of intense and invincible curiosity. I had penetrated again into the psychical world, into the realm of the unseen and real existences that surround us.

Precisely then, while those impressions took form and coherence in my mind, the conductor came up the stairs. Simultaneously the bell sounded, and as the bus slackened speed and stopped, he leant over the side by me, so that I saw his face very clearly. In another moment he stamped, signalling the driver to go on again, and turned to me with hand out for my fare. He punched a two-penny ticket for me, and then walked forward along the gangway towards the front seat where the unexplained passenger sat. But halfway there he stopped and turned back again.

'Funny thing, sir,' he said. 'I thought I saw another fare sitting there.'

He turned to go down the stairs, and, watching him, I saw, just before his head vanished, that he looked forward again along the roof, shading his eyes with his hand. Then he came back a couple of steps, still look-ing forward, then finally turned and left me alone on the top there—or not quite alone. . .

After leaving Hyde Park Corner a somewhat grosser darkness per-vaded the streets, but still I believed that I could see faintly the outline of the bowed head of the man who sat on the front seat of the bus. But in that dim, uncertain light, flecked with odd shadows, I felt that my certainty that it was still there faded, as I strained my eyes to pierce the ambient dimness.

Looking forward eagerly and intently then, I was suddenly startled again by the feeling that somebody (or something) brushed by me. Instantly I started to my feet, and with one step got to the head of the stairs leading down. Certainly there was no one on them, and equally certainly there was no one now on the front seat, or on any other seat.

A fine rain had begun to fall, blown stingingly by the wind that was increasing every moment, and having completely satisfied myself that there was no one there, I descended from the top of the bus to go inside if there was a seat to be had.

I was delayed, still standing on the stairs, by the stream of passen-gers leaving the bus, and when I got down to the ground floor I found that as I had had the top to myself on the first part of my journey, I was to enjoy an untenanted interior now. I sat close to the door, and presently beckoned to the conductor.

'Did anyone leave the top of the bus,' I asked, 'just before we stopped here?'

He looked at me sideways a little curiously.

'Not as I know of, sir,' he said.

We drew up, and a number of cheerful soldiers invaded the place.

For some reason I could not get the thought of this dim, inconclusive experience out of my head. It was not at all impossible that all I had seen—namely, the head and shoulders of a man seated on the front bench of the bus—was accounted for by the tricky shadows and veiled light of the streets; or, again, it was within the bounds of possibility that in the darkness a real living man might have come up there, and in the same confusion of shade and local illumination have left again.

It was conceivable also that the same queer lights and shadows deceived the conductor even as they had deceived me; while, as for the brushing against my arm and leg, which I thought I had twice experienced, that might possibly have been the stir and eddy of some draught on this windy night buffeting round the corner by the stairs. And yet with every desire to think reasonably about it, I could not make myself believe that this was all. Deep down in me I knew I was convinced that what I had seen and felt was not on the ordinary planes of perceptible things. Furthermore, I knew that there was more connected with that figure on the front seat that should sometime be revealed to me. What it was I had no idea, but the sense that more was coming, some development which I felt sure would be tragic and terrible, while it filled me with some befogged and nightmarish horror, yet inspired me with an invincible curiosity.

Accordingly, next evening I stationed myself at the place where I had boarded this particular bus some quarter of an hour before the time that it passed there the previous night. It appeared probable that the phantom, whatever it was, was local; that it might appear again (as in a haunted house) on the bus on which I had seen it before. I guessed, furthermore, that, its habitat being a particular bus, the locality of its appearance otherwise was between the Ritz Hotel and the top of Sloane Street.

My knowledge of the organization of the traffic service was *nil*, it was but guesswork that led me to suppose that the conductor would be on the same bus tonight as that on which he had been the evening before. And, after waiting ten minutes or so, I saw him.

Tonight the bus was moderately full both inside and on the top, and it was with a certain sense of comfort that I found myself gregariously placed. The front seat where it had sat before, however, was empty, and I placed myself on the seat immediately behind.

Just on my right were a man in khaki and a girl, uproariously cheerful. The sound of human talk and laughter made an encouraging music, but in spite of that, I felt some undefined and chilly fear creeping over me as we bounced down the dip of Piccadilly, while I kept my eyes steadily on the vacant couple of seats in front of me. And then I felt something brush by me, and, turning my head to look, saw nothing that could account for it. But when I looked in front of me again, I saw that on the vacant seat there was sitting a man with coat collar turned up and head bent forward. He was not in the act of sitting down—he was there.

We stopped at that moment at Hyde Park Corner; the rain had begun to fall more heavily, and I saw that all the occupants of the top of the bus had risen to take shelter inside or in the Tube station; one alone, sitting just in front of me, did not move.

At the thought of being alone again with him, a sudden panic seized me, and I rose also to follow the others down. But even as I stood at the top of the stairs, something of courage, or at least of curiosity, prevailed, and instead I sat down again on the back seat (nearer than that I felt I could not go) and watched for what should be. In a moment or two we started off again.

Tonight, in spite of the falling rain, there was more light; behind the clouds, probably the moon had risen, and I could see with considerable distinctness the figure that shared the top with me. I longed to be gone, so cold was the fear that gripped my heart, but still insatiable curiosity held me where I was.

Inwardly I felt convinced that something was going to happen, and, though the sweat of terror stood on my face at the thought of what it might be, I knew that the one thing even more unfaceable was to turn tail and never know what it was.

On the right the leafless plane-trees in the Park stretched angled fingers against the muffled sky, and below, the pavements and roadway gleamed with moisture. Traffic was infrequent, infrequent also were the figures of pedestrians; never in my life had I felt so cut off from human intercourse.

Close round me were secure, normal rooms, tenanted by living men and women, where cheerful fires burnt and steady lights illuminated the solid walls. But here companionless, except for the motionless form crouched in front me, I sped between earth and sky, among dim shadows and fugitive lights. And all the time I knew, though not knowing how I knew, some dreadful drama was immediately to be unrolled in front of me. Whether that would prove to be some re-enactment of what in the world of time and space had already occurred, or whether, by the stranger miracle of second-sight, I was to behold something which had not happened yet, I had no idea. All I was certain of was that I sat in the presence of things not normally seen; in the world which, for the sake of sanity, is but rarely made manifest.

I kept my eye fixed on the figure in front of me, and saw that its bowed head was supported by its hands, which seemed to hold it up. Then came a step on the stairs, and the conductor was by me demanding my fare. Having given it, a sudden idea struck me as he was about to leave the top again.

'You haven't collected the fare from that man in front there,' I said.

The conductor looked forward, then at me again.

'Sure enough, there is someone there,' he said, 'and can you see him, too?'

'Certainly,' said I.

This appeared to me at the moment to reassure him; it occurred to me also that perhaps I was utterly wrong, and that the figure was nothing but a real passenger.

What followed happened in a dozen seconds.

The conductor advanced up the bus, and, having spoken without attracting the passenger's attention, touched him on the shoulder, and I saw his hand go into it, as it plunged in water. Simultaneously the figure turned round in its seat, and I saw its face. It was that of a young man, absolutely white and colourless. I saw, too, why it held its head up in its hands, for its throat was cut from ear to ear.

The eyes were closed, but as it raised its head in its hands, looking at the conductor, it opened them, and from within them there came a light as from the eye of a cat.

Then, in an awful voice, half squeal, half groan, I heard the conductor cry out:

'O my God! O my God!' he said.

The figure rose, and cowering as from a blow, he turned and fled before it. Whether he jumped into the roadway from the top of the stairs, or in his flight fell down them, I do not know, but I heard the thud of his body as it fell, and was alone once more on the top of the bus.

I rang the bell violently, and in a few yards we drew up. Already there was a crowd round the man on the road, and presently he was carried in an ambulance, alive, but not much more than alive, to St George's Hospital.

He died from his injuries a few days later, and the discovery of a certain pearl necklace concealed in the clothes of his room, about which he gave information, makes it probable that the confession he made just before he died was true.

The conductor, William Larkins, had been in gaol on a charge of stealing six months before, and on his release, by means of a false name and forged references, he had got this post, with every intention of keeping straight. But he had lost money racing, and ten days before his death was in serious want of cash.

That night an old acquaintance of his, who had been associated with him in burglaries, boarded the bus, heard his story, and tried to persuade him to come back into his old way of life. By way of recommendation, he opened a small dressing-bag he had with him, and showed him, wrapped away in a corner, the pearl necklace which subsequently was discovered in Larkins' room. The two were alone on the top of the bus, and, yielding to the ungovernable greed, Larkins next moment had his arm over the passenger's face, and with a razor out of his dressing-bag had cut his throat.

He kept his wits about him, pocketed the pearls, left the bag open and the razor on the floor, and descended to the footboard again.

Immediately afterwards, having ascertained that there were no blood stains on him, he ascended again and instantly stopped the bus, having discovered the body of a passenger there with his throat cut and the razor on the floor. The body was identified as that of a well-known burglar, and the coroner's jury had brought in a verdict of suicide.

THE FRIEND IN THE GARDEN

JACK DENNISON was not one of those to whom the capacity for happiness had never been given. By birthright it had been his, that royal and supreme gift which, with the magic of Midas, turns into gold the dullest and most leaden of happenings, and lights a rainbow in the most trivial of experiences. But he had lost it, as utterly and irretrievably as if it had never been his, and this evening as he strolled up and down the short velvet of the lawn behind his house, waiting for his sister and her husband, he remembered that today was the anniversary of his loss, which had turned the sweet waters to bitterness, making Marah of the pleasant fountains of his life. The blow had descended on him without warning of any sort. He had been married not quite a year to the woman to whom he had dedicated his entire life and love, and on an evening in early June three years ago, when, as tonight, the brakes were a-bubble with the liquid raptures of the mated nightingales, he came home to find that she had left him with the friend whom, after her, he had most loved and trusted in all the world. Thus happiness died for him, and its ghost wailed ever beside him.

He had pleasures in plenty: there was nothing that he liked which was not within his power to attain. He was still scarcely thirty, and his health retained the serene vigour of youth; he had many intellectual interests and the sensitive perceptions of the true artist, and inheriting, as he did, one of the largest private fortunes in England, he had means to possess himself to the beautiful things he so intelligently admired. Yet in all the pleasure they gave him there was no grain of happiness; his empty and cheated heart was incapable of that, and he neither forgave nor wished to forgive those who had wrought its desolation.

After his wife's betrayal of him, he had shut up his immense country house in Derbyshire and his town house in Berkeley Square, and spent his years, generally alone, in this more moderate mansion perched high on Paulton Hill and overlooking one of the loveliest reaches of the Thames. Round the house were some six acres of garden, sufficient to give him the complete privacy he desired, yet not so large that he could not be on intimate terms with every yard of it. The house itself, long and low and creeper-clad, stood in the middle of its garden, which was framed in noble trees of secular growth; at the back of it, where he now strolled, was built out a broad flagged terrace, where at this moment dinner was laid, for the evening was hot and calm. Half a dozen steps led down from it on to the lawn, which was set in deep flower-beds. At the far end a shrubbery flaming with laburnums screened the stables from the garden.

His sister and brother-in-law, Dick Ainger, had come down to spend two or three weeks with him, thus combining, as Helen said, the pomps of the season in town with the pleasures of the country and his society. Half an hour in the motor sufficed to take anyone to the centre of things, and tonight Helen and (possibly, though improbably) her husband were going up after dinner to the great fancy-dress ball at Fortescue House. She, in whose superb vitality there still flourished a child's love of mystery, had kept the manner of her impersonation a secret both from her husband and Jack. All that they knew was that the ball in question was geographical; Canada and India and Africa's golden fountains would no doubt be suitably represented, but she had given them no hint at all of the land of her choice, except that she was not Mount Everest, and that she might just be considered geographical. It may be added that she was tall enough for Mount Everest.

Ten minutes later they were seated at dinner, and she was explaining why she had not dressed first, as she had intended.

'It would have taken half an hour more,' she said, 'and I was exceedingly hungry. Also, some of it would have come off, I think. I shall dress afterwards. Dick dear, do settle whether you are coming or not; you've been shilly-shallying all day. It is time this indecision ceased. I want another piece of melon.'

Dick, amiable and very red-faced and elephantine, followed his wife's example with regard to the melon.

'It has ceased,' he said. 'I shall not go. I am cool for the first time today, and I shall remain so. There will be no Red Sea, unless another genius has thought of it.'

Helen laughed.

'Well, it's something to have made up your mind,' she said, 'though you sacrifice quite a good joke and quite a good dress. And as you are poor and joke with difficulty, darling, it is rather a serious loss. You shall stop and cheer up Jack. Oh! but, Jackie, you oughtn't to want cheering up. I hear you have found a Karl Huth which completes your collection of miniatures. Aren't you awfully happy?'

Jack considered this.

'I was awfully pleased for an hour or two,' he said. 'And now, as a matter of fact, I feel rather flat. Isn't there something in the Psalms about that sort of thing? He gave them their desire, and the leanness of it withal entered into their souls.'

'Darling, you can prove anything you please if you quote the Psalms,' said she. 'There are all sorts of abominable sentiments there.'

She gave a little scream.

'Oh, there's a creepy-crawly on the tablecloth,' she said. 'Do put a glass over it.'

Jack inverted a wineglass over an innocent earwig and watched it.

'Poor little devil!' he said; 'in prison like the rest of us.'

Helen gave a rather elaborate little sigh of impatience.

'Jack, you've got creepy-crawlies inside you tonight,' she said. 'Besides, if we are in prison, as you so cheerfully suggest, we shall have to die in order to get out. I should not like that at all.'

Jack looked at her brilliant, eager face.

'No, dear,' he said; 'and may you have many happy years in prison yet. I hope you have got an enormously long sentence.'

'So do I,' said Helen fervently. 'Oh, I wish I could buy years and years from the people who don't care about it all.'

The black bitterness welled up in Jack again.

'You might have all mine without charge,' he said.

'Oh, Jack, don't!' she cried. 'You have no manners. It spoils my pleasure to think you are unhappy; it does really, dear old boy. And now I must go to dress. You will have to guess what I am, and I shall be vexed if you can't guess, and a little vexed if you can, because then it will seem to be obvious. May I order the motor to be ready in half an hour?'

Jack passed the decanter of port to his brother-in-law, who settled himself down for a quiet evening with evident relief.

'Thanks,' he said. 'I make a rule to have only one glass of port, and then I prove it very often by having two. Now, my dear fellow, we haven't had a good talk for a year or more. Tell me about yourself.'

Jack considered this request.

'I've got a Karl Huth,' he said. 'That's all. I'm just the same, and likely to be. It's a pleasant prospect, with the probability of so many years in front of me.'

Stout, pleasant Dick moved his chair a little more round.

'I'm sorry, I'm sorry,' he said. 'Can't you manage to—what is it they call it in the City—manage to have a good healthy reconstruction?'

'Excellent advice,' said Jack. 'But you might as well say to a plain woman, ''Have a reconstruction and be beautiful.'' '

'And she'd take that advice if she were sensible,' said Dick. 'She'd get a bit of eyebrow, and a touch of rouge, and some more hair, and what not. There's no woman so plain and no job so bad that you can't make the best of it, instead of the worst. You are young and still—'

'I am as old as the devil,' said Jack.

'Well, he gets about still, and shows no signs of impaired activity, they tell me. You have artistic tastes and can gratify them.'

'You can't build happiness out of pleasures,' said Jack. 'It's no use talking, my dear fellow. There's only one thing I look forward to in life, and that is the end of it.'

They sat silent for a little, and round them the night deepened and the stars grew more brilliant. Then over the fields to the left the moon rose large and tawny. Somewhere not far off a dog began to howl, and Dick frowned.

'I hate hearing a dog howl at night,' he said, 'though I'm not really superstitious. They say it means death.'

'To oneself?' asked Jack.

'Oh, I don't go so far as that.'

'Well, we know that there's death going on among other people whether a dog howls or not,' remarked Jack. 'I think it's only howling for the moon.'

Quite suddenly the howling ceased.

'There! he's got it,' said Jack. 'Lucky dog. Good heavens!'

He turned quickly round, considerably startled. Helen had come silently out of the door into the house, and was standing close by him. She was dressed from head to foot in white with silver embroideries, her face and even her lips were whitened also, and high up in her powdered hair was set one huge diamond star.

'Well, Jack,' she said. 'Guess!'

Jack looked up and down the cold, radiant figure for a moment or two.

'Ah, I see,' he said. 'You are the Pole Star.'

Helen applauded.

'You dear,' she said. 'You had to think first, and then you guessed right. Shall I do?'

'But admirably. You are superb. But I nearly guessed wrong. At first I thought you were Death.'

'Is this your idea of Death?' she said. 'I thought Death was supposed to be a skeleton in black.'

Suddenly the moonstruck dog lifted up his mournful voice again. Helen raised her hand dramatically.

'You, who say you are in prison,' she said in a low, even voice; 'I have come to release you.'

Jack caught her mood.

'I have waited for you,' he said. 'I have long wanted you.'

She shook her head.

'You don't play up,' she said in her natural voice. 'You aren't frightened.'

'I know I'm not. But that is because I am playing up.'

Helen turned to take her cloak from her maid who had just come out with it, and they heard her laugh and stifle her laughing. The cloak was white also, and a hood came over her head.

'Well, I'm ready,' she said. 'But I shan't be back till very late, Jack. How am I to get in? Will somebody sit up?'

'Oh, there's no need. You can come through the garden and in at this door; it's always left open.'

'God bless me! don't you lock up at night?' asked Dick.

'No. Burglars can always get in if they are determined to, and it only annoys them to have to pick locks. But I dare say I shall be up, Helen; I don't go to bed till very late.'

'Well, goodnight, dear, in case I don't find you up. Dick, I know I shan't see you.'

'I, too, am quite certain of that,' said he. 'I shall go to bed in half an hour.'

The motor was already waiting, and Helen set off.

'She's up to some trick tonight,' said Dick when she had gone. 'Did you hear her laughing to herself? She's going to play some practical joke upon you.'

Jack laughed.

'I shouldn't be the least surprised,' he said. 'As likely as not she'll drive about for an hour instead of going to the ball, and then come in through the garden gate and pretend she is Death. When we were little she was always making apple-pie beds and turnip ghosts.'

'That was an apple-pie laugh,' remarked Dick. 'She made a ghost for me the other night just outside the smoking-room. Frightened me out of my wits.'

'She won't frighten me. I shall take her Death as seriously as a judge. I shall pretend she is Death. And then, when it has gone on long enough, I shall say to her very suddenly, "Excuse me, but there's a creepy-crawly on your cloak," Upon which she will scream loudly, and hurry off to her ball.'

They talked on for half an hour or so, and then Dick gave a wide and unconcealed yawn.

'Well, I think I shall leave you to entertain your white friend alone,' he said. 'Bedtime for me. What a night! Moon and stars all in their places and shining like old winkie. I like to see the solar system working smoothly. It sets an example to one's own inside.'

Jack looked at his good-humoured, healthy face.

'I'm sure yours follows it,' he said. 'Goodnight, Dick. I shall sit up for my friend in the garden.'

Jack sent the servants to bed, and sat alone in the windless, moonlit dusk. In the trees once again the nightingales poured their love-song into the sleeping night, rising from rapture to rapture. The sense of this bitter anniversary lay heavy on him, and whether he looked forward or backwards, the bitterness seemed irreparable. Often he had tried to forgive; as often he had felt that forgiveness lay outside his powers; he did not even now wish to forgive. A black stain of hatred covered him, body and soul; as long as his life lasted he knew it would be there. He could not, while he lived, look forward to the fading of it into grey indifference. As for life itself, he had no joy in it; at any moment he would have put himself cheerfully and calmly and even eagerly into the cool hands of death.

For a moment his mouth uncurled itself into a smile at the thought of the prank which it seemed quite possible Helen would play on him. He thought it more likely than not that presently he would see her tall, white figure glimmer among the bushes, and then come out into the moonlit space of the lawn. She was perfectly capable of sacrificing an hour of her ball to 'pull off,' as she would say, so splendid a joke, hoping to frighten him. She well knew his spiritualistic leanings; she would think it easily possible that he would take quite seriously a white figure coming towards him out of the night. They had often witnessed extraordinary materializations together, heard voices that purported to come from the shadowy and unknown confines of the spirit world; and on his side, in case she came, he was more than ready to fool her in response to her fooling of him, and induce her to believe that he believed in the reality of her impersonation. If she came, it would help to pass an hour of the night that was always too long.

Then that distraction passed, and once again the hatred and bitterness of his life gripped and shook him.

'Oh God! if I could die!' he said.

Once again the unseen dog began to howl, and Jack felt a drowsiness or torpor of some kind settle in his limbs and in his brain. He did not trouble to analyse it, or think whether it was a mental or a physical fatigue that had so strangely wearied him. And at that moment he saw a tall, white figure gleaming among the trees at the end of garden. He knew it must be Helen, and he roused himself, or tried to rouse himself, into a keener interest. He had to 'play up,' as she had said, to make a success of the joke which was costing her golden minutes of her ball.

The figure came slowly across the lawn and mounted the steps of the terrace where he sat. She had put her hood over her face, so that her face was quite hidden. Hidden, too were her hands in the folds of the long white cloak.

Jack stood up, still feeling drowsy, but determined to play his part in a farce that had entailed so large a sacrifice on the side of his sister.

'Who are you?' he said in a voice that he made to tremble. 'What are you?'

He was answered in a very even, quiet tone.

'The friend you want,' she said. 'The friend who is to complete and end your life.'

Jack recollected his recorded attitude.

'I suppose you are Death, then,' he said. 'Certainly our lives are very incomplete without you. I am so glad to see you. Have you come to take me away? I think that is charming of you. Will you take anything, or shall I? Perhaps you have some morphia, or strychnine, or, at any rate, a razor with you. And you came in through the garden gate. I call that friendly. A friend in the garden. Have you come from town?'

'From there and from many other places,' said the friend.

Certainly Helen was playing beautifully, thought he. Her voice was a miracle of inexorable quiet. And she stood quite still, without tremor of movement. It was necessary to play up to this perfection of acting, and Jack, still drowsy, did his best.

'You must travel a great deal.'

'Yes, I travel over the whole world. Wherever man has trod, there go I, and erase his footsteps. I go to the ice of the southern pole, and to where the pole star of the north looks down from the zenith.'

This seemed almost a hint that Helen had had enough.

But Jack delayed his catastrophe point of the creepy-crawly a little longer. She was acting so wonderfully.

'And you always travel without a maid and without any luggage,' he said. 'Of course, you don't need either. Nor shall I when I come with you. We came naked into the world, and we shall go without any belongings. Do tell me what it feels like to be you. I should like to know that first, before I come with you.'

She still sat absolutely motionless. Her voice came from beneath the hood that hid her face, quiet and clear and inexorable. It was not like Helen's voice.

'There is little to tell,' she said. 'I am exceedingly simple. My whole duty is just to kiss those to whom I am sent, and then they follow me. I am glad you are not afraid of me, and that you welcome me. I generally come as a friend, and it is as a friend I have come to you. I never come unless I am sent. I am not a mistress, hard or cruel, but just a servant of Him who is infinitely kind. I will tell you, if you wish, a little about myself before we go. But sit down. Those whom I visit almost always receive me sitting or lying. It is more natural. Very few receive me standing.'

Jack still felt that he knew it was Helen. But her acting was something transcendent. As he sat down, still drowsy, he felt a little quiver of his heart, a tribute to her power.

'I heal all diseases of the body and of the soul,' she said. 'Those who are tortured with bodily torment turn their faces to me, and I kiss them, and their torment is over. Those who suffer more cruelly, those who have hatred and remorse at their hearts, are equally helped by me and comforted. Those who have gone wrong in this weary life find their wanderings over when I come to them.'

Her cloak had fallen back a little, so that one of her hands was exposed. Jack saw that it was quite white. He remembered Helen's very thin dress, and was anxious for her.

'Do come indoors,' he said; 'I am sure you are cold. It would be a bore to have you laid up.'

He felt it was time that this excellently played farce ended.

'Excuse me,' he said, 'there's a creepy-crawly climbing up your arm. Oh! Helen—'

She had not moved.

'Helen, I knew it was you,' he said, but his voice faltered.

Then in a flash all his drowsiness left him, and it left him awed and quiet and aware.

'Death, dear friend!' he said.

She took the hood from her face. It seemed rather that the hood gently moved aside, and he saw a face, young and inexorable and kind; but not Helen's face.

'I comfort the broken-hearted,' she said, 'and by my very act I forgive all sin and all hatred in those who are sorry. I am rest to the weary, to the sad I am consolation. All your life you have been in the hands of my Master, and yours, but I make you realize better in what loving hands you are!'

Jack had sat at her bidding. Now he tried to rise, but found he could not.

'And you are not afraid now?' she asked.

'No, I am not afraid,' he said. 'Perhaps my foolish flesh is a little afraid, but I am not.'

She rose.

'Then look round once more, dear Jack,' she said, 'before you come with me. You have not looked on the glory and the wonder of the world enough in these last three years. You have shut your eyes and ears to the voices and sights of joy.'

'Then you know all about me?' he asked. 'I need make no confession of the blackness and uncharity of my heart?'

'Nobody's heart is black,' she said, 'if he says it is black. So look round once more, quietly and gratefully. See how the myriad worlds above are awake over this sleeping earth and how they shine in the dawn of the everlasting day.'

Jack leaned back in his chair. His flesh, his body, and bones ached with a drowsy yearning to ache no more. Something within him beat like a hammer, and longed to stop beating.

'Oh, kiss me quickly, my friend,' he said.

'Then say, "God bless everything." Those who sin from too much passion, and those who sin from too little. Those who are are afraid, those who hate, those who spoil their own lives, and those who spoil the lives of others. Those who lie, and those who cheat. Bless them all, dear Jack. Make peace with them all. And with your wife; include her!'

He gave a startled movement.

'I can't,' said he.

'I think you can. You must learn to love again.'

Jack lay half reclined in his chair. A wonderful prospect of rest and peace had come to him. Everything that had happened to him in past years, all he had suffered, and all his hate, melted and receded and vanished in face of this wonderful offer of peace.

'God bless them all,' he said.

She bent forward and kissed him on the forehead. He gave out a little shudder, and was still.

Next moment he was alone on the terrace, with folded hands and quiet face. A sudden little breeze sprang up in the garden, and as it passed the nightingales burst into a torrent of song. And the dog ceased howling. Then the intense quiet of midsummer night descended on the garden again.

Ten minutes later a white-robed figure crossed the lawn. Helen saw Jack sitting very still and quiet in the moonlight, and wondered if her colossal practical joke had been guessed. But she had delayed her appearance as Pole Star at Fortescue House for an hour, and it was incumbent on her now to attempt to pull it off. She drew her hood over her face and concealed her hands.

'And is this all my welcome?' she said in a low, rather terrible voice. 'You said you would so welcome me. Wake, I have come for you.'

He sat quite still, and a sudden misgiving seized her.

'Oh, Jack, I think you guessed,' she said. 'You said you wouldn't be frightened, and you are not. But you rather frighten me.'

Once more she paused.

'Jack, wake up!' she said quickly, and took one of his nerveless hands in hers.

Instantly she dropped it.

'Jack,' she said, 'why don't you answer me? I give up. I wanted to play a joke—'

Then her voice suddenly rose to a scream.

'Dick, Dick!' she cried. 'Come here—come, somebody. I don't know what is the matter.'

The household had not yet gone to bed. Lights were awakened, and hurrying steps responded to her call.

But Jack did not move. He had found his friend.

THE RED HOUSE

Hugh Fairfax had been accustomed for the last six or seven years to spend his summer holiday with his wife and their two young children—babies when they first were perambulated about the place—at the sequestered town of Olcombe, near the south coast of Kent. This had once been a considerable port, but in process of three centuries, the sea had thrown up, or perhaps left by its retreat, so large an acreage of sandy grass-covered dunes that it was a port no longer, and stood at the distance of some two miles from the highest tides.

This loss of sea-going traffic was partly atoned for by the game-playing instincts of the late nineteenth century, and Olcombe had recovered some measure of its former prosperity by virtue of the army of golfers who made it so densely populous at all holiday seasons of the year. Satiated by the invigoration of exercise and long hours in open air, they were mostly content with narrow lodgings, and Hugh Fairfax, when first I made his acquaintance there, had a frankly odious little villa on the outskirts of the town, hemmed closely in by the gas-works and the railway station.

Our acquaintance soon ripened into friendship, things prospered with him in the city, and last year he told me that he had bought that red-brick Georgian house near the top of the hill on which Olcombe stands, at which he had long cast envious glances. He proposed that I should come and camp in it with him for the last week of July, in order to worry it into habitable shape for the triumphal entry of his family in the first week in August. As a bribe or reward for my services, he hoped that I would spend that month with them, and rejoice in the comfort which our joint exertions should have produced. This suited me admirably, and I at once accepted.

Bells and electric light had already been installed when we arrived, but for the first few nights, till the bedrooms were habitable, we put up at the hotel. These days were abominably wet, and in consequence we spent most of our time in industrious pullings about of the furniture as it arrived in vans from town.

The house itself was charming in the matter of the size of its rooms and general amenities; though unlived in for the last six months it was in excellent repair, and it was clear that at the price Hugh had paid for it he had secured a tremendous bargain.

The previous possessor had been a certain Mr Arthur Whitfield, a retired solicitor, who dabbled in chemistry. We had both of us seen him dozens of times at the club-house on the golf links, where he used to take tea after his half round, which he always played with his wife. He was a sedate, middle-aged man, eminently polite and respectable, and eminently forgettable. She, so we vaguely knew, had been ordered south for the winter, and had left Olcombe late in the previous autumn. Shortly before Easter, some four months later, he (again we were vague and uninterested in the matter) had left also, after selling all his furniture, and putting the house into the hands of the agent for immediate disposal at a reserve price extraordinarily low.

That was all Hugh knew about the matter, and, having secured possession of the house, he cared not at all what its previous history had been.

The house, long and two-storied, with attics in the roof, fronted the street. The door opened into a spacious flagged hall, from which a broad-banistered staircase of dark oak led to the upper landing.

On each side of the hall were fine rooms, the left-hand one of which, on entering, was clearly indicated as suitable for the dining-room, since it was near the kitchen. This and a big sitting-room, destined for the drawing-room, which looked out on to the high-walled garden at the back, were oak-panelled, as was the hall.

On the right of the door was a rather smaller room, which Hugh instantly divined was his. Here there was no panelling; the walls were of unpapered plaster, painted an agreeable dark red. The condition of the paint made it appear that this decoration had been lately done.

It happened that the furniture for this room arrived, with that of the drawing-room, in the first van that came down, and after spending the morning and the early afternoon—for the day was too wet to dream of going out—in making tentative arrangements of it, we were sitting on a book-case in Hugh's room, enjoying a recuperative cigarette after our labours, and awaiting the arrival of the second van load, for which the men had gone to the station. As we sat there we both heard the ringing of an electric bell in the basement, and, supposing that the second van had come, I strolled to the window, wondering how it was that we had not noticed its advent, while Hugh went to open the front-door. To my surprise, I saw that the street was empty, and at that moment he came back from the hall.

'What bell could that have been then?' he asked.

Even as he spoke it sounded again, faint and far away, but certainly in the house.

'Let's go to the switchboard and look,' I suggested, and together we went down the kitchen passage. There was the switchboard, and the indicator of the room called 'Study' was still faintly oscillating.

'But that's the room where we were sitting,' said Hugh. 'Odd that the bells should have got out of order already.'

It did appear rather odd, but it was certainly insignificant, and neither of us paid, as far as I know, any further attention to it, for on the moment we heard the unmistakable rumbling of the fresh van, and the electric bell sounded again, while the indicator opposite 'Front door' agitated itself.

'So that's in order, anyhow,' he said.

The unpacking of this second van, and the disposal of its furniture occupied us till it grew dark, but after the men had returned with it empty to the station, Hugh and I laboured on for another hour, with the help of the electric light. Then we let ourselves out into the rain-streaked evening, locked the front door behind us, and, desirous of a little fresh air, though it was accompanied by fresh water, walked for a mile or two out of the town before going to our hotel.

On our return, our way lay by the Red House (for Hugh had decided on this strictly veracious description, instead of soaring into the region of Laburnums or Blenheims, which abounded in Olcombe), and as we came opposite to it on the other side of the street he waved his stick at it.

'Look at it!' he said. 'All mine! I burst with jealousy of myself. Why—'

He stopped suddenly.

'But there's a light in my room,' he said.

That appeared to be so. The curtains were drawn across the windows (I had done it myself in order to observe the effect), but between them there certainly showed a thin line of light where they were not completely pulled together.

'We must have left the light burning,' he said. 'Lucky I saw it.'

There was no other explanation, nor any need for one. But in my mind I felt quite certain I had put the light out. The switch had been a little stiff; I could have sworn I remembered handling it.

It was the next day that we made the great discovery. Hugh and I had been performing a mystic dance with the bookcase in his room—a staggering dance, for it was heavy—moving it to a fresh position. As we dumped it into its new place, the corner of it struck the wall sharply, and brought off a big flake of plaster, that rattled down behind it.

I apologized, for it was clearly my fault, and, looking at the damage, saw that below the plaster was what looked like dark wood. The possible glory of the discovery led Hugh to forgive me, and himself to chip off a fresh piece of it.

That put the matter beyond doubt. Behind the plaster there was certainly oak panelling similar to that in the other sitting-rooms. Instantly this introduced a new feature into our decorative campaign.

The person who plumbed probably knew how to plaster, and Hugh, with the reminiscence of a shop that looked as if it harboured such characters, ran out, and shortly returned with a mild and apathetic workman.

He looked a little surprised at the order given him, and in explanation told us that not six months ago he had been employed on the job of putting up the plaster that was now to be removed.

But this was all in the way of business, and he promised that, if he could get to work at once, his job should be finished by next day. Getting to work at once implied the removal into the middle of the room of all the furniture we had put in place.

That day and the next the abominable weather continued, and we spent our entire time in the Red House, which became populous with the representatives of various trades.

In the study the plasterer had finished his work, the walls had been denuded down to the old oak panels, and the furniture was back in its place. With the arrival of a couple of servants next day, the house was clearly habitable, and Hugh and I were to move in from the hotel on the following morning.

I was wandering round the study that evening as dusk fell, admiring the restored panelling, when something rather curious about it struck me. It was regular all the way round, with the exception of a piece in the middle of the wall opposite the door.

Here smaller panels took the place of the large ones, and, looking more closely, I saw that the lines accounted for by the possible presence of a door. Then I perceived that the conjecture must be correct, for some three feet from the ground was a small circular inlay of wood, where, no doubt, the handle had been.

Further investigation showed the complete join of the door, and the mark of hinges; the crack was filled up with plaster, painted to resemble the tone of the wood.

Five minutes' excited plying of kitchen skewers by myself and Hugh sufficed to free the plastered join, and soon the door swung open, disclosing inside a largish closet, the walls of which were papered. It was all rather fun, and Hugh left me alone in order to return the skewer to the kitchen.

We were just about to start for our hotel, and, having closed the door of this newly discovered cupboard, I went into the hall to wait for him, conscious for the first time of a perfectly unreasonable repugnance for the room. How that repugnance had got there, I had no idea whatever, but for that reason, I think, I preferred to wait in the hall.

I opened the front door, and stood there looking out into the street, when suddenly I felt something push by me, for all the world as if an invisible presence had come in from outside.

It was so startling that, though I knew there was no one there, I looked into the dusk of the hall to assure myself that it was empty. Something had certainly brushed past me. But the hall was untenanted; so, too, was the street. And then down in the basement an electric bell sounded; simultaneously I heard Hugh's foot on the stone stairs from below.

I had shut the front door, and must have stood, invisible to him, in the shadow, for he crossed the hall, whistling, and entered the study.

'You needn't be so impatient—' he began.

Then he stopped, seeing, I suppose, that he spoke to an empty room.

I advanced to the door of the study; on the sound of my footsteps he had turned round.

'Why impatient?' I asked.

'Oh, there you are!' he asked. 'Why did you ring. I was only looking round the kitchen.'

He paused a moment.

'Or was it only that bell that is out of order?' he asked.

'Only that.'

'And no one at the front door?'

My mind, I am bound to say, went back to that impression of being brushed against by some presence.

'No,' I said; 'I have been standing there.'

He turned on the light in the study, as he stood by the door, and looked round.

'I'll have a handle put on that cupboard door tomorrow,' he said, 'and a lock. Convenient place for putting papers.'

Even as he spoke the door swung slowly open, quite noiselessly. Then, and I confess to a curious shiver of the flesh as I saw it, it swung back again till it was quite closed. It irresistibly suggested that it had been pulled to, after some presence that had entered, from within. Yet nothing had entered, nor had anything entered two minutes before when I stood by the door into the street.

I thought Hugh glanced at me as if to see whether I had noticed it. Then he walked across the room, pulling the curtains together as he went, and picking up a couple of books that lay on the floor. Finally, he pulled a chair across the cupboard door, setting it close to the wall.

'Well, we may as well go,' he said. 'The servants will come tomorrow morning, and they'll be ready for us by dinner-time. I hope it will be fine; I should like a day on the links.'

That night the ill-temper of the skies was conjured away, and we spent an azure day at golf. But there was present to my mind, through every moment of it, the sense, ominous and oppressive, of some dark nightmarish background to the hours. I knew that I dreaded the return, not to the rather gaunt hotel, but to the comfortable red-brick house.

There was something queer about it, something ambushed there, that had at present only faintly stirred in its lurking-place, so that its movement might have been mistaken for the action of draughts of air or defective electric wires. All that evening while we played picquet in Hugh's study, I felt as if someone stood by me, awfully and malignantly watching, and when, at the close of our game, Hugh busied himself with utilizing the cupboard, and storing in it what had accumulated on the floor, papers, and tennis rackets, and boxes of golf balls, I felt that my uneasiness was somehow localized there. But nothing disturbed the tranquillity of the evening. And when, after making these dispositions, his yawning suggested that it was bedtime, I was almost disposed to sit up a little longer, with the express purpose of convincing myself by a lonely vigil that my fears were unfounded. But it was evident that a host's duties on this first night made him sit up for me, and we went upstairs together. He was the last to leave the room, and I noted in my mind that he put out the lights.

I got into bed at once, and instantly fell asleep. I slept well and dreamlessly, but awoke with the sense that some sudden noise had aroused me. What it was I did not know, for when I got possession of my senses, all was perfectly still again.

Through the curtains there came the faint light of early morning, and feeling that the room was rather hot, I went to the window to open it wider, and looked out. The street was dark and empty, but lying across it, coming from the study below my bedroom, shone two thin streaks of light.

I cannot describe with what horror that sight struck me, nor with what relief I heard immediately human footsteps coming down the passage from Hugh's room.

I went to my door and opened it, just as he came opposite to it. 'Did you hear the bell?' he asked.

'I believe it woke me. And there's a light in the room downstairs.'

'How do you know?' he asked.

'I saw it across the street from my window.'

He had turned on the electric light that lit the stairs. Together we went down, and entered the study. There was burning just one light near the cupboard; the chair which he had placed against it was moved away, and the door was open. But the room was perfectly quiet and empty.

'It's all utter nonsense, you know,' Hugh said irritably, turning out the light. 'But the electrician comes tomorrow; he shall see to it.'

Whether the electrician had much to do with it or not, I cannot say, but certainly no further disturbance occurred for some days after that. Margaret Fairfax and the children came down next afternoon, and for a week or so, whatever it was that had caused those queer disturbances, harassed us no more.

Hugh, after asking me not to hint at these things to Margaret (which was inconsistent with his triumphant assurance that the electrician had put everything to rights), did not allude to them again, and appeared to forget about them. But both in his mind and in my own, I think there was, so to speak, a little black seed planted, which was now monstrously sprouting in the dark soil.

One day, after a morning round on the links, we were in the club-house where we had lunched. I had just taken up the local paper and was walking across to an armchair in the window to glance at it before we started again, when a man, somehow familiar to me, but only vaguely so, crossed the square of grass outside on his way into the clubhouse. For one second I cudgelled my memory as to who he was, without success, and turned to my paper.

The first paragraph I saw related to the identification of the body of a suicide at Folkestone as that of Mr Arthur Whitfield, retired solicitor of Olcombe, and instantaneously I recollected who was the man whom I had seen crossing the square of grass outside.

We arrived back at the Red House, after our second round, just as it was growing dusk. As we came in, Daisy, the six-year-old girl, came out of Hugh's study. She ran up to her father.

'Daddy, who is that funny lady in your study?' she asked, 'I don't like her.'

Hugh went into the room, and next moment he called out:

'Daisy, you little liar, there isn't any funny lady.'

Daisy peered round the door.

'Well, then, she's gone,' she said. 'But she was here just this minute.'

'What was she like? What was she doing?' asked Hugh.

'She was standing by the cupboard door, where you keep the tennis things. And I didn't like her. I came to put back a racquet Mummy and I had been playing with.'

'Perhaps she has gone inside,' said Hugh, and went across the room to the door. Daisy suddenly rushed up to me, and clung to my coat.

'No, no!' she said. 'Don't let her out. I don't like her.'

'Nonsense, darling', said Hugh, and opened it.

Instantly he fell back a pace, beating wildly with his hands in the air. A crowd of big flies, shrilly buzzing, poured out of the opened door; there must have been hundreds of them, because, for a moment, Hugh's head was almost invisible among them.

Then quite suddenly the buzzing ceased, as if they had all settled about the room. I was standing close to the door with Daisy, who shrieked aloud.

'Unclean brutes,' said Hugh. 'How on earth did they get in there? Turn on the light, will you? We must get them out of the room.'

I did as he told me, and we looked about to see where they had settled, while Hugh went to the windows and opened them wide. But there was not a fly to be seen anywhere.

We searched the walls, we flapped with Hugh's mackintosh at the inaccessible corners by the ceiling, we brushed the carpet. They had completely and utterly vanished.

'Run to your mother, Daisy,' said Hugh. 'And don't say anything to her about the funny lady. Mind, not a word. It's our secret.'

Daisy lingered a moment.

'Yes, daddy,' she said. 'And the flies? They were funny, weren't they?'

'Yes, dear, awfully funny. But don't say anything about them either.'

After the child had gone, Hugh went back to the cupboard door and threw it wider. He remained there a couple of minutes, poking and peering about, and then, banged the door and locked it.

'What do you make of it all?' he said to me. 'I don't attach any importance to the funny lady; the child probably saw some queer shadow. But the flies; they came out by the hundred. And what happened to them?'

He came across the room to me.

'Is there something queer, do you think?' he asked.

At that moment Margaret came into the room. She closed the door quietly behind her.

'Hughie, there's a man in the hall,' she said. 'Has he come to see you? I asked him what his business was, and he didn't answer me.'

Hugh, with a quickness which I inwardly applauded, did not hesitate.

'Yes, dear,' he said. 'I was expecting him.'

He went out, and Margaret sat down by me in the window-seat.

'Good game?' she asked. 'Oh, by the way, I saw rather a dreadful thing in the paper. I wonder if Hugh knows.'

As she spoke Hugh came back into the room. The light fell, I suppose, rather oddly on his face, for Margaret looked at him with a sudden curiosity.

'Hughie, is anything the matter?' she said. 'You look so white.'

'Matter? Why should there be? There isn't, anyhow.'

He sat down in his armchair, purposely, as I thought, with his back to us.

'I was just saying there was rather a dreadful thing in the paper today,' she said in a minute. 'Mr Arthur Whitfield—'

Instantly Hugh wheeled round.

'Well, what about him?' he said.

'His body was identified at the police-court at Folkestone. He committed suicide. And I thought you told me he had gone abroad to join his wife.'

Hugh spoke with a voice that was not characteristic of him; it was quite level and slow.

'Mr Whitfield must have come back, then,' he said.

Margaret went upstairs to dress immediately afterwards, and I noticed that Hugh went out into the hall with her. But he returned at once.

'There is something queer,' he said to me. 'For the man in the hall was Whitfield, I would swear to it.'

'And what happened?' I asked.

Hugh, with the first sign of nervousness that I had seen in him, looked quickly round the room.

'I thought he came in here,' he said.

'I didn't see him,' said I. 'But I saw him after lunch today crossing the grass plot outside the club-house.

I stopped suddenly, for I knew, in a way that is inexplicable but unmistakable, that he was there then, close to us. But I saw nothing.

I got up.

'Let's go out of this room,' I said in a whisper. 'He is here.'

Even as I spoke I saw him with absolute distinctness of vision. He was standing by the cupboard door, and once more the cupboard door was opened. I heard nothing of its opening, but I suppose Hugh did, for he looked up.

'There's that beastly door opening again,' he said, and went towards it.

I felt my voice strangled in my throat.

'Don't go there,' I gasped. 'He's there.'

Hugh came close to me.

'Do you see him now?' he said.

'Yes, yes. He's going inside. Now he's gone.'

We finished our conversation upstairs in my bedroom, and made our plans, and when Marget had gone to bed, we proceeded to execute them. A carpenter came in to help us, and first we took out of the cupboard all that Hugh had stored there, took down the shelves, and stripped the paper from the walls.

It was clear that at the back of the cupboard was a hollow space some seven feet high; the walls on either hand, however, were solid. As the paper came off the cupboard and the room began to fill with a curious aromatic smell. Soon, as we stripped the corners where the back of it joined the sides, we saw that the whole back was a panel.

The carpenter examined this professionally.

'Looks as if it slid sideways, sir,' he said.

We worked at this (there was only room for two at a time in the cupboard) for a minute or two without success. Then suddenly it yielded, and ran swiftly to the left. Behind it there was standing up a tall swathed thing. Hugh and I had barely time to spring aside when it tottered and fell forward, tumbling out into the room with a soft, heavy thud...

It was the body of a woman.

By degrees, the story of the Olcombe murder, and the suicide of the murderer, was pieced together, as subsequently known to the world. The wretched woman, without doubt, had been killed by her husband, carefully embalmed, and walled up. We must suppose that terror began to gain on him—remorse perhaps—and that, first, he had found intolerable the house that concealed his crime, and later, life itself became intolerable also.

In pieces to us also came the mysterious psychical evidence, the ringing of the bell, the horrible incident of the flies, the sight to Daisy of the woman, and to Margaret, her husband, and myself, the sight of the murderer. Now one of us, now another, got into communication with the unseen world, arbitrarily it would seem, but when for some dim reason each of us happened to be in tune with it. And these fragmentary, inexplicable messages, I suppose, did the work for which they were sent, for since then the Red House has been untroubled.

THROUGH

RICHARD WAGHORN was among the cleverest and most popular of professional mediums, and a never-failing source of consolation to the credulous. That there was fraud—downright, unadulterated fraud—mixed up with his remarkable manifestations it would be impossible to deny, but it would have been futile not to admit that these manifestations were not wholly fraudulent. He had to an extraordinary degree that rare and inexplicable gift of tapping, so to speak, not only the surface consciousness of those who consulted him, but, under favourable circumstances, their inner or subliminal selves, so that it quite frequently happened that he could speak to an inquirier of something he had completely forgotten, which subsequent investigation proved to be authentic.

So much was perfectly genuine; but he gave, as it were, a false frame to it all by the manner in which he presented these phenomena. He pretended, at his *séances*, to go into a trance, during which he was con-tolled sometimes by the spirit of an ancient Egyptian priest, who gave news to the inquirer about some dead friend or relation, sometimes more directly by that dead friend or relation, who spoke through him. As a matter of fact, Waghorn would not be in a trance at all, but per-fectly conscious, extracting, as he sat quiescent and with closed eyes, the knowledge, remembered or even forgotten, that lurked in the mind of the sitter, and bringing it out in the speech of Mentu, the Egyptian control, or the lost friend or relative about whom inquiry was being made.

Fraudulent also (as coming from the intelligence of discarnate spirits) were the pieces of information he gave as to the conditions under which

those who had 'passed over' still lived, and it was here that he chiefly
brought consolation to the credulous, for he represented the dead as
happy and busy, and full of spiritual activities. This information, to
speak frankly, he obtained entirely from his own conscious mind. He
made it up, and we cannot really find an excuse for him in the
undoubted fact that he sincerely believed in the general truth of all
he said when he spoke of the survival of individual personality.

Deeply dyed, finally, with fraud, and that in crude, garish colours,
were the spirit rappings, the playing of musical boxes, the appearance
of materialized spirits, the smell of incense that heralded Cardinal Newman; all that bag of conjuring tricks, in fact, which disgraces and makes
a laughing stock of the impostors who profess to be able to bring the
seen world into connection with the unseen world. But, to do Waghorn justice, he did not often employ those crude contrivances, for his
telepathic and thought-reading gifts were far more convincing to his
sitters. Only occasionally his powers in this line used to fail him, and
then, it must be confessed, he presented his Egyptian control in the
decorations of the Egyptian Hall as controlled by Messrs Maskelyne
and Cooke.

Such was the general scheme of procedure when Richard Waghorn,
with his sister as accomplice in case mechanical tricks were necessary,
undertook to reveal the spirit world to the material world. They were
a pleasant, handsome pair of young people, gifted, both of them, with
a manner that, if anything, disarmed suspicion too much, and while
futile old gentlemen found it quite agreeable to sit in the dark holding
Julia's firm, cool hand, similarly constituted old ladies were the
recipients of thrilling emotions when they held Richard's, the touch
of which they declared was strangely electric. There they sat, while
Richard, deeply breathing and moaning in his simulated trance, was
the mouthpiece of Mentu and told them things which, but for his
indubitable gift of thought-reading, it was impossible for him to know,
or if the power was not coming through properly they listened, hardly
less thrilled, to spirit rappings and musical boxes and unverifiable information about the conditions of life where the mortal coil hampers no
longer.

It was all very interesting and soothing and edifying. And then there
suddenly came an irruption of something wholly unexpected and
inexplicable . . .

Brother and sister were dining quietly one night after a busy but

unsatisfactory day, when the tinkling summons came from the telephone, and Richard found that a quiet voice, belonging, so it said,
to Mrs Gardner, wanted to arrange a sitting alone for the next day.
No address was given, but he made an appointment for half-past two,
and went back without much enthusiasm to his dinner.

'A stranger,' he said to his sister, 'with no address and no reference
of introduction. I hope I shall be in better form tomorrow. There was
nothing but rappings and music today. They are boring, and also they
are dangerous, for one may be detected at any time. And I got an
infernal blow on my knuckles from that new electric tapper.'

Julia laughed.

'I know. I heard it,' she said. 'There was quite a wrong noise in one
of the taps as we were spelling out "silver wing." '

He lit his cigarette, frowning at the smoke.

'That's the worst of my profession,' he said. 'On some days I can
get right inside the mind of the sitter, and, as you know, bring out the
most surprising information; but on other days, today, for instance—
and there have been many such lately—there's a mere blank wall in
front of me. I shall lose my position if it happens often; nobody will
pay my fees only to hear spirit rappings and generalities.'

'They're better than nothing,' said Julia.

'Very little; they help to fill up, but I hate using them. Don't you
remember when we began investigating, just you and I alone, how often
we seemed on the verge of genuine supernatural manifestations? They
appeared to be just round the corner.'

'Yes; but we never turned the corner. We never got beyond mere
thought-reading.'

He got up.

'I know we didn't, but there always seemed a possibility. The door
was ajar; it wasn't locked, and it has never ceased to be ajar. Often
when the mere thought-reading, as you call it, is flowing along most
smoothly, I feel that if only I could abandon my whole consciousness
a little more completely, something, somebody would really take control
of me. I wish it would, and yet I'm frightened of it. It might revenge
itself for all the frauds I've perpetrated in its name. Come, let's play
picquet and forget about it all.'

It was settled that Julia should be present next day when the stranger
came for her sitting, in order, if Richard's thought-reading was not
coming through any better than it had done lately, that she should help

in the rappings and the luminous patches and the musical box. Mrs Gardner was punctual to her appointment, a tall, quiet, well-dressed woman, who stated her object in wishing for a *séance* and her views about spirit communication with perfect frankness.

'I should immensely like to believe in spirit communications,' she said, 'such as I am told you are capable of producing, but at present I don't.'

'It is important that the atmosphere should not be one of hostility,' said Waghorn in his dreamy, professional manner.

'I bring no hostility,' she said. 'I am in a state, shall we say, of benevolent neutrality, unless'—and she smiled in a charming manner—'unless benevolent neutrality has come to mean malevolent hostility. That, I assure you, is not the case with me. I want to believe.'

She paused a moment.

'And may I say this without offence?' she asked. 'May I tell you that spirit rappings and curious lights and sounds of music do not interest me in the least?'

They were already seated in the room where the *séance* was to be held. The windows were thickly curtained; there was but a glimmer of light from the red lamp, and even this the spirits would very likely desire to have extinguished. Waghorn felt that he and his sister had wasted their time in adjusting the electric hammer (made to rap by the pressure of the foot on a switch concealed in the thick rug underneath the table) behind the sliding panel, in stringing the invisible wires, on which the luminous globes ran, across ceiling, and making ready all the auxiliary paraphernalia in case the genuine telepathy was not on tap, if their visitor took no interest in such things. So, with voice dreamier than before and slower utterance, as he was supposed to be beginning to sink into trance, he just said:

'I can't foretell the manner in which They may choose to make their presence known.'

He gave one loud rap, which perfectly conveyed the word 'No' to his sister, indicating that the conjuring tricks were not to be used. Subsequently, if really necessary, he could rap 'Yes' to her, and the music and the magic lights would be displayed. Then he began to breathe quickly and in a snorting manner, to show that the control was taking possession of him.

'My brother is going into trance very quickly,' said Julia. And there was dead silence.

Immediately almost a clear and shining lucidity spread like sunshine, after these days of cloud, over Waghorn's brain. Every moment he found himself knowing more and more about this complete stranger who sat with hand touching his. He felt his subconscious brain which had lately lain so befogged and imperceptive, sun itself under the brilliant clarity of illumination that had come to it, and in the impressive bass in which Mentu was wont to give vent to his revelation, he said:

'I am here! Mentu is here!' He felt the table rocking beneath his hands, which surprised him, since he had exerted no pressure on it, and he supposed that Julia had not understood his signal, and was beginning the conjuring tricks. One hand of his was in hers, and by the pressure of his finger-tips in code, he conveyed to her 'Don't do it.' Instantly she answered back 'I wasn't.'

He paid no more heed to that, though the table continued to oscillate and tip in a very curious manner, for his mind was steeped in this flood of images that impressed themselves on his brain.

'What shall Mentu tell you today?' he went on, with pauses between the sentences. 'Someone has come to consult Mentu... It is a lady; I can see her... She wears a locket round her neck with a piece of black hair under glass between the gold.'

He felt a slight jerk from Mrs Gardner's hand, and in finger-tip code said to Julia:

'Ask her.'

Julia whispered across the table:

'Is that so?'

'Yes,' said Mrs Gardner; and Waghorn heard her take her breath quickly. He just remembered that she was not in mourning, but that made no difference. He knew, not guessing, that Mrs Gardner wanted to know something from the man or woman on whose head that hair once grew, which was contained in the locket that rested unseen below her buttoned jacket. Then next moment he knew also that this was a man's hair. Thereafter the flood of sun and certain mental impressions poured over him in a spate of sunlit waters.

'She wants to know about the boy whose hair is in the locket... He is not a boy now... He is, according to Earth's eyes, a grown man... There is a D. I see a D—not Dick, not David... There is a Y. It is Denys—not Saint Denys, not French—English Denys—Denys Bristow.'

He paused a moment, and heard Mrs Gardner whisper:

'Yes; that is right.'

Waghorn gave vent to Mentu's jovial laugh.

'She says it is right,' he said. 'How should not Mentu be right?. . .
Perhaps Mentu is right, too, when he says that Denys is her brother. . .
Yes; that is Margaret Bristow who sits here. . . Not Margaret Bristow
any longer—Margaret. . .'

Waghorn saw the name quite clearly, but yet he hesitated. It was
not Gardner at all. Then it struck him for the first time that nothing
was more likely than that Mrs Gardner had adopted a pseudonym.
He went on:

'Margaret Forsyth is Denys's sister. . . Margaret wants to know
about Denys. . . Denys is coming. . . . He will be here in a moment. . . .
He has spoken of his sister before. . . He did not call her Margaret. . .
He called her Q. . . He called her Queenie. . . Will Queenie speak?'

Waghorn felt the trembling of her hand; he heard her twice try to
speak, but she was unable to control the trembling in her voice. Then:

'Can Denys speak to me?' she said in a whisper. 'Can he really come
here?'

Up to this moment Waghorn had been enjoying himself immensely,
for after the days in which he had been unable to get into touch with
his rare and marvellous gifts of consciousness-reading, it was blissful
to find his mastery again, and, besieged with the images which
Margaret Forsyth's contact revealed to him, he had been producing
them in Mentu's impressive voice, revelling in his restored powers. Her
mind lay open to him like a book; he could read where he liked on
pages familiar to her, and on pages which had remained long unturned.
But at this moment, sudden as some qualm of sickness, he was aware
of a startling change in the quality of his perceptions. Fresh knowledge
of Denys Bristow came into his mind, but he felt that it was coming
not from her, but from some other source. . . Some odd buzzing sang
in his ears, as when an anaesthetic begins to take effect, and, opening
his eyes, he thought he saw a strange patch of light, inconsistent with
the faint illumination of the red lamp, hovering over his breast. At the
same moment he heard, though dimly, for his head was full of confused noise, the violent rapping of the electric hammer, and, already
only half conscious, felt an impotent irritation with his sister for employ-
ing these tricks. He struggled with the oncoming of the paralysis that
was so swiftly invading his mind and his physical being, but he struggled
in vain, and next moment, overwhelmed with the onrush of a huge
enveloping blackness, he lost consciousness altogether. The trance that
he had so often simulated had invaded him, and he knew nothing more.
He came to himself again, with the feeling that he had been recalled

from some vast distance. Still unable to move, he sat listening to the quick panting of his own breath before he realized what the noise was. His face, from which the sweat poured in streams, rested on something cold and hard, and presently, when he opened his eyes, he saw that his head had fallen forward on to the table. He felt utterly exhausted, and yet somehow strangely satisfied. Some amazing thing had happened . . .

Then, as he recovered himself, he began to remember that he had been reading Mrs Gardner's or Mrs Forsyth's mind when some power external to himself took possession of him, and on his left he heard Julia's voice, speaking very familiar words:

'He is coming out of his trance,' she said. 'He will be himself again in a moment now.'

With a sense of infinite weariness he raised his head, disengaged his hands from those of the two women, and sank back in his chair.

'Draw back the curtains,' he said to Julia, 'and open the window. I am suffocating.'

She did as he told her, and he saw the red rays of the sun near to its setting pour into the room, while the breeze of sunset refreshed the air. On his right still sat Mrs Forsyth, wiping her eyes and smiling at him, and having opened the window Julia came back to the table, looking at him with a curious, anxious intentness.

Then Mrs Forsyth spoke:

'It has been marvellous,' she said. 'I cannot thank you enough. I will do exactly as you, or, rather, as Denys told me about the test, and if it is right, I will certainly leave my house tomorrow, taking my servants with me. It was like Denys to think of them too.'

To Waghorn this meant nothing whatever. She might have been speaking Hebrew to him. But Julia, as she often did, answered for him.

'My brother knows nothing of what happened in his trance,' she said.

Mrs Forsyth got up.

'I will go straight home,' she said. 'I feel sure that I shall find just what Denys described. May I telephone to you about it at once?'

'Yes, pray do,' said Julia. 'We shall be most anxious to hear.'

Richard got up to show her out, but, having regained his feet, he staggered and collapsed into his chair again. Mrs Forsyth would not hear of his attempting to move just yet, and Julia, having taken her to the door, returned to her brother. It was usual for him, when the sitting was over, to feign great exhaustion, but the realism of his acting today had almost deceived her into thinking that something not yet experienced in their *séances* had occurred. Besides, he had said such strange, such detailed and extraordinary things. He was still where she had left him, and there could be no reason, now that they were alone, to keep up this feigned languor.

'Dick,' she said, 'what's the matter? And what happened? I couldn't understand you at all. What did you say all those things for?'

He stirred and sat up.

'I'm better,' he said. 'And it is you who have to tell me what happened. I remember up to a certain point, and after that I lost consciousness completely. I remember thinking you were rocking the table, and I told you not to.'

'Yes; but I wasn't rocking it. I thought you were.'

'Well, it was neither of us, then,' said he. 'I was vexed because Mrs Gardner—Mrs Forsyth—had said she didn't want that sort of thing, and I was reading her as I never ready anyone before. I told her about the locket and the black hair. I got her brother's name. I got her name and her nickname, Queenie. Then she asked if Denys could really come, and at that moment something began to take possession of me. I think I saw a light as usual over my breast, and I think I heard a tremendous rapping. Did you do either of those? Or did they really happen?'

Julia stared at him a moment in silence.

'I did neither of those,' she said. 'But they happened. You must have pressed the breast-pocket switch, and trod on the switch of the hammer.'

He opened his coat.

'I had not got the breast-pocket switch,' he said. 'And I certainly did not tread on the hammer switch.'

Julia moved her chair a little closer to him.

'The hammer did not sound right,' she said. 'It was ten times louder than I have ever heard. And the light was quite different somehow. It was much brighter. I could see everything in the room quite distinctly. Go on, Dick.'

'I can't. That's all I know until I came to, leaning over the table and bathed in perspiration. Tell me what happened.'

'Dick, do you swear that is true?' she asked.

'Certainly I do. Go on.'

'The light grew and then faded again to a glimmer,' she said, 'and then suddenly you began to talk in a different voice; it wasn't Mentu any longer. Mrs Forsyth recognized it instantly, and I thought what wonderful luck it was that you should have hit on a voice that was like her brother's. Then it and she had a long talk; it must have lasted half an hour. They reminded each other how Denys had come to live with her and her husband on their father's death. He was only eighteen at the time, and still at school. He was killed in a street accident, being run over by a bicycle two days before her birthday. All this was correct, and I thought I never heard you mind-reading so clearly and quickly; you hardly paused at all.'

Julia was silent a moment.

'Dick, don't you really know what followed?' she asked.

'Not in the smallest degree,' he said.

'Well, I thought you had gone mad,' she said. 'Mrs Forsyth asked for a test, something that was not known to her and never had been known to her, and you gave it instantly. You laughed, Denys laughed, the voice that spoke laughed, and told her to look behind the row of books beside the bed in the room that was still known as Denys's room, and she would find tucked away a little cardboard box with a gold safety-pin set with a pearl. He had bought it for her birthday present, and had hidden it there till the day came. He was killed, as I told you, two days before. And she, half sobbing, half laughing, said: "Oh, Denys, how deliciously secretive you used to be." '

'And is that what she is going to telephone about?' asked Waghorn.

'Yes. Dick, what made you say all that?'

'I don't know, I tell you. I didn't know I said it. And was that all? She said something about leaving her house tomorrow, and taking the servants. What did that mean?'

'You got very much distressed. You told her she was in danger. You said—'

Julia paused again.

'You said there was something coming—fire from the clouds and a rending. You said her country house, which I gathered was down somewhere near Epping, would be burst open by the fire from the clouds tomorrow night. You made her promise to leave it, and take the servants with her. You said her husband was away, which again is the case. And she asked if you meant Zeppelins, and you said you did.'

Waghorn suddenly got up.

' "You meant," "you said you did," ' he cried. 'What if it's "He meant," "he said he did"?'

'It's impossible,' she said, 'utterly impossible.'

'Good Lord, what's impossible?' he asked. 'What if I really am that which I have so long pretended to be? What if I am a medium, one who is the mysterious bridge between the quick and the dead? I'm frightened, but I'm bound to say I'm horribly interested. All that you tell me I said when I was in trance never came out of Mrs Forsyth's mind. It wasn't there; she didn't know about the pearl pin; she had never known it. Nor had I ever known it. Where did it come from then? Only one person knew—the boy who died ten years ago knew it.'

'It yet remains to be seen whether it is true,' said she. 'We shall know in an hour or two, for she is motoring straight down to her house in the country.'

'And if it turns out to be true, *who* was talking?' said he.

The sunset faded into the dusk of the clear May evening, and the two still sat there waiting for the telephone to inform them whether the door which, as Waghorn had said, had seemed so often ajar and never quite closed was now thrown open, and light and intelligence from another world had shone on to his unconscious mind. Presently the tinkling summons came, and with an eager curiosity, below which lurked that fear of the unknown, the dim, mysterious land into which all human creatures pass across the closed frontier, he went to hear what news awaited him.

'Trunk call,' said the operator, and he listened.

Soon the voice came through.

'Mr Wagorn?' it said.

'Yes.'

'I have found the box in exactly the place as described. It contained what we had been told it would contain. I shall leave the house, taking all the servants away, tomorrow.'

Two mornings later the papers contained news of a Zeppelin raid during the night on certain Eastern counties. The details given were vague and meagre, and no names of towns or villages where bombs had been dropped were vouchsafed to the public. But later in the day private information came to Waghorn that Forsyth Hall, near Epping, had been completely wrecked. No lives, luckily, were lost, for the house was empty.

THE BOX AT THE
BANK

THE beginning of these things, which I shall set forth in this plain narrative, happened on the evening of November 2, 1922, and the conclusion of them on the evening of the same calendar day in the year 1927. But it seems to two out of the three people concerned (and possibly to the third as well, though at present we have no further news from her) that what I have called 'the conclusion of them' is really only the first step in what may prove to be their subsequent development, and the reader, if he perseveres to the end of this short account, may possibly agree with us. But, as he will see, any further development has to be waited for, as far as Hugh Lister and I are concerned: the most we can do is to get ready for it. Again, if it comes, it may come to someone who is a total stranger to us. That is partly the reason why I am thus broadcasting, so to speak, through the Press the story of what has already happened in the hope that, should any such development occur in the experience of someone who has glanced at these pages, he will communicate the same to me.

On the evening of November 2, 1922, two friends of mine were dining with me in the house in which I am now sitting. One of these was Hugh Lister, already referred to, the other Dorothy Crofts, who married a cousin of mine, Norman Crofts, and was then a woman of nearly seventy years old and long widowed. She still preserved that insatiable interest in the concerns of daily life, which is the only secret of keeping young, and she was equally insatiable in her curiosity as to what would happen to her after death, to which, though she enjoyed life quite enormously, she looked forward just as we look forward to travel in an unknown country. She had extraordinary gifts as a purely physical medium: time and again, if she would consent to 'concentrate,' I have seen objects, such as tables and chairs, move towards her, and I have heard the room resound with rappings, or, if we sat in the dark, scintillate with lights. But she strongly disclaimed from such phenomena any so-called psychical origin: she maintained, quite rightly, so I believe, that they had nothing to do with spirits, but were the manifestation of some purely material law of which we knew nothing. She called them her conjuring tricks, and had not the slightest idea how they were done, or what they would be.

Originally we were to have been a party of four, with a view to bridge after dinner, which Dorothy plays with strangely misguided enthusiasm, in which case there would probably have been no beginning of things at all. But at the last moment I got a telephone message to say that our fourth had caught a very bad chill, and this diversion was therefore denied us. The day had been one of those preposterous *macedoines* of weather which sometimes occur at this time of year; the morning had dawned clear and cold and frosty, about midday a gale had sprung up, the temperature had risen violently, and during the afternoon we had been regaled by a thunderstorm. In the evening papers it was reported that an earthquake had been felt in the northern counties.

Whether these vagaries of climate were responsible for the wayward behaviour of a small wireless set which I had lately installed, or whether I was awkward in its adjustments, I do not know, but when I turned it on after dinner I could get nothing but squeals and mutterings and broken voices, and Dorothy suggested that we were inexplicably in touch with some agitated zoological gardens.

'That was certainly a hyena,' she said, 'and there's the keeper remonstrating with it. The earthquake has upset the poor thing. What a hideous row; do switch it off.'

I was just about to do so, when this menagerie of noises ceased altogether, and there was dead silence. Dorothy thought I had switched off.

'Thanks. That's more peaceful,' she said.

'But it's still on,' said I.

'Then the animals have calmed down and gone to sleep. But how magical those machines are even when they misbehave. And to think that we should be able to hear quite clearly in this room what is going on in some theatre or music-hall miles away! Sometimes I half expect that something different in kind will come through. It wouldn't be really much more astounding.'

'What sort of thing do you mean?' I asked.

'You'll laugh at it as being fanciful,' she said. 'But just consider; as far as we know there's no sound reaching our ears this moment except the sound of my voice talking and the flapping of the flames in the fire. But if your machine was working properly we might be listening to a band somewhere or a lecture. We are sure that we can now hear nothing of either of them, but they, and a thousand other noises, all the noises in the world in fact, are actually in this room, and we've only got to tune into them by some purely mechanical means in order to hear them. Our ears, you would say, cannot conceivably hear that band and that lecture, and yet when you turn a little handle, they do. We hear things that are not audible to our corporeal senses.'

'I see what you mean,' said Hugh. 'There are probably whole kingdoms of other sounds which exist, though they are inaudible to our senses. Is that it, Dorothy?'

'Yes. I went to *The Merchant of Venice* last night, and that struck me when the lines came:

' "Such harmony is in immortal souls.
But while this muddy vesture of decay
Doth grossly close us in, we cannot hear it." '

'But those aren't material sounds,' said I.

'How do you know they are not?' she asked. 'Why shouldn't the stars be singing? On a frosty night they look as if they were. And why shouldn't some mechanical means pierce our muddy vesture, so that we can hear them? Your machine can do it to some extent, and let us hear what is going on at the music-hall. A hundred years ago any scientist would have said it was quite impossible that we in this room should hear the band at the Savoy. But it's not only possible, but perfectly easy. And what to us today seems purely fantastic will be a chapter in an elementary science-primer a hundred years hence.'

'And is that all you meant?' I asked.

'No, my dear, of course not,' said she. 'All our advance in science at present, and perhaps for years to come, is only the running of the man who gets up speed for his leap. It is all solid ground, and then comes the jump across what seems to us the unbridgeable gulf. Perhaps it will be the final achievement of science to penetrate and establish communication with what lies beyond.'

'But what if nothing lies beyond?' said Hugh.

'I know that you don't feel sure of it,' said Dorothy, 'and I allow it would be comfortable to have some definite proof of it, however small.

Something, I mean, that can't be accounted for any other way than by the explanation that it did come from the other side of that gulf of death. How I longed for such a manifestation after my Norman died! We made a compact, he and I, that whichever of us passed over first should do all that was possible to get into communication with the one who was left. But nothing ever happened that convinced me that it came from him.'

'Did you try mediums?' asked Hugh.

'Didn't I, indeed. I tried them by the score, and they most of them professed to have got into touch with him at once and sent all sorts of rather sentimental and edifying messages from him that he was very busy and very happy. There was a sort of Sunday-school piety about them all which was quite unlike Norman, and if they were from him he must have changed very much, and I felt I should scarcely recognize him when I join him. Once or twice, again, I was told things that the medium could not have known: things about his life on earth which were quite true and which were known probably only to me. But then they *were* known to me, and it is just as likely that the medium obtained them by thought transference from me, as that she obtained them by spiritual communication from him. The only evidence which would be satisfactory would be if a medium told one something which was not known to anybody on this earth, but which turned out to be true. Anything else may be thought-transference between the living. Deeply interesting and most inexplicable. But then my conjuring tricks are that, and they are not evidence of the survival of the human spirit.'

She laughed.

'But I've long given up mediums,' she said. 'I don't like sitting in the dark with a man or a woman who presently goes into a trance and is made the spokesman for an Egyptian princess or Cardinal Newman. Mediums are usually inspired by such terribly distinguished people. Snobbishness is out of place in the spiritual world.'

'Go on about science being like a man running to get up speed for his leap,' said I.

'That's how I believe the gulf will be bridged,' said she, 'in spite of the opposition of the majority of scientists, who refuse to investigate anything psychical, and deride, as a mixture of fraud and fancy, phenomena of which they know nothing and which they will not investigate. They have none of them the slightest idea what the material world is made of and turn their backs on the quarter from which light may come. But in spite of that, they are being forced to run, and they will have to leap out over the final edge of the material world into what they call the supernatural.'

'Supernatural!' said Hugh. 'There isn't such a thing.'

'Now what do you mean by that?' asked Dorothy.

Hugh frowned at the fire for a moment.

'I mean that there can be no break anywhere,' he said. 'There is no final edge of the material world. It runs out like a promontory into the great unknown sea of psychical things. And the sea runs in, with countless bays and estuaries, into the land... The whole caboodle, whatever it is, must be one.'

'So that if,' I ventured to interrupt, 'a ghost, a figure of someone who was dead and whom once you knew, began to form itself in the air between us, you wouldn't call it supernatural, but only a natural phenomenon, appearing in concordance with some natural law of which we know practically nothing.'

'Exactly. I daresay it wouldn't be bounded by time and space in the way that we think we are, but it's our mistake to imagine that we are bounded like that. Time, at the utmost, is a little fog immediately surrounding us, and we are in eternity also. Time and space alike can be only a small wisp of cloud in the infinite. Life, whatever life is, can never have begun. There must have been a creative impulse, however far you go back; you can never get back to nothingness, and therefore you can never, however far you go on, get into nothingness.'

Dorothy laughed again.

'For heaven's sake don't let us be abstract,' she said. 'Abstractions make my brain reel, for I'm a practical woman. Let's go back to our subject. There does seem to be a break in existence, and we call it death. But I can't believe it is a real break. We move on a little out of sight, and I've been devising a test which would demonstrate to you two, after I'm dead, that I've only moved on. I want to show you something practical, not give you vaguely pious assurances that I'm busy and happy and working away with Cardinal Newman and Egyptian princesses. And I think I've made up a test which, if it comes off, will be convincing.'

'Impossible', said I. 'You can't make any communication to us, after you're dead, which we couldn't have guessed or conjectured from our knowledge of you while you were alive.'

'My dear, do be quiet and listen,' said she. 'I'm going to take a nice little box and place in it certain material objects. No one shall know, except myself, what they are: there may be a key, or a flower, or a ring, or a piece of paper with words written on it, or a pencil, or a photograph, or an elastic band, or a boot-lace, or a coin, or a card, or a pebble, or a tie-pin, or a biscuit, or a book... I have everything portable in the world to choose from. Well, when I have made my selection, I shall seal the packet up and send it to my bank, and I shall leave directions in my will that it is to be delivered to either of you when you go and claim it. But you must both promise me that you will not claim it unless you are convinced that I, from the other world, or so we call it, have conveyed to you what it contains. Then you will open it and see if you are right. Nobody on this earth can possibly know what is inside it, so if, out of all the multiplicity of objects which I can put in it, you find that you have chosen precisely those that I have put there, it will be pretty good evidence that the knowledge has come to you from me.'

'Not a bad idea,' said Hugh. 'What a pity you won't be here, Dorothy, to see the success of your experiment.'

'My dear, I shall be *there*,'' said she. 'If in my future existence after death I can send you, by some means or other, a correct message of what is in that box, I imagine I shall know that I've done so. And, anyhow, you will have the satisfaction of knowing that you have learned from me on the other side of death what was unknown to anyone living. Surely that will be a good, sound, practical proof that I am in existence, still with an individual memory of the earth.'

The idea was an interesting one, and for some quarter of an hour we discussed it, trying to foresee subsequent objections (given that the test seemed to have succeeded) which might invalidate it as a proof. An obvious precaution to be taken was that before claiming and opening the packet we must write down and witness and date our solution, however conveyed to us, of what the packet contained.

'But there's more than that,' said I. 'Hugh often has extremely curious and vivid dreams. He might, after your lamentable death, dear Dorothy, dream that you had told him what was in the packet. And then if we opened it and found its contents bore no relation to what he had dreamed, a most ingenious test would be lost. I think we must rule out dreams. Not good enough to risk opening it.'

'I agree,' said Hugh, 'and I should like to rule out mediums. We shall both of us probably imagine what is in your posthumous packet, and by thought-transference a medium might get at it. I vote against dreams and mediums.'

'We aren't leaving many routes for communications,' said I.

'We don't want to,' said Dorothy. 'If, after death, I find it is possible to get through to you, I'll manage it without dreams or mediums. How, I don't know.'

'And then there's another thing,' said I. 'Isn't is possible that after death our memory of earth affairs may be very dim and vague? It often happens at séances that the communicating spirit can't get the names right even of those they knew best and want to speak to. The medium says, 'Is there a Henry here?' And then they try Charles.'

Dorothy got up, warming herself at the fire.

'If I forget what I've put in that packet,' she said firmly, 'I must have lost all individuality. Dorothy Crofts (that's me) simply can't forget the amazing things she will stow there. If she does, she has ceased to be. And individual survival is what we want to get at.'

She was wearing a collar of moonstones, and as she turned her head, I saw that one of them was missing.

'There's a stone gone out of your collar,' I said.

'I know. It dropped out while I was dressing. But I picked it up: it's quite safe. But how cold it's got.'

'This charming climate,' said I. 'Do some conjuring tricks to warm you.'

The room certainly had got icy, though the fire prospered, and, having put more coal on it, I went to the window and drew the curtains aside, to see if any pleasant little surprise in the shape of a snowstorm had been brewed for us. But the night was clear and I pulled the window open. A current of warm mild air poured in: it was certainly far colder in the room in spite of the fire than it was outside.

Dorothy had seated herself at the card-table, which had been put in anticipation of bridge.

'Snowing, I suppose?' she said.

'Not a bit. Much warmer outside than in.'

'That's odd,' she said. 'I've known that happen once or twice at séances, when something really came through. It isn't actually cold here. You won't find that the thermometer is low.'

There was one on the wall away from the fire, and Hugh peered at it.

'Sixty-five', he said, 'but I feel it bitter. The result of our spooky conversation, I suppose. By the way, it's All Souls' Day.'

'Bless them!' said Dorothy. 'Now I'll just do some conjuring tricks for five minutes and then I must get home.'

'What are they going to be?' I asked.

'That's exactly what I don't know. That's the joy of them. But I know something will happen. I can always feel when the steam is up.'

She sat back in her chair at the card-table, on which were pencils and markers and two new packs of cards, just resting her hands on the edge of the table and relaxing herself. For two or three minutes she sat thus, both of us watching her, and then a couple of sharp raps came apparently from the loud-speaker, which stood on the piano a few feet away. Simultaneously one of the packs of cards spread itself out over the table just as if someone had smoothed them out for cutting, and then reversed itself so that the faces of the cards were exposed. The top one was the joker.

'That's a beauty,' said Hugh.

He had hardly spoken, when Dorothy pushed her chair back.

'There's something coming,' she said, 'but it's nothing to do with me; it's from outside my range.'

There came a sound from the loud-speaker, as of someone whispering. Then I heard articulated words in a voice that I knew had been once familiar.

'Dorothy, can you hear me? Can you hear me, Dorothy?'

She ran to it.

'Ah, yes, yes,' she cried. 'It's you, Norman! Oh, at last! Now what is it, my darling? I'm here.'

There was silence, and then once more very faintly came the whisper: 'It's difficult,' it said, 'but I've done it, my dear.'

There was no more, and presently Dorothy turned to us, wiping her eyes.

'Thank God for that,' she said. 'That was Norman's voice: shouldn't I recognize it out of a thousand? Now I must go. No more conjuring tricks after that.'

She and Hugh went off together, and when I came back, after seeing them into their taxi, the room which, five minutes ago, had seemed so cold, was almost oppressively warm. Certainly that impression of cold occurred sometimes, as Dorothy had said, at séances, when some manifestation was at hand, and it was curious that immediately after we had all felt it there came through the loud-speaker the voice which she recognized as her husband's. I, too, had recognized it as familiar, and when she said it was his, I had the conviction that she was right. But it had been such a fragment that it was worth little as evidence: all that I was quite sure about was that something was seriously amiss with the transmission tonight. Then suddenly the loudspeaker poured forth a riot of jazz, and I turned it off. It was time to go to bed, and I gathered up the cards, which still lay spread fanwise on the table. But the joker which, I clearly remembered seeing lying on the top of them was gone, and I searched everywhere for it, but without success.

I saw Dorothy again a few days after this meeting, and she told me that she had made up the packet and sent it to the bank with full directions. Without conscious intention, I began to wonder what she had put in it, and instantly the missing joker from my cards seemed a likely object. Again, when a month or two later I saw that the moonstone which had dropped out of her collar had not been replaced, I fixed on that as having gone into the packet, and the disappearance of a minute china cat from her writing-table, which had long been a mascot there, indicated a similar destination. I thought, in fact, that Dorothy had made up her packet rather obviously, and one day I mentioned my conjectures to her. She laughed.

'Very sharp of you,' she said, 'and it all sounds most probable. But I can't make up another packet, and we must just leave it as it is. You may see some day just how right or how wrong you were, but that won't be till I'm dead, and perhaps not then. In the meantime forget about it all as much as you can. I don't feel the least like dying yet.'

Time went on. Dorothy took to spending the greater part of the year at the little place her husband had left her in Cornwall, taking a niece of Norman's to live with her, and during the year which preceded the incident with which, for the present, my story closes, I had seen very little of her. I heard from her, however, on the morning of November 2, 1927, a happy, chatty letter, promising, as usual, that she would come up to London before long and suggesting that I should go down to her for Christmas. By pure chance—if there is such a thing as chance in this world of elaborate design—Hugh was dining with me that night, and it was not till he had reminded me of the fact that it came into my head at all that it was just five years ago to the day that we had talked over the packet which was to be left at the bank.

'I had half forgotten about it,' said I, 'but it's vivid enough now you mention it. There was a joker missing from a pack of cards that night, and a moonstone missing from Dorothy's collar, and subsequently a little mascot cat missing from her writing-table. I feel sure she put all those into the packet, and for that reason it has ceased to be a good test. May it remain many years in the bank, without the possibility of either of us claiming it, but if she dies before I do there will be in the world the knowledge, because it really comes to that, of certain objects which are sealed up there.'

'I had half-forgotten about it, too,' said he, 'but I was reminded of it today. I went to sleep after lunch, which I haven't done for ever so long, and I had the most extraordinarily vivid dream about it.'

'But we settled dreams shouldn't count,' said I, 'and besides Dorothy is quite alive. I heard from her today.'

'I know that,' said he, 'but I intend to tell you my dream all the same, for it has haunted me ever since. I dreamed that you and she and I were sitting here in this room, and she said, 'Now I'm going to tell you both what's in the packet.' I begged her no to, because it would quite spoil it as a test, and she said, 'On the contrary, it will establish it. There's nothing in the packet at all. It's just an empty box. Nothing in it. Empty. You'll open it quite soon now and then you'll see.' And then I woke, rather annoyed with her, and found myself sitting close up to the fire and shivering with cold.'

He pulled a half-sheet of paper out of his pocket.

'The whole thing was so vivid,' he said, 'that I wrote it down, just as I've told you, and dated it with the day and the hour. Just glance through it, and if it's correct, sign the note I made at the bottom.'

'I never heard such nonsense,' said I. 'Supposing I dream tonight that the packet contained something else? Besides, as I say, the whole thing is worthless at present. She's not dead, bless her. Your dream can't have come from her on the other side.'

'That's true. But sign it all the same,' said Hugh.

I looked through the few lines, and found they contained just the account he had given me. At the bottom he had written, 'Hugh Lister told me this dream on the evening of November 2, 1927.'

'I may as well give the hour, too,' I said, and added 9.25 p.m. and signed it.

'And now confess what rubbish it all is,' said I.

'Rather. But I like rubbish. I've got lots of dreams written down.'

We talked for a while, but by degrees I got more and more occupied with my new wireless set, which had arrived only the day before, and was the last word in the inventions on the market. What particularly fascinated me was fishing blindly for some wandering voice in the air, and having switched the two controls across to 2,000, I put one of the dials at 100 and the other at zero, and began softly turning the latter.

'You can't tell what will come through,' I said, 'and usually nothing does. But there's romance about it: it's much more exciting than tuning in to a station you know. Just like fishing: you throw a fly over a waste of waters, and from the unknown something rises to it.'

But it seemed as if nothing was rising from the unknown tonight; whistlings from the machine occasionally heralded the vicinity of something coherent, but never could I get more than mutterings.

'It wants humouring,' I said. 'I don't know its ways yet. Machines aren't mere inanimate affairs: there is almost a living sensitiveness about them sometimes. They answer to one hand and not to another.'

'I'll try mine in a moment,' said Hugh, 'but I must get warm first. I've felt cold ever since I woke from my nap this afternoon.'

'Put some coal on,' I said. 'It does seem chilly.'

Hugh rattled a shovelful of coal on to the fire and poked it up into a blaze.

'Like that night five years ago,' he said, 'when Dorothy thought she heard Norman's voice. Queer thing that was.'

He walked to the stool on which my wireless stood, independent and complete in itself, and brought it on to the hearthrug.

'That will encourage it,' he said. 'And now we'll see what my magic touch will do. Am I to twirl those dials about?'

'Yes, and go slow when it whistles.'

With a hand on each of the dials, he moved them about this way and that. Suddenly there came a whistle, and immediately afterwards a voice:

'Nothing in it,' it said. 'Empty.'

Then again the whistle came, and with something, I hardly knew what, twanging in my brain, I sprang up.

'Get back to that again,' I said. 'Something got through.'

'I'm back exactly where I was,' said he in an odd choked voice.

'You can't be. Move the dials by a fraction of an inch. Just stroke them.'

For ten minutes more first he and then I tried to get back to that hair's-breadth of an adjustment, but it was no use.

'Perhaps that was all,' he said. 'And what do you make of it?'

We knew what was in each other's minds then.

'And what do you make of it?' I answered.

He drew the paper I had signed from his pocket.

' "Nothing in it. Empty," is exactly the phrase which I dreamed that Dorothy used to me this afternoon,' he answered.

'And what then?' I asked sharply. I knew I was frightened, and that my nerves were a-jangle.

'Now pull yourself together,' he said. 'I know what's in your mind, and you know what's in mine, namely that Dorothy—'

Before he could say anything more, the door opened, and my servant came in.

'Telephone, sir, a trunk call,' he said.

I went down the half-flight of stairs to where the telephone stood. It was Dorothy's niece who wanted to speak to me. She had only just got hold of my address and telephone number from a letter of mine which she found among a pile of papers on her aunt's table. Her news was that Dorothy had died quite suddenly that morning.

I went down to Cornwall for the funeral, and it was not till my return that Hugh and I talked over what had happened that night. That odd vivid dream of his had come to him after Dorothy's death, so also of course, had the message—if it was a message—from her on the wireless. We settled to wait for another ten days in order to see whether any further sign or intimation reached us, but there was none, and at the end of that time we went together to the bank where the packet was deposited and asked for it. All was in order, and there was handed to us a box wrapped up in paper and heavily sealed: with it was a letter directed to me. We took them to my house, and opened the letter first. It was quite short.

'My dear, I have been very cunning,' it ran. 'I took away that joker from your pack of cards, and I put away the little china cat that used to stand on my table, and the moonstone which was missing from my collar. All to mislead you. I knew you were wondering what would be in the packet, and these would give you false scents. By now the packet will be in your hands, and perhaps you will have opened it, for you and Hugh would not have claimed it unless you thought that since my death I had managed to communicate with you. I wish I was there to see you open it, but possibly—who knows?—I shall be. I do hope you will have got my message correctly, though how I shall be able to send it I can't yet guess. Love to you both. Dorothy.'

I read this aloud.

'That's so like her,' said Hugh, 'and now we'll open the packet. Luckily there can't be the slightest mistake about it. If there's anything whatever in the box, the test is a complete failure.

I broke the seals and cut the string, and took off the paper in which the box was wrapped. It was made of varnished wood with a catch to shut it, and I raised the hinged lid.

The box was empty.

That, for the present, is the end of my story. As far as Hugh and I can see, the test was completely successful: and Dorothy some hours after her death conveyed to us both that there was nothing in the packet. From the other side of death she came through to us. And, since she has done so once, she may get through again. But in our ignorance of what the conditions of communication are, she may choose next time to get through not to us, to whom now she has made a convincing demonstration, but to others who are strangers to us. If, therefore, whether by wireless or by automatic script or by dreams any message, apparently from her, arrives, we hope that the recipient will kindly inform us of it.

THE LIGHT IN THE GARDEN

THE house and the dozen acres of garden and pasture-land surrounding it, which had been left me by my uncle, lay at the top end of one of those remote Yorkshire valleys carved out among the hills of the West Riding. Above it rose the long moors of bracken and heather, from which flowed the stream that ran through the garden, and, joining another tributary, brawled down the valley into the Nidd, and at the foot of its steep fields lay the hamlet—a dozen of houses and a small grey church. I had often spent half my holidays there when a boy, but for the last twenty years my uncle had become a confirmed recluse, and lived alone, seeing neither kith nor kin nor friends from January to December.

It was, therefore, with a sense of clearing old memories from the dust and dimness with which the lapse of years had covered them that I saw the dale again on a hot July afternoon in this year of drought and rainlessness. The house, as his agent had told me, was sorely in need of renovation and repair, and my notion was to spend a fortnight here in personal supervision. I had arranged that the foreman of a firm of decorators in Harrogate should meet me here next day and discuss what had to be done. I was still undecided whether to live in the house myself or let or sell it. As it would be impossible to stay there while painting and cleaning and repairing were going on, the agent had recommended me to inhabit for the next fortnight the lodge which stood at the gate on to the high road. My friend, Hugh Grainger, who was to have come up with me, had been delayed by business in London, but he would join me tomorrow.

It is strange how the revisiting of places which one has known in youth revives all sorts of memories which one had supposed must have utterly faded from the mind. Such recollections crowded fast in upon me, jostling each other for recognition and welcome, as I came near to the place. The sight of the church recalled a Sunday of disgrace, when I had laughed at some humorous happening during the progress of the prayers; the sight of the coffee-coloured stream recalled memories of trout fishing; and, most of all, the sight of the lodge, built of brown stone, with the high wall enclosing the garden, reawoke the most vivid and precise recollections. My uncle's butler, of the name of Wedge—how it all came back!—lived there, coming up to the house of a morning, and going back there with his lantern at night, if it was dark and moonless, to sleep; Mrs Wedge, his wife, had the care of the locked gate, and opened it to visiting or outgoing vehicles. She had been rather a formidable figure to a small boy, a dark, truculent woman, with a foot curiously malformed, so twisted that it pointed outwards and at right angles to the other. She scowled at you when you knocked at the door and asked her to open the gate, and came hobbling out with a dreadful rocking movement. It was, in fact, worth the trouble of going round by a path through the plantation in order to avoid an encounter with Mrs Wedge, especially after one occasion, when, not being able to get any response to my knockings, I opened the door of the lodge and found her lying on the floor, flushed and tipsily snoring... Then the last year that I ever came here Mrs Wedge went off to Whitby or Scarborough on a fortnight's holiday. Wedge had not waited at breakfast that morning, for he was said to have driven the dogcart to take Mrs Wedge to the station at Harrogate, ten miles away. There was something a little odd about this, for I had been early abroad that morning, and thought I had seen the dogcart bowling along the road with Wedge, indeed, driving it, but no wife beside him. How odd, I thought now, that I should recollect that, and even while I wondered that I should have retained so insignificant a memory, the sequel, which made it significant, flashed into my mind, for a few days afterwards Wedge was absent again, having been sent for to go to his wife, who was dying. He came back a widower. A woman from the village was installed as lodge-keeper, a pleasant body, who seemed to enjoy opening the gate to a young gentleman with a fishing-rod... Just at that moment my rummaging among old memories ceased, for here was the agent, warned by the motor-horn, coming out of the brown stone lodge.

There was time before sunset to stroll up to the house and form a general idea of what must be done in the way of decoration and repair, and not till we had got back to the lodge again did the thought of Wedge re-occur to me.

'My uncle's butler used to live here,' I said. 'Is he alive still? Is he here now?'

'Mr Wedge died a fortnight ago,' said the agent. 'It was of the suddenest; he was looking forward to your coming and to attending to you, for he remembered you quite well.'

Though I had so vivid a mental picture of Mrs Wedge, I could not recall in the least what Wedge looked like.

'I, too, can remember all about him,' I said. 'But I can't remember him. What was he like?'

Mr Harkness described him to me, of course, as he knew him, an old man of middle height, grey-haired, and much wrinkled, with the habit of looking round quickly when he spoke to you; but his description roused no response whatever in my memory. Naturally, the grey hair and the wrinkles, and, for that matter, perhaps the habit of 'looking round quickly,' delineated an older man than he was when I knew him, and anyhow, among so much that was vivid in recollection, the appearance of Wedge was to me not even dim, but had no existence at all.

I found that Mr Harkness had made thoughtful arrangements for my comfort in the lodge. A woman from the village and her daughter were to come in early every morning for cooking and housework, and leave again at night after I had had my dinner. I was served with an excellent plain meal, and presently, as I sat watching the fading of the long twilight, there came past my open window, the figures of the woman and the girl going home to the village. I heard the gate clang as they passed out, and knew that I was alone in the house. To cheerful folk of solitude, such as myself, that is a rare but pleasant sensation; there is the feeling that by no possibility can one be interrupted, and I prepared to spend a leisurely evening over a book that had beguiled my journey and a pack of Patience cards. It was fast growing dark, and before settling down I turned to the chimney-piece to light a pair of candles. Perhaps the kindling of the match cast some momentary shadow, for I found myself looking quickly across to the window, under the impression that some black figure had gone past it along the garden path outside. The illusion was quite momentary, but I knew that I was thinking about Wedge again. And still I could not remember in the least what Wedge was like.

My book that had begun so well in the train proved disappointing in its development, and my thoughts began to wander from the printed page, and presently I rose to pull down the blinds which till now had remained unfurled. The room was at an angle of the cottage; one window looked up to the little high-walled garden, the other up the road towards my uncle's house. As I drew down the blind here I saw up the road the light as of some lantern, which bobbed and oscillated as if to the steps of someone who carried it, and the thought of Wedge coming home at night when his work at the house was done re-occurred to my memory. Then, even as I watched, the light, whatever it was, ceased to oscillate, but burned steadily. At a guess, I should have said it was about a hundred yards distant. It remained like that a few seconds and then went out, as if the bearer had extinguished it. As I pulled down the blind I found that my breath came quick and shallow, as if I had been running.

It was with something of an effort that I sat myself down to play Patience, and with an effort that I congratulated myself on being alone and secure from interruptions. I did not feel quite so secure now, and I did not know what the interruption might be. . . There was no sense of any presence but my own being in the house with me, but there was a sense, deny it though I might, of there being some presence out-side. A shadow had seemed to cross the window looking on to the garden; on the road a light had appeared, as if carried by some noc-turnal passenger, and somehow the two seemed to have a common source, as if some presence that hovered about the place was striving to manifest itself. . .

At that moment there came on the door of the house, just outside the room where I sat, a sharp knock, followed by silence, and then once more a knock. And instantaneous, as a blink of lightning, there flashed unbidden into my mind the image of the lantern-bearer who, seeing me at the window, had extinguished his light, and in the dark-ness had crept up to the house and was now demanding admittance. I knew that I was frightened now, but I knew also that I was hugely interested, and, taking one of the candles in my hand, I went quietly to the door.

Just then the knocking was renewed outside, three raps in quick succession, and I had to wait until mere curiosity was ascendant again over some terror that came welling up to my forehead in beads of mois-ture. It might be that I should find outside some tenant or dependent of my uncle, who, unaware of my advent, wondered who might have business in this house lately vacated, and in that case my terror would vanish; or I should find outside either nothing or some figure as yet unconjecturable, and my curiosity and interest would flame up again. And then, holding the candle above my head so that I could look out undazzled, I pulled back the latch of the door and opened it wide.

Though but a few seconds ago the door had sounded with the knockings, there was no one there, neither in front of it nor to the right or left of it. But though to my physical eye no one was visible, I must believe that to the inward eye of soul or spirit there was apparent that which my grosser bodily vision could not perceive. For as I scrutinized the empty darkness it was as if I was gazing on the image of the man whom I had so utterly forgotten, and I knew what Wedge was like when I had seen him last. 'In his habit as he lived' he sprang into my mind, his thick brown hair not yet tinged with grey, his hawk-like nose, his thin, compressed mouth, his eyes set close together, which shifted if you gave him a straight gaze. No less did I know his low, broad shoulders and the mole on the back of his left hand, his heavy watch-chain, his dark striped trousers. Externally and materially my questing eyes saw but the empty circle of illumination cast by my candle, but my soul's vision beheld Wedge standing on the doorstep. It was his shadow that had passed the window as I lit my lights after dinner, his lantern that I had seen on the road, his knocking that I had heard.

Then I spoke to him who stood there so minutely seen and yet so invisible.

'What do you want with me, Wedge?' I asked. 'Why are you not at rest?'

A draught of wind came round the corner, extinguishing my light. At that a gust of fear shook me, and I slammed to the door and bolted it. I could not be there in the darkness with that which indubitably stood on the threshold.

The mind is not capable of experiencing more than a certain degree of any emotion. A climax arrives, and an assuagement, a diminution follows. That was certainly the case with me now, for though I had to spend the night alone here, with God knew what possible visitations before day, the terror had reached its culminating point and ebbed away again. Moreover, that haunting presence, which I now believed I had identified, was without and not within the house. It had not, to the psychical sense, entered through the open door, and I faced my solitary night with far less misgiving than would have been mine if I had been obliged now to fare forth into the darkness. I slept and woke again, and again slept, but never with panic of nightmare, or with the sense, already once or twice familiar to me, that there was any presence in the room beside my own, and when finally I dropped into a dreamless slumber I woke to find the cheerful day already bright, and the dawn-chorus of the birds in full harmony.

My time was much occupied with affairs of restorations and repairs that day, but I did a little private thinking about Wedge, and made up my mind that I would not tell Hugh Grainger any of my experiences on the previous evening. Indeed, they seemed now of no great evidential value: the shape that had passed my window might so easily have been some queer shadow cast by the kindling of my match; the lantern-light I had seen up the road—if, indeed, it was a lantern at all—might easily have been a real lantern, and who knew whether those knocks at the door might not have been vastly exaggerated by my excitement and loneliness, and be found only to have been the tapping of some spray of ivy or errant creeper? As for the sudden recollection of Wedge, which had eluded me before, it was but natural that I should sooner or later have recaptured the memory of him. Besides, supposing there was anything supernormal about these things, and supposing that they or similar phenomena appeared to Hugh also, his evidence would be far more weighty, if it was come at independently, without the prompting of suggestions from me.

He arrived, as I had done the day before, a little before sunset, big and jovial, and rather disposed to reproach me for holding out troutfishing as an attraction, when the stream was so dwindled by the drought.

'But there's rain coming,' said he. 'Can't you smell it?'

The sky certainly was thickly overcast and sultry with storm, and before dinner was over the shrubs outside began to whisper underneath the first drops. But the shower soon passed, and while I was busy with some estimate which I had promised the contractor to look at before he came again next morning, Hugh strolled out along the road up to the house for a breath of air. I had finished before he came back, and we sat down to picquet. As he cut, he said:

'I thought you told me the house above was unoccupied. But I passed a man apparently coming down from there, carrying a lantern.'

'I don't know who that could be,' said I. 'Did you see him at all clearly?'

'No, he put out his lantern as I approached; I turned immediately afterwards, and caught him up, and passed him again.'

There came a knock at the front door, then silence, and then a repetition.

'Shall I see who it is while you are dealing?' he said.

He took a candle from the table, but, leaving the deal incomplete, I followed him, and saw him open the door. The candlelight shone out into the darkness, and under Hugh's uplifted arm I beheld, vaguely and indistinctly, the shape of a man. Then the light fell full on to his face, and I recognized him.

'Yes, what do you want?' said Hugh, and just as had happened last night a puff of wind blew the flame off the candle-wick and left us in the dark.

Then Hugh's voice, suddenly raised, came again.

'Here, get out,' he said. 'What do you want?'

I threw open the door into the sitting-room close at hand, and the light within illuminated the narrow passage of the entry. There was no one there but Hugh and myself.

'But where's the beggar gone?' said Hugh. 'He pushed in by me. Did he go into the sitting-room? And where on earth is he?'

'Did you see him?' I asked.

'Of course I saw him. A little man, hook-nosed, with eyes close together. I never liked a man less... Look here, we must search through the house. He did come in.'

Together, not singly, we went through the few rooms which the cottage contained, the two living rooms and the kitchen below, and the three bedrooms upstairs. All was empty and quiet.

'It's a ghost,' said Hugh; and then I told him my experience on the previous evening. I told him also that I knew of Wedge, and of his wife, and of her sudden death when on her holiday. Once or twice as I spoke I saw that Hugh put up his hand as if to shade the flame of the candle from shining out into the garden, and as I finished he suddenly blew it out and came close to me.

'I thought it was the reflection of the candle-light on the panes,' he said, 'but it isn't. Look out there.'

There was a light burning at the far end of the garden, visible in glimpses through a row of tall peas, and there was something moving beside it. A piece of an arm appeared there, as of a man digging, a shoulder and head...

'Come out,' whispered Hugh. 'That's our man. And what is he doing?'

Next moment we were gazing into blackness; the light had vanished.

We each took a candle and went out through the kitchen door. The flames burned steady in the windless air as in a room, and in five minutes we had peered behind every bush, and looked into every cranny. Then suddenly Hugh stopped.

'Did you leave a light in the kitchen?' he asked.

'No.'

'There's one there now,' he said, and my eye followed his pointing finger.

There was a communicating door between our bedrooms, both of which looked out on to the garden, and before getting into bed I made myself some trivial excuse of wanting to speak to Hugh, and left it open. He was already in bed.

'You'd like to fish tomorrow?' I asked.

Before he could answer the room leaped into light, and simultaneously the thunder burst overhead. The fountains of the clouds were unsealed, and the deluge of the rain descended. I took a step across to the window with the idea of shutting it, and across the dark streaming cave of the night outside, again, and now unobscured from the height of the upper floor, I saw the lantern light at the far end of the garden, and the figure of a man bending and rising again as he plied his secret task... The downpour continued; sometimes I dozed for a little, but through dozing and waking alike, my mind was delving and digging as to why out there in the hurly-burly of the storm, the light burned and the busy figure rose and fell. There was haste and bitter urgency in that hellish gardening, which recked nothing of the rain.

I awoke suddenly from an uneasy doze, and felt the skin of my scalp grow tight with some nameless terror. Hugh apparently had lit his candle again, for light came in through the open door between our rooms. Then came the click of a turned handle, and the other door into the passage slowly opened. I was sitting up in bed now with my eyes fixed on it, and round it came the figure of Wedge. He carried a lantern, and his hands were black with mould. And at that sight the whole of my self-control was shattered.

'Hugh!' I yelled. 'Hugh! He is here.'

Hugh came hurrying in, and for one second I turned my eyes to him.

'There by the door!' I cried.

When I looked back the apparition was no longer there. But the door was open, and on the floor by it fragments of mud and soaked soil...

The sequel is soon told. Where we had seen the figure digging in the garden was a row of lavender bushes. These we pulled up, and three feet below came on the huddled remains of a woman's body. The skull had been beaten in by some crashing blow; fragments of clothing and the malformation of one of the feet were sufficient to establish identification. The bones lie now in the churchyard close by the grave of her husband and murderer.

DUMMY ON A DAHABEAH

I HAD been awake some time, wedged tight in my berth, with a knee against the wall and a foot against the iron rail, which prevented my falling bodily on the floor, listening lazily to the drumming of the screw. We had passed through very rough weather the day before, and the boat was still rolling heavily. From time to time I could see the horizon, bearing Crete on its rim, swing into sight across the glass of the port-hole, and now and then a great blue transparency of wave would fling itself against the window, darkening the cabin for a moment. Then the boat righted itself, and the bright reflection of the water cast on the roof scudded along again till another big wave took us in hand. But it was a glorious morning, and though I would willingly have pro-longed those delicious moments which lie on the borderland between sleeping and waking, I felt it my duty to wake Tom. He stretched himself lazily and sat up.

'It is good to be at sea,' he said. 'When do we get in to Alexandria?'

'About one.'

'Well, it's time to get up. Shall I get up first or you? How this old tub is rolling! There's not room for us both to dress together.'

'You,' said I promptly.

Tom rang the bell and ordered his bath.

'Hot and salt,' said he.

He staggered into his dressing-gown, plunged at his slippers, and sidled out of the cabin. I found to my disgust that I was too much awake to continue not thinking, and read the directions for putting on the lifebelt, according to the principles of the P and O. Drowning was a horrible death! People who had been nearly drowned were supposed to say that it was delightful, like going slowly to sleep. Well, perhaps it was better than some deaths. And then, by a natural transition, my thoughts wandered to where I was going, and what I was going to do.

Tony and I were on our way to join Harry Brookfield. Six months ago he had lost his wife. She had been dressing for a ball in London and her dress caught fire. She died in a few hours.

Since then he had been abroad, and this winter he was in Egypt. He had written to me saying that he was going up the Nile in a daha-beah for a few months, and would Tom and I join him. And, we for our vices and virtues, being people of leisure, said we would. Harry had been in Cairo for a few days already, and we hoped to join him there in the evening.

But the rough weather detained us, and we did not get into Alexan-dria till after the express for Cairo had left. Alexandria is not a partic-ularly attractive place, but it has the smell of the south about it, and to me no place is without merit provided it smells of the south.

After dinner we sat in the open garden of the Hotel Abbat and smoked. Smoking begets silence, and silence thought, and thought speech; and after a little while Tom began to speak of a thing which had several times been in the background of my mind since the receipt of the letter which asked us to come to Egypt.

'It's odd Harry coming out to Egypt again, isn't it?' he said.

'Why?' I asked, because I knew and did not wish to say.

'His wife, you know. He spent his honeymoon on a dahabeah up the Nile.'

'Yes, and on the same dahabeah as that on which we are going now.'

'Have you seen him since—since it happened?'

'Yes, I met him in Florence in November, and he came with me from there to Athens before you came out.'

'How does he bear it?'

'He never mentions her name, and tries never to think of her,' I said.

'That makes it all the odder, his taking his dahabeah.'

'Yes, unless he has succeeded in never thinking of her.'

Harry met us next day at Cairo station, and we were both, I think, surprised to see him looking so extremely well and prosperous. Great sorrow—and his sorrow had been very great—usually leaves some trace behind, often some little nervous trick of manner, or, more generally, when the mind is unoccupied, a haunted, anxious look. But he was, in every respect, his old cheery self. The traditional English plan of travelling in order to forget, which reverses the *'coelum non animum'* proverb, had evidently vindicated itself in his case.

'Delighted to see you,' he said. 'Tom, you are growing fat. You shall sit in the sun till you are as dry as a grasshopper. As for you,' he went on, turning to me, 'you simply look absurdly well. People like you have got no business to spend a winter in Egypt. We'll go straight to the dahabeah. She's ready, and we can start in an hour. Cairo is hateful—cram full of the refuse of English-speaking people. One always sees on Shepheard's veranda some eight or ten of the people one hoped never to see again.'

And before three o'clock we were off.

At this point in my story I must give a word of warning. I make no defence for what I am going to tell you, except the very unsatisfactory and unconvincing one that I declare that what I record as happening to me is true. Tom Soden is also willing to declare that what is recorded of him is true. Harry Brookfield died last year, and I can no longer make him a witness. But many people who, before his death, played whist with him and Tom will tell you that they have often heard him say to Tom, 'Why can't you play your hand as you played your dummy's up the Nile?' And when he asked this question Tom not unfrequently would turn rather pale and ask for a whisky and soda.

That is all my defence.

We started with a good north wind which took us quickly along, the great sail stretched taut and firm, and the water rising from the forefoot in a thin feather. That evening we got to Memphis, and as the moon was full we took donkeys and rode out to Sakharah, on the edge of the desert. There is an Arab proverb, 'He who smells the desert once, smells it when he dies,' and sometimes in London, which smells quite different, I have felt, on hot June evenings, when the air seemed to be dying with the want of breath, that I should be almost willing to die if I could smell the desert once more. The truth is that the desert alone, of all things created, does not smell at all, and our sense of smell, the most delicate and keen sense we possess, finds it infinitely restful to draw in warm, unused air that smells of nothing at all. Perhaps that is what the Arab proverb means. The moon was at its full; Jupiter, blazing low on the horizon, cast a shadow of its own; the seen Pleiades, distinct and unblurred, hung high, freed of their silver net; and low in the north the Great Bear swung slowly to its setting, upside down. To the west, the desert stretched away, silent and sombre, across a continent.

Even Tom, who is not given to have 'feelings,' felt its spell.

'I should like,' he said, 'to walk straight into it for ever, if only it was always moonlight.'

The false dawn was already beginning to glow faintly in the east when we got back to the dahabeah, and a couple of hours after we had gone to bed we weighed anchor, and still followed by the north wind slid on our course.

For several days we had a delicious, uneventful life, reading not at all, talking not much, only sitting in the sun and charging our bodies with stores of superfluous health. But towards the end of the week Harry began to get rather restless, and it occurred by degrees to all of us that we might perhaps do well to employ ourselves, however lazily, while we sat in the sun. The wind still held good, and it was a pity to stop the boat and go shooting, for the best shooting ground lay farther up the river, and in all human probability, we should have plenty of days on which we could not move, so that it was best to go on while we could. And one afternoon, while we were dozing after lunch, Tom said lazily:

'Why not play cards?'

Brookfield jumped up at once.

'The very thing,' he said. 'Have any of you fellows got cards? We'll play whist with dummy. Whist is the only game one doesn't get tired of. Three years ago we used even to play double—' and he stopped suddenly.

Brookfield was among the best whist players in England, but, as far as can remember, his wife used to play even better than he. He, I know, always used to consider that she was the better player of the two. Personally, I play moderately well, but I have none of those instantaneous intuitions which mark a first-rate player's intuitions, which he will probably be able to justify by rule if he thinks, but which seem to dictate to him directly. Tom contrasted finely with Brookfield. He often had extraordinary promptings in his mind to play absolutely fatal cards, and his justification for following such promptings was a thing to make angels weep.

That night, after dinner, and for twenty-five successive nights, we played together, and sometimes also in the afternoon. On each occasion we cut for playing with dummy, and on each occasion, oddly enough, the cards determined that Tom should do so. We meant to write to the press about it till more extraordinary events put it out of our minds.

On the whole this was the best arrangement, for Brookfield would not have cared for the game if he had played with Tom, and as it is a slight advantage to play with dummy, it was better that Tom should do so than he. We played small points—a shilling, I think—and we played the same all the time.

For the first few nights, as was natural, Tom lost steadily, but slowly, for the cards favoured him. He played his usual inconsequent game, if possible leading a singleton, starting a rough at once, and after making a few tricks having his trumps cleared out by a couple of rounds, and losing the majority of the remaining tricks.

But on the fourth or the fifth night he quite suddenly played a game correctly, or, to be accurate, he made his dummy play correctly. I had dealt and his dummy was to lead. Dummy's hand contained four trumps, six spades, two diamonds, and one heart, and Tom's horny fist was, as usual, stretched across the table to pick up the heart. But instead of playing it he suddenly changed his mind and led a small trump, holding queen, ten, and two small ones. He himself took the first trick with the king and led them back. He hesitated a moment before playing dummy's card, but eventually played the ten, not the queen, and Brookfield took it with the ace. A round of diamonds fell to dummy, and he led the queen of trumps, capturing my knave. In other words, Tom, the illiterate, uneducated Tom, had executed a successful finesse—a simple one, it is true, but a correct and justifiable one.

Dummy was now left with the thirteenth trump. He established his spades after two rounds, lost one trick in hearts, roughed the next round with his remaining trump, and made four tricks in spades. Tom was already, then, up, and thus got out. Though dummy's hand was a good one, Tom himself held no cards except the king of trumps, and the only way to get out was to play the hand exactly as dummy had played it.

Now, it was a simple enough hand to play for anyone who knew anything about whist, but you must remember that Tom knew nothing about whist. That he had generalized from watching our play was almost impossible, for he had invariably nailed his colours to the single one lead before that, and indeed the last time he had done so he had scored heavily, for both Harry and I happened to be very weak in common suits, and had been unable to get the lead till the single rough had developed into a double.

Harry gathered up the cards and made them while Tom dealt for dummy.

'You played that hand correctly,' he said. 'Why didn't you lead dummy's single card as usual?'

'Well, you fellows always tell me it's wrong,' he said, 'and it seemed hard luck on dummy to make him play badly. Ace of hearts,' he added, turning up the trump card. Oddly enough, the next deal very closely resembled the last, but Tom held the sort of hand which dummy held before. He got the lead in the third round and led his single card, spoiled his triumph by roughing, let us in on clubs, and lost the odd.

Harry gathered up the cards with a laugh.

'So you've gone back to the old tactics,' he said.

'You had too many clubs, and, besides, the trumps went badly for us,' said Tom, meaning, I suppose, that he had only one club and had used his trumps to rough.

'The trumps lay just as they lay before when you scored off us by finessing,' said Harry. 'You could have done exactly the same thing again.'

'What's finessing?' asked Tom.

Harry stared.

'You finessed when you made dummy play the ten of trumps instead of the queen, two rounds ago.'

'Did I?' said Tom. 'It must have been a mistake. Don't argue, Harry. Whose deal?'

There were two candles on the table where we were playing, and a big lamp on the dining-table. Once or twice Tom looked up quickly, as if something had startled him, and then got up and moved the lamp away. All evening he seemed rather on edge, and when a moth flew in at the open window, and immolated itself in the candle, he started to his feet, dropping his hand. He continued to play with his usual cheerful disregard of anything but the current trick.

We played that night for about two hours, and though nothing interrupted the monotonous imbecility of Tom's play, I noticed several times that he played dummy's hand rather well. But about eleven he said he was sleepy, and yawned his way to bed, while Harry and I went on deck to smoke the last cigarette of the day.

We had stopped for the night just below a small Arab village. A late rising moon showed the mud huts huddled together on the bank, a few palm trees cutting the sky with their incisive fronds, and on either side the long line of the desert. It was very hot, and now and then a truffle of wind blew across the stream; a dry, scorching wind, without health in it. A dog sat on the edge of the river, howling lugubriously. The moon was so bright that one could hardly resist the illusion that its light was hot, and, indeed, Harry moved his chair into the shade, with a sudden, impatient exclamation. Then there was silence again.

After a while he spoke slowly, and weighing his words.

'It's very strange,' he said to me, 'but tonight I have felt again what I have not felt for nearly six months. You know for a week after she died—I am speaking of my wife—I used constantly to think that she was somewhere close to me. Now, tonight, all through that game of whist, I felt it strongly. I suppose it is only the associations I have with this dahabeah. Oddly enough, it is the same one that we came up in for our honeymoon. I tried to get another one instead, but I couldn't.'

He was silent a moment and then went on.

'You know I have always tried to avoid thinking of her,' he said. 'It is best to do so. It is no use keeping a wound open. Death is death, whatever you may say.'

He flicked the ash off his cigarette, which was nearly burned out, and lit another from the stump.

'I have always to root those memories out of my mind,' he went on, 'and I mean to go on trying. But tonight that feeling was so strong, the feeling, I mean, that she was there, that I had to speak of it. It is a great relief to speak of things. If one bottles them up inside one, they go bad, so to speak. And now I have told you, and I feel better.'

He touched a bell and the Arab servant came up.

'Whisky and soda,' said Brookfield. 'Have one, too, Vincent. Two sodas.'

He shifted his chair again, as if showing that the subject was to be changed.

'The moon is as big as a bandbox tonight,' he said. 'Don't you always imagine the moon to be as big as some small object? In England it varies between soup plates and half-crowns, but in the south it extends to bandboxes. It was almost a sin to sit in the cabin tonight, but the cards would have blown about here. By the way, did you notice Tom's play once or twice? He actually played intelligently.'

'Yes,' said I, 'but the funny thing was that he never played his own hand intelligently. It was always dummy's hand that he managed well.'

'That's odd. I didn't notice it. Usually, it is the other way round. Even a good player often spoils his dummy's hand for the sake of his own. At least a good player will often run a risk with his dummy's hand which he wouldn't with his own. Do you know Bertie Carpuncle? He plays a cautious game himself, but if he ever plays with dummy he makes his dummy do rash and brilliant things. It's the oddest thing to see.'

The whisky and soda arrived. We both silently blessed Mr Schweppe and were just preparing to turn in when Tom appeared in pyjamas.

'Greedy boys,' he remarked. 'Give me some, too. It's as hot as blazes below. My cabin had been shut up and it was stifling. By the way, which of you uses Cherry Blossom scent? My cabin smelt strongly of it.'

I saw Harry's eyes grow large and startled for a moment in the darkness, but he replied almost immediately:

'Cherry Blossom fiddlesticks! It's the bean fields. You can smell them here.'

Tom sniffed the hot night air.

'I can't. Well, here's my whisky. One long drink and then I go to bed.'

We all went down again in a few moments, but as I passed Harry's cabin he called me in.

'You never use Cherry Blossom, do you?' he asked.

'No, nor any other. I thought you said it was the bean fields.'

'Of course it was. I forgot. Well, goodnight.'

Next evening brought us to Assiout, and we spent an hour or two in the bazaars, which seemed to be full of cheap Manchester cottons. Tom thought them very native and characteristic, and bought several yards of a flimsy sort of calico, stamped with the leaves of date palms in red. He was delighted with them till he found S No 2304 in the corner. We pointed out to him that they were just as pretty whether they had S No 2304 on them or not, but he was dissatisfied.

That night, and on every night during the next week, we played whist after dinner. Each time, as I have said, Tom played with dummy, and his own play remained consistently bad, while his dummy play consistently improved. Often he would take up a bad card to lead, drop it again, and substitute a good one. It almost seemed as if one particular part of his brain played dummy and another, his normal brain, played his own cards; or as if another will was superimposed on his when playing for dummy. Harry and I laughed at it, and got accustomed to it, but Tom was always curiously unlike himself while he was playing. He was preoccupied and rather irritable. On one occasion, when it was dummy's lead, he sat looking at the cards so long that I was just going to remind him that he had to lead, when he suddenly looked up across the table, then at me, and said:

'Her lead, isn't it?'

A moment afterwards, even before Harry had time to burst out laughing, he looked at us confusedly and said:

'I beg your pardon. I don't know what I have been thinking about.

Dummy to play. Small heart.'

Harry put down his cards.

'Our Thomas is asleep,' he said, 'and has been dreaming about Her. What's her name, Tommy, and when is it going to come off?'

But Tom had turned suddenly pale.

'It's stifling in here,' he said, 'and I wish to goodness one of you two wouldn't use Cherry Blossom. Scents are not meant for men.'

'It's She,' said I. 'Who is she, Tommy?'

Once again Harry's eyes grew large and startled.

'Come on,' he said, 'it's your turn, Vincent.'

That night, for the first time, I began to feel vaguely uncomfortable. At the moment when Tom said, 'Her lead, isn't it?' I found myself looking towards dummy's place quite seriously and quite instinctively. No doubt his very matter-of-fact tone had led me to do it. Of course I saw nothing there. The cards were arranged in suits on the table, and a chair, which happened to be put in such a position that if we have been playing four Tom's partner would have been sitting in it, was, of course, empty. Then Harry's laugh broke in, and I wondered what I had looked up for.

Once again Harry and I stopped up on deck for a few minutes, and he said to me:

'Do you remember me telling you a few nights ago that I had determined not to think of her? I made a great effort, and I have not failed. Ah!' he sniffed the air—'bean fields again. That accounts for Tom's Cherry Blossom.'

That night I did not get to sleep for a long time. Every now and then I dozed a little, but was recalled to my senses by a sudden whiff of some faint smell passing by me. My cabin was separated from Tom's only by a curtain, and I thought I could hear him stirring. At length I got up, and he, too, as far as I could judge by faint, rustling sounds that came from his cabin, was moving about, and I drew the curtain aside and looked in. The moonlight streamed in through the window, and by its light I could see that he was lying on his back, fast asleep.

Of course, there were a hundred explanations. He was restless in his sleep; or it was the curtain over his door that had been rustling, for a strong wind was blowing up the pasage that led from the saloon to the cabins; and I went back to bed again.

Cherry Blossom! Cherry Blossom! What dim chord of memory twanged in my mind at the thought of it? Where had I smelt it? I could not remember what Cherry Blossom smelt like. Rather sickly, I should think. I dozed off again, thinking about it vaguely and dreamily, and suddenly awoke with a start. That was the smell, the smell that I could perceive in my cabin now, the smell which Harry had said was bean fields. And then, in a moment, I remembered where I had smelt it before. A crowded ball-room—a band playing a Strauss waltz—Harry's voice saying. 'Hallo! I never expected to see you here! We are just back from Egypt. Come and see my wife.' Then, finding myself on the balcony overlooking the square, where a tall, pale woman was sitting talking to half a dozen men. She saw me and smiled to me, putting out her hand, and I advanced towards her. Then a little breeze shook the awning and wafted towards me the delicate scent—not sickly—of the smell I had perceived in my cabin when I awoke. Once again that evening, when I was dancing with her, she dropped her handkerchief and I picked it up for her. Her handkerchief smelt of Cherry Blossom.

I was frightened, and fright is tiring. Soon I fell asleep.

The dragoman we had with us on the boat had taken the Brook-fields up on their honeymoon, and next morning, as I was on deck, he came up to me and asked if we wanted to stop at Grigeh. There was nothing to see there, he said, and when he had been up with Mr and Mrs Brookfield before they had gone straight on. A sudden idea struck me, and I asked him which cabin Mrs Brookfield had had.

He thought for a moment and then said:

'No 3. I am sure it was No 3, and Mr Brookfield the one opposite.'

No 3 was Tom's cabin.

In the next few nights, I can only remember one thing that struck me as curious, excepting, of course, the constant improvement in Tom's dummy play, and the slight deterioration, if anything, in his own. It was this:

One night, dummy held a long hand of trumps, and it was Tom's lead. He opened with the king and ace of a common suit. Dummy only had two, the eight and the four, and Tom played out the eight first and then four. He then led another of the same suit for dummy to rough. Harry burst out laughing.

'It is pathetic,' he said. 'You make dummy call for trumps and then don't lead them to him! Poor, ill-used dummy!'

Tom looked puzzled.

'I wanted him to trump,' he said.

'Then why didn't you make him call for trumps?'

'Call for trumps? Oh, that's when you play a high one and then a low one, isn't it? He never called for trumps.'

But both Harry and I had noticed it.

Though nothing else strange happened for two or three days, an odd change had begun to come over Tom. During the day he was himself, but after dinner he always became curiosly nervous and agitated. One night after I had gone to bed he came into my cabin half-undressed, and sat for an hour there. He said his cabin was so close and stuffy; though it was the coolest cabin on the boat, and for the last day or two the heat had decreased considerably. And while we were playing whist he would constantly glance up quickly and nervously, and more than once I saw him focus his eyes at the empty air in front of him, just in that some disconcerting way which dogs sometimes have towards dusk, as if they saw something which we could not see. Meanwhile, we had gone steadily on. We had passed Grigeh, and if the wind held we expected to be at Luxor, where we were to stop for a time, before the end of the week.

One night after dinner Tom and I were sitting on deck. The moon had not yet risen, but by the keen, clear starlight we could see the broad river stretched out in front of us like plate of burnished metal. To the left rose high, orange-coloured rocks, which gave out the heat they had been baked in during the day, and on the right lay the brown expanse of desert. An Arab below was chanting some monotonous native song, and the echo was returned from the rocks in a curious plaintive whine. Suddenly the wind dropped altogether, and the great sail flapped against the mast. The current took us slowly back, and as we neared the shore the anchor was thrown out, and we stopped for the night.

Suddenly Tom caught my arm.

'There, did you not see it?' he said.

I looked quickly round in the direction of his finger, but there was only the pale, glimmering deck, and behind the circle of the sky.

'It came last night to fetch us to play whist,' he said. 'I am frightened. Let us go quick, or it will come again.'

'My dear Tom, what do you mean?' I asked.

'Never mind, it is nothing,' he said. 'Come quickly. It will be all right then.'

And he literally dragged me downstairs.

'Harry, where are you?' he called. 'Come and play whist, it's getting late.'

'Well, I've been waiting for you,' shouted a voice from the saloon. Again we cut for dummy, and again it fell to Tom. For the last week he had won steadily. That night, whether it was that Tom's strange terror had affected my nerves, I do not know, for though I had at present neither seen nor heard anything peculiar, from the moment I began to play I felt that there was something living in the room besides ourselves, and when on one occasion I looked round and found the soft-footed dragoman, who had entered the room to get orders for next day without my hearing him, standing at my elbow, I could have shrieked aloud.

It must have been about nine when we began. Harry, as usual, was absolutely absorbed in the game, but Tom's eyes went peering nervously about the cabin, and, as for me, I confess to having been absolutely upset. But the game went on quietly, and by degrees I recovered myself. Tom was playing even worse than usual, and the dummy had not much opportunity to distinguish itself. But at length there came a hand—I cannot remember all the details of it—in which, towards the end, dummy held three suits, his trumps being exhausted, in two of which, diamonds and spades, Harry and I were both over him. Tom had already run out of spades, and held only one small diamond. He led the ace of hearts, in which suit dummy held the king and knave. Tom took up the knave to put on third hand, hesitated, and played the king instead. He then led the queen, which drew the knave, and after that the ten. He was four up already, and this secured him the odd trick. Then said Tom:

'What a fool I was to play the king. I can't think what made me do it.'

Harry gasped.

'Why, man, if you'd played any other card, you'd have lost the odd. Don't you see, if dummy had not played the king, the lead would have been placed in his hand next round, and he would have had to play a diamond with a spade. You had to unblock.'

Tom said frankly that he did not understand, and the game went on. The next round dummy played the grand coup, the opportunity for which seldom occurs, and is still seldom recognized. But Tom saw it at once.

Two rounds afterwards I had just picked up my cards and was sorting them, when—it takes longer to describe than it did to take place—I was suddenly conscious of something seen out of the corner of my eye on my left. Also, I could no longer see the white flash of cards where dummy's hand was laid on the table. I saw a glimmer as of a white dress, a faintly outlined profile, and at that moment a little breeze blowing in through the open window wafted across me a faint smell of Cherry Blossom. The whole thing was instantaneous, and I looked up from the hand I was sorting. There was nothing there—dummy's cards were laid on the table, the chair was empty, and the little puff of wind had passed. Then looking at Tom, I saw that he was looking fixedly at the opposite side of the table. Moist beads of perspiration stood on his forehead, and one hand was clutching the tablecloth. Then he gave a long-drawn breath of horror, and his head fell forwards on the table.

We raised him, and soon brought him round. He had complained all day of headache, and he said he thought he had had a touch of the sun. He was sorry to break up the game, but he thought he had better go to bed. No doubt he would be all right in the morning, and— and would Harry mind his moving into the other empty cabin?

Next morning he seemed better, but nervously anxious not to be left alone. Harry spent the morning in writing letters, and Tom and I sat on the deck. I expected he would speak of something—I did not know what—and before long he did.

There had been a silence, and Tom broke it.

'Did you see nothing?' he said.

It would have been mere affectation to pretend not to know what he meant.

'I hardly know if I did nor not,' I said.

'But her face—her face,' he went on almost in a whisper. 'There was a horrible scar across it, a bar of raw, burned flesh. What happened then? I fainted, did I not?'

'Something rather like it.'

He threw himself back in his chair despairingly.

'I can't tell Harry about it,' he said. 'Besides, I don't think he knows she is there. She does not come to see him, but only to play whist. It is horrible. Even if I don't see her, I know she is there. Wait a minute.'

He got up out of his chair and ran downstairs.

Five minutes later he returned.

'Stand up,' he said, 'and look at the water behind us.'

I looked closely at the broken wake of the boat.

Thirty yards behind us in the water was covered with a quantity of little white specks.

'Why, have you thrown the cards overboard?' I asked.

'Yes, it is worth trying.'

That evening, for the first time for twenty-six nights, we did not play whist. The boat was ransacked for the cards, but they had vanished. Harry was furious, but we never told him what we had done. And with the cards vanished the Thing which had taken dummy's place.

THE RETURN OF FRANK HAMPDEN

D R ARTHUR BANNERMAN was, as all the world knows, the supreme and final authority on the functions and diseases of the brain and nervous system when, still quite a young man, he retired from regular practice. His reason for so doing was thoroughly characteristic of his nature, for he complained that he had no time to learn while he was engaged in teaching.

He had begun to distrust the methods that had already earned him so brilliant a career; or, at any rate, had had glimpses of huge fields and expanses of possibilities which would utterly put out of date all that was now surmized about the origin of such evils as he combated.

For two years, up to the time when the following strange incident happened, Arthur Bannerman devoted himself to occult study. Nothing was too extravagant for his attention—witchcraft, spiritualism, Satanism, demoniacal possession—all possible and exploded sources of the disorders and sicknesses of the soul were the material of his investigations. Often he found nothing to be gleaned; but as his work went on he became more and more convinced of his theory—that the source of all mental and physical trouble lies behind the mind, in that mysterious and unexplored cave where essential vitality abides. He groped, as he said of himself, in a twilight full of dim horrors, among which he walked undismayed, and flashed his bull's-eye into the mists. . . So much then of prologue.

There was a light behind the drawn blinds of Dr Bannerman's sitting-room one day last week as I passed his house on my way home from dinner, and since it had long been a constant custom between us (for we lived but a few doors apart) to smoke the 'go-to-bed' cigarette together, I rang and asked if he would let me come in for a quarter-of-an-hour.

In answer, his servant told me that he had already sent a note to me begging me to do so, if I returned while the night was still decently young, and accordingly I took off my coat, and followed on his heels upstairs.

Arthur Bannerman was not alone; there was sitting on the sofa by the side of the fireplace a young man whom I had never seen before. As I came in he turned towards the door, and I looked on the handsomest and most diabolical face I had ever seen. Simultaneously Bannerman got up.

'I hoped you might come in,' he said. 'Let me introduce my cousin, Mr Hampden, who is staying with me for a day or two.'

As young Hampden got up, I saw that Fifi, Bannerman's fox-terrier, a lady whose amiability almost amounted to idiocy, slunk away from where she had been sitting by her master's chair into a far corner of the room, where she sat with bristling hackles, and eyes that gleamed with terror and were stale with hate, watching the young man. His right arm was in a sling, and he held out his left hand to me.

'You will excuse me,' he said, 'but I am only just recovering from a broken arm.'

Somehow I had a repugnance that was almost invincible against touching his hand. The feeling was quite inexplicable, but—but I knew precisely what Fifi was feeling. However, we shook hands, and he looked over his shoulder at the dog.

'My cousin's terrier doesn't approve of me,' he said with a laugh.

'Yes, it's very odd,' said Banneran. 'Call her, Frank.'

Frank Hampden clicked his fingers together with an encouraging sound.

'Fifi, Fifi dear,' he said.

For a moment I thought this most confiding of young ladies was going to fly at him. But apparently she had not the courage, and retreated behind the window-curtains.

'And I'm so fond of dogs,' said Hampden to me.

Instinctively I knew he lied. I can no more account for that than I can account for the impression of hellish evil that his face conveyed. He was quite young—two or three and twenty as I guessed, and yet below the youthful softness of his features there lived a spirit malign and mature, an adept in horror.

Then, looking across to Bannerman, I saw that he was observing his cousin with that intense and quiet scrutiny that doctors give to a patient who puzzles them.

'And are you friends with Fifi?' asked Hampden. 'See whether she will come to you if I stand by you.'

Fifi had half emerged from her ambush behind the curtains, and I called to her. But she did not move; she gave a little apologetic whine, as if to signify that I was asking an impossible thing, and beat her stumpy tail on the carpet.

'Now stand away from him, Frank,' said Bannerman.

Fifi needed no further invitation; she danced across the room to me, with her slim body curled to a comma, wriggling and squealing with delight. But on Hampden's taking a step towards me, she snapped and fled.

He laughed.

'Well, I think I shall go to bed,' he said, 'now that you have come to keep Arthur company. By the way, where is your cat, Arthur? I haven't seen her all day.'

'I haven't either,' said he. 'Perhaps—perhaps she's out in the garden.'

Hampden laughed again.

'Cats like gardens,' he said. 'But she has been there a long time. Well, goodnight. Goodnight, little angelic Fifi. You don't know how I love you.'

Bannerman waited till the door had closed on his exit, and then instantly spoke.

'You haven't received my note, then?' he said. 'But it doesn't matter; you have done what I wanted, which was to observe my cousin. Now, what do you think of him? I want just your impression.'

'Unreservedly?' I asked.

'Of course.'

'I think he is the most terrible man I ever saw,' said I. 'It was all I could do to remain in the room with him.'

'Terrible? How terrible?'

'Murderous; hardly human. I felt like Fifi.'

'I thought you did,' said he. 'Now did you hear him ask about my cat?'

'Yes.'

'Well, he killed her last night, and buried her in the garden.'

Somehow this quiet and horrible announcement threw me off my balance.

'What do you *mean?*' I asked.

'Exactly what I tell you. It so happened that I slept very badly last night, because, as a matter of fact, I was thinking about Frank, and how—how to get at him. About three in the morning I heard the door into the garden being opened, whether from outside or from within, I did not know. The idea of burglars occurred to me, and without turning up my light I leant out of the window.

'There was bright star-light, enough to distinguish objects, and I saw Frank come out of the house carrying something dark under is arm. He put it down to fetch a spade from the tool-house, and I saw what it was.

'You remember my blue Persian? He dup up a couple of plants with lumps of soil round their roots, buried the cat, and very carefully replanted the Michaelmas daisies above it. It took him some time to do this, for he could work with one arm only. And as he worked he laughed to himself—a sort of dreadful giggling.'

'But he's a fiend,' said I.

'Yes—at present. What he said tonight, by the way, used to be perfectly true. He was devoted to dogs, and, indeed, to all animals. But about last night. He was in a dressing-gown over his night-wear. Well, when he went out today, I examined his dressing-gown. There was a quantity of cat's hair on it. Also, I dug up the Michaelmas daisies again. Below was the body of my poor cat. He had cut its throat... He would kill Fifi if he could. He is longing to. Afterwards, he will pass on to other killings—bigger killings.'

'He's insane, then,' said I; 'he's a dangerous lunatic.'

Bannerman did not reply for a moment.

'It isn't he at all,' he said suddenly. 'You saw Frank Hampden's body. But somebody else is in possession.'

Again he paused.

'Do you want to hear the wildest and most extravagant tale, which I yet believe is perfectly true?'

'Naturally.'

'Good! Then listen. I shan't disappoint you.'

He settled himself in his chair and spoke, as he so often does, with his hands over his eyes, so as to shut out all external distractions.

'Three weeks ago,' he said, 'a man called James Rollo was hung at Beltonborough for the most atrocious murder of his wife. The deed, apparently, was quite objectless. He was fond of her, there had been no quarrel, and after it was done he appeared much distressed at her loss, but not at his crime.

'The question naturally arose as to his sanity, and the doctor who had watched him after he had been condemned asked me to come down and give my opinion. We could neither of us find any point in which he was not otherwise perfectly sane.

'But there was an idea that came into my mind about the history of the case, and one day when I was talking to him I quite quietly asked him this question: "Did you begin by killing flies?" In general he was a sullen, silent man, but when I asked him this, his eyes brightened, and he said: "Yes; how did you know? Flies first, then cats and dogs.". . . Now do you see?'

'You mean that there is the same kind of disease, you would call it, developing in your cousin?'

He nodded.

'Just that. I feel convinced that poor Frank is suffering from an early stage of James Rollo's malady, for which, as it was impossible to say that he was not sane, James Rollo was hung. But I mean much more than that. I mean that the hanging of James Rollo was directly responsible for this development in Frank, though no one could have foreseen that.'

'Responsible for it?' I asked.

'So I soberly believe. Now I am going to advance to you the wildest and most preposterous theory. But I hope to prove that my theory is correct, and I hope to cure Frank.'

Bannerman had sat up, and was looking at me as he said this. Then he sank back in his chair again, and covered his eyes with his hands as before.

'There's a steep hill at Beltonborough,' he said, 'with a sharp corner just outside the prison-gate. A quarter-of-an-hour after James Rollo had suffered the extreme penalty, Frank came tearing down the hill on his motor-cycle to catch an early train. He skidded and fell just outside the prison. At that very moment I was leaving the prison on my way back to town. Frank had sustained compound fracture of his right arm, and the less he was moved till that was set the better.

'So I brought him into a room in the prison infirmary, gave him chloroform, and the prison-surgeon set his arm. It was a very difficult job, and he was under the anaesthetic for a considerable time. And when he came round, he was changed. It seemed as if another soul had entered his body. And that soul is in possession of it still.'

Bannerman sat up again, and looked at me.

'It seems quite certain,' he said, 'that under some conditions, such as deep mesmeric trance or during the unconsciousness that accompanies an anaesthetic, the bonds that seem so indissolubly to unite a man's soul with his mind and his body are strangely relaxed.

'The condition is almost one of temporary death; often the heart's beat is nearly suspended, often the breathing is all but extinct, the connection between soul and body is almost severed. This happened twice during Frank's unconsciousness.

'And there is another theory, proved to my mind beyond all doubt, that at the moment of death, particularly of sudden death, the soul, though severed from the body, does not at once leave its vicinity, but remains hovering near its discarded tenement.

'Well, at that hour when Frank's soul was loosened, was relaxed in its hold on his body, another soul, I believe, was close at hand, a disembodied soul—just disembodied. And I believe that the soul of James Rollo entered and took possession of my cousin's body.'

For a long moment there was dead silence, and I heard footsteps passing to and fro in the room above—Frank Hampden's no doubt. It seemed that Bannerman joined his mind on to my thought, and moved further with it.

'Frank's footsteps,' he said. 'He walks up and down like that for hours while It within him makes plans. It is thinking about Fifi.'

It was useless for me to tell myself that this wild tale made commonsense revolt. That went without saying. But that did not dispose of the tale. Here, at any rate, was by far the most eminent of brain specialists, the most careful and exact of students, gravely (and with what impressive gravity!) advancing a theory that defied reason. But did it defy reality?

'What are you going to do?' I asked.

'Investigate a little further first,' said he. 'In fact, I am expecting Reid, the medium, to arrive any minute. I have often been in *séance* with him, and I believe him to be honest. In any case, he will have no opportunity for being dishonest, for he has never seen Frank.'

'But how can a medium help you?'

'In this way. If Frank's body is possessed by the spirit of James Rollo, Frank's own spirit, houseless, will almost certainly be hovering near its rightful habitation. We will ask Reid if he can materialize for us the spirit of Frank Hampden. That is all I shall tell him. Ah, there is Reid! I told my servant to go to bed.'

The bell had sounded, and Bannerman left the room. In a moment he came back with the medium, a perfectly commonplace, rather under-sized man, with a high, bulging forehead. Then I looked at his eyes, and thought him commonplace no longer. They seemed to look out and beyond. I cannot express it otherwise.

In a couple of sentences Bannerman told the medium what was wanted—namely, the materialization of a certain Frank Hampden. Reid asked only one question.

'Has the body of Frank Hampden been long dead?'

Bannerman did not hesitate.

'I believe his spirit left it some three weeks ago,' he said.

Reid sat down.

'We will try,' he said.

The electric light was put out, but the glow from the fire was sufficiently bright to enable me, when we had sat for a couple of minutes round the table which Bannerman placed in front of the medium, to distinguish quite clearly the furniture and occupants of the room. I could see the profile of Reid, the full face of Bannerman, the chairs, the table, glints of reflected flame on the glass of pictures, and with complete distinctness I observed that Fifi had curled herself up contentedly on the hearthrug. Above our heads the footsteps still went up and down the room.

Almost immediately the medium went into trance. I saw his head bowed over his chest, and heard his breathing go slow. For some time nothing whatever happened; then the table began to creak under our joined hands, and there came from it a very loud rap. Instantly the medium's breathing grew quick and short. Then Bannerman said:

'Is that the spirit of Frank Hampden?'

Three loud raps answered.

'Come to us visibly, if you can,' he said.

Again we sat long in silence. Then from the direction of the door there came a very cold current of air, so palpable that I looked round fully expecting to see that the door was open. But it was closed. Fifi, I think, felt it also, for she sat up, sneezed, and drew herself a little nearer to the fire. But, though the door was closed, I knew that something—someone—had entered. And I heard Bannerman say below his breath: 'It is coming!'

Then it came.

Close beside the medium there began forming in the air whorls and spirals of grey mist-like texture, curling and interweaving, and growing thicker every moment. It was not so much material that became visible, but shape; it was like a silver-point drawing of a man that thus took form. Then above that there began to grow the shape of a head; features outlined themselves on it, dark hair crowned it, and in a little while there stood almost at my elbow the complete figure of the man whose footsteps still went gently to and fro above our heads.

The face was absolutely distinct and quite unmistakable; but instead of the diabolical cruelty that I had seen there before, there was on it an expression of so hopeless an anguish that my throat worked when I looked. The whole apparition swayed slightly to and fro as it stood there, like the flame of a candle in a draught.

Then Bannerman spoke, and in the trembling of his voice I guessed what emotion he was feeling.

'Is that you, my dear Frank?' he said.

The head bowed, the lips moved, but I heard nothing.

'Why are you not in the body, Frank?' he asked.

This time there came a whisper, just audible.

'I can't—I can't,' it said. 'Someone is there—someone horrible. . . For heaven's sake, help me!'

The white, agonized face grew more convulsed. 'For the love of heaven!' it repeated.

I looked away for a moment down at the hearthrug, where a sudden noise attracted my attention. Fifi was sitting bolt upright looking at the figure which stood close to her, and the noise that I had heard was the thumping of her tail.

Then she came cautiously forward, still looking up at the face, the image of which an hour before had so filled her with rage and terror. But now she emitted little pleased, anxious whines, seeking attention. Finally she gave a sharp little bark, and presented her white paw, as was her custom when she demanded notice of some friend. And those instinctive, unsought advances of Fifi quite suddenly convinced me that, monstrous and incredible as it all was, the real Frank Hampden, visible to her eyes as to ours, stood there woeful and imploring.

Once more Bannerman spoke.

'Be patient, my poor Frank,' he said. 'We will help you.'

The figure slowly faded, and before long the medium stirred and awoke, breathing slowly again and drenched with sweat.

'Did he come?' he asked.

'Yes; sit quiet and rest a while,' said Bannerman, turning on the electric light.

He sat for some time buried in thought, while Reid—in all appearance a little, commonplace fellow—drank some whisky-and-soda, and chatted negligibly about current topics.

Fifi, pleased and excited, was nosing about the room as if searching for traces of a friend. Once she seemed to listen to the footsteps that still moved in the room above, and gave an angry snarl. Then Bannerman seemed to come to some conclusion with himself.

'I won't keep you any longer now, Mr Reid,' he said, 'but I shall certainly want you again—tomorrow, probably. I will telephone to you. I hope you may be able to come without fail.'

The moment he had gone, Bannerman turned to me.

'I'm going to risk it,' he said; 'I'm going to do all that I can to restore poor Frank. For I don't doubt now, for a moment, that it was Frank—his essential self—that was made manifest to us. It is a human soul, dispossessed, that sees the house of its body defiled by that murderous regent. I *can't* doubt that it is so. But what a tale to tell at the coroner's inquest if I fail!'

'You mean you risk Hampden's death?'

'Necessarily. A strong and desperate spirit has to be got out of that poor boy's body. It will cling hideously to the house it has entered; it may shatter it sooner than emerge. But any risk is right, when we consider the stake we play for, the rehabilitation of that kind, jolly boy—for so he was. But how—how can we do it?'

He got up and began pacing up and down the room, thinking aloud.

'Frank—Frank's body, I mean,' he said. 'We've got to loosen the ties between his body and the spirit that is possessed of it before we can hope to drive it out. It got in, you see, when Frank was under that anaesthetic... but on what excuse can I get him to take an anaesthetic?

'By jove! there's that drug, that hyocampine. It seems safe; I've used it several times for violent maniacs, and it produces the sleep that comes nearest of all to death. It seems to attack and stupefy the very self. Hyocampine—you've heard of it? It's quite tasteless; you can mix it in coffee, for instance, and it acts almost instantaneously. Then when he has taken it, we'll have our good Reid again, and see if through his mediumship we can get the materialization of the murderer... It's a chance... After lunch tomorrow—yes, I'll get Reid to come then... Risk? It's the biggest risk I've ever taken.'

He stood quite still a moment, and then, as his habit was when his mind was made up, the whole burden of his perplexity and hesitation was lifted from him.

'And about you?' he said. 'Will you come and see the end of this? Frankly, I should like you to. But you must choose for yourself; the final scene, if all goes well, is bound to be appalling, for there will be here visible in the room the spirit of James Rollo. Appalling, too, will be his exit from poor Frank's body. But I should like another will working with mine.'

As I went downstairs with Bannerman, I heard the door of the room above open.

'Is that you, Arthur?' asked Frank Hampden's voice. 'How late you are.'

He signed to me to be quiet.

'Do you want anything, Frank?' he asked.

'Nothing particular. But I was wondering whether, when you come upstairs, you would bring Fifi to my room. I like a dog in my room.'

Bannerman glanced at me, then laughed.

'I should recommend your making friends with Fifi first,' he said.

I arrived, as we arranged, at Dr Bannerman's house next afternoon immediately after lunch, on the ostensible errand of taking him out for a walk. He and Hampden had just had coffee.

'Yes, do take him out for a walk,' said the latter, 'and leave me to amuse myself. In fact, I was thinking of going down to the home for cats in Chelsea and getting one for Arthur as a present. I hear nothing has been seen of his jolly blue Persian.'

'That's very nice of you,' said Bannerman, watching him. Frank yawned.

'I'm not sure that I shan't have a nap first,' he said. 'I feel fearfully drowsy. Too much lunch, I suppose. Sorry to be rude, but I really must have a snooze.'

He went across to the sofa, put his hands behinds his head, and closed his eyes.

'Then the cat's home,' he muttered, 'and I've got to make friends with Fifi. Make friends . . .'

We waited a moment; then Bannerman called the sleeper by name, and finally shook him by the shoulder, but the drug already was strongly in operation, and he roused no sign of consciousness. Then he brought in Reid, who had just arrived, shutting out the light from the window by drawing the curtains. But the firelight leapt brightly on the walls, and I could see with distinctness all that passed. Fifi, I noticed, came into the room with them. Then Bannerman spoke to the medium.

'We want you, if you can,' he said, 'to produce for us the spirit of James Rollo, who was hung for murder three weeks ago. We have reason to believe that he is near us.'

Reid did not answer immediately.

'Dr Bannerman,' he said at length, 'I should like to know that it is for good and not for evil or for idle curiosity that you ask this.'

'It is for the sake of a soul that is in utter wretchedness,' said he.

In a very few minutes the medium fell into deep trance, with head fallen forward. For a little while his breathing grew slow; presently it quickened into short, rapid respirations. Then I heard a noise as of rustling leaves from where Frank Hampden lay, and saw that the sofa with its chintz skirts was all a flutter beneath the violent trembling of his body, which till now had lain so utterly motionless. Presently, not from the direction of the door, but from the sofa, a cold strong wind below, making the pictures rattle on the walls, and Bannerman called on the spirit of James Rollo.

'Come from where you are,' he said, 'and be made manifest.'

Suddenly Hampden began to groan, and the groans rose louder, shrilling into dreadful cries. Terrible convulsions seized his limbs, distortion and a rending agony began to work in his face; the body, haunted and possessed by that murderous ghost of a man who had been hung for his atrocious crime, writhed and bent like a sapling in a storm.

Then round it there grew a pale greenish light, the halo of some hellish psychical emanation, brightest round the open mouth. This light grew upwards, column-like from him, lines and curves began to wreathe themselves in it, and slowly, horribly it fashioned itself into the likeness of a man. As it approached completion, the convulsions and groanings subsided, till, at the end, when this wraith with face of murderous and sullen hate hung swaying in the air above the sofa, the body from which it had come but twitched and shook, and then lay as if dead.

Once again Bannerman spoke.

'In the name of the Holiest,' he cried, 'and by the power of the Highest, I bid you go to the place He has appointed for you!'

Then . . . I can only describe what happened by saying that a stupendous shock overwhelmed every sense. The room leapt into a blaze of light, a noise more appalling than any thunderclap rent the air; the chair, where I sat, and the table rocked as if some earthquake wave passed through the house. And yet I felt that this cataclysm came not from outside, but from within, was conveyed to the senses by the spiritual crisis that raged round us. Then succeeded silence as of the Polar night, but above the couch no longer floated the phantasm of James Rollo.

Then again I heard Bannerman speak in a hoarse whisper.

'Keep absolutely still,' he said.

Just opposite me was the sofa where Frank Hampden's body lay. It was quite motionless, and the limbs were curled into monstrous shapes, and the face was still distorted with its dying agony.

Presently I saw that a light, rosy and exquisite, like sunrise on Alpine summits, began to glow round it; it stirred a little, stretching itself out like a tired child; the face, irradiated by that celestial glow, grew composed, the mouth shut, the eyelids quivered and unclosed for a moment, then fluttered and fell again. The light faded, and I knew that I had looked on the most wonderful thing that mortal eyes had ever seen, for into the body that had lain there, lifeless and dead, the spirit had entered again. After a while the medium began to move; very slowly and wearily he raised his sunk head.

'It is over,' he said.

Bannerman got up and drew back the curtains—and Fifi, crawling out from under the sofa, sat and looked at the young man who lay sleeping there. Then she gave a little whine, and gently licked the hand that dangled over the side of the couch.

It was not till late that evening that Frank Hampden came to himself again. We were still watching by him when suddenly he sat up, and looked round, puzzled, smiling, wondering . . . I have never seen a face so instinct with charm and kindliness.

THE SHUTTERED ROOM

Hugh Lister and his wife had come down from London to attend the funeral of his uncle, that strange old hermit of a man who had lived for the last year utterly recluse and indeed practically unseen in the charming Georgian house and high-walled garden, which, at his death, had now come into possession of his nephew. Two bachelor brothers, so Hugh remembered, had originally bought the place, and for some years had lived together there. But he knew almost nothing of their history, though he could recollect seeing them both, as a boy, when they spent the night at his mother's house in town on their way abroad for some piece of holiday-travel in which they annually indulged: grim, odd-looking men, much alike, who quarrelled about the price of their tickets, and seemed considerably to dislike each other. They lived together, it appeared, because a joint establishment was cheaper than two separate houses, and they had a strong community of tastes in their love of money, and their dislike of other people. . .

Hugh's fugitive recollection had now, after the funeral, been reinforced and amplified by a talk with Mr Hodgkin, his uncle's solicitor, and he had learned more of these queer brothers. They had lived entirely withdrawn from the local life of this little town of Trenthorpe: no guest ever crossed their threshold, nor did they set foot at all in the houses of their neighbours. Seldom were they ever seen outside their house and garden, and, indeed, not often within, for their domestic requirements were provided by a woman who went in for a few hours every morning to make their beds and lay their breakfasts, and cook some food for their dinner, but she would be busy in the kitchen when they came downstairs, and sometimes for days together she never set eyes on either of them. Except for her, the only human being who for the last four or five years had had access to any portion of the premises was the man who had charge of the furnace in the back yard behind the house which heated the radiators through its rooms and passages. Every day throughout the year he must come in the morning and consult the thermometer which hung in a shaded nook on a wall there, and should it register below 60° Fahrenheit, the furnace must be lit, and stoked twice during the day, before he paid his final visit at ten o'clock at night, and made up a fire that would keep the house warm till morning again.

No window ever appeared to be opened in that hermitage, and seldom cleaned; the meals were of the most frugal; an overheated house and complete solitude were all that the brothers asked of life. The man and the woman who looked after their needs went for their wages every week to Mr Hodgkin, who also discharged for the brothers their bills and paid for them the rates and taxes of the freehold house. But this dismal frugality and joylessness was not the consequence of insufficient means, for they each had an income of five or six hundred a year, of which they spent not half. The rest merely accumulated at the bank, for they made no investments. One or other of them was occasionally seen in the early morning walking by the bank of the tidal river that swept under the hill on which Trenthorpe stood, and debouched into the sea a mile or two away, but he would have returned to the house before nine in the morning, and thereafter appeared no more.

Most of this was news to Hugh and Violet: then Mr Hodgkin went on to speak of an event which they knew had occurred, though the details had not reached them.

'That was the manner of life of your two uncles,' Mr Lister,' he said, 'until a year ago when the mysterious disappearance of the younger, Mr Henry, took place. I had just come downstairs one morning, and was beginning my breakfast when Mr Robert, whose funeral we have just attended, was announced. He had found the front door of his house, which, as you will presently see when we visit it, is secured by a multitude of bolts and locks and chains, standing wide open. It had not been forced from outside, for the bolts had been withdrawn from within. He called to his brother, but got no answer, and ascending to his room, found that it was empty. His bed had been slept in, his instruments of toilet had been used, but there was no trace of him anywhere either in the house or the garden. It seemed most likely, therefore, that it was he who had gone out, leaving the door wide, but this was so extraordinary a thing for him to have done that Mr Robert instantly came round to tell me about it. It struck me also as so odd that I rang up the police office, search and enquiries were made, and within an hour a cloth cap, which Mr Robert indentified as belonging to his brother, was found on the bank of the river, where sometimes he walked, and next day his walking-stick was found at low tide on a sand-shoal a mile farther down. The tide—it was one of the big spring-tides— had been at the flood about five o'clock in the morning on which he disappeared, and assuming that he left the house soon after that, it must have been running very strong to the sea, and the river was dragged without result. Then came further evidence, for a labourer in the town who had gone out to work at daybreak, said that he had seen a man, answering to the description which was circulated, crossing the bridge above the bank where the cap was found.'

'Was it supposed to have been an accident?' asked Hugh.

'There was not sufficient evidence to make that clear. It is possible that Mr Henry might have slipped while walking along the bank, for the ground was very miry: on the other hand, Mr Robert, in the statement he made to the police, said that for several days his brother had been very queer in his behaviour, and possibly it was suicide, but there could, of course, be no inquest, since the body was never found. Death was presumed after the due legal period, and by the will which both your uncles had made, which was in my keeping, and by which the survivor of the two was named as the heir of the deceased, Mr Henry's property passed to his brother. That was completed only a few days ago. Previously to that, Mr Robert, as you know, had made a further will under which you inherit.'

Mr Hodgkin paused a moment, but Hugh had no question to put to him, and he continued in the same even voice.

'After Mr Henry's disappearance,' he said, 'your surviving uncle became more recluse than ever, and once only, as far as I am aware, he left his house and garden, and that was when he came to see me to make his will. The charwoman continued to go in every morning, but now she hardly ever saw him. He moved from the bedroom upstairs next to Mr Henry's both of which looked out on to the garden, and occupied a small room on the ground floor looking out on to the street, and the two bedrooms upstairs were locked and the keys were in his keeping. He similarly locked the two corresponding rooms on the ground floor which look on to the garden, though he used them him-self, and the charwoman left his food on a small table in the hall outside, and he took it in after she had gone, putting the plates and utensils he had used in the same place for her to wash up next day. Her range, in fact, was entirely confined to the kitchen and your uncle's bedroom, from which he had always gone into one of the locked rooms on the ground floor before she arrived. If he wanted anything ordered for him, there would be a note for her on the table by his bed stating his requirements. So it went on till last Thursday, the day of his death.'

Again the lawyer paused.

'It is a painful and terrible account I have to give you, Mr Lister,' he said. 'She went to his bedroom as usual, and found him crouching in a corner of the room, and he screamed out with fright, she said, when he saw her, and kept crying out: "No, no! have mercy on me, Henry!" Like a sensible woman she ran straight for the doctor, and as she went past his window, she heard him still screaming. Dr Soleham was in, and came at once: your uncle was still in some wild access of terror, and he slipped by them, and ran out into the street. Then quite suddenly he spun round and collapsed. They brought him back into the house, and in a few minutes it was all over.'

Such was the grim manner in which Hugh Lister entered into his inheritance: it was all horrible and mysterious enough, but no question of personal grief or loss came into it, since he was practically a stranger to these queer relations of his. Mr Hodgkin went into other business matters with him; there was a considerable sum of money which was his, also this house and garden, of which the house, so the lawyer told him, was in a state of the most hideous dilapidation and disrepair. Of the garden he knew nothing, for though it stood in the middle of the little town, its high brick walls screened it from all scrutiny of the houses round, and the rooms which looked on to it from the house had long been kept locked. Hugh and his wife slept that night at an inn, and next morning Mr Hodgkin called to take them over the property.

Pitiable indeed was the neglect into which his charming and dignified little mansion had fallen. The roof leaked in a dozen places, the mildewed paper was peeling off the walls, the carpets were rotted by damp and drip: here they were faded by the sun, here they were mere rags and ribands. The casement bars of the windows were perished, the panes so crusted with dust and spiders' webs that scarce a glimpse of the street outside could be seen; doors sagged on their hinges; a litter of sticks and straws from the nests of starlings that had built in the chimneys littered the hearths; pictures had fallen from the walls and lay in fragments of splintered glass and broken frames on the floor. Then there were the four locked rooms which looked on to the garden, two upstairs and two below, to be explored. A bunch of keys was found in the bedroom below, which Robert Lister had used, and they began their investigations upstairs, starting with the first door on the landing: this was the room, the charwoman told them, which Mr Henry had occupied, and which had been locked ever since his disappearance.

The key grated rustily in the boards, but soon the door stood open, and they saw that the room was quite dark, for the windows were shuttered. A little fumbling revealed the fastenings, and Hugh, throwing them open, gave an exclamation of surprise. For the room, though long closed and neglected, with sagging ceiling and damp-stained walls, bore all signs of use: the bed-cloths, coverlet and blankets and moldy sheets were still on the bed, half-turned back, as if its occupant had only just left it. On the washstand were sponge and toothbrush, and beside it on the floor stood a brass hot-water can, green with verdigris: in the window was a dressing-table with a looking-glass, blurred and foggy, and by it a pair of hair brushes and a shaving brush, and a rusty razor with the dried stain of soap on the blade. There were a couple of pairs of boots, efflorescent with gray mildew below it; the chest of drawers was full of clothes. Nothing had been touched since the morning when Henry Lister left it, not to return.

Violet felt a sudden qualm of misgiving, coming from she knew not what secret cell in her brain. The room, with its dead air and vanished occupant, was still horribly alive. She moved across to the window, with the notion of throwing it open, so that the wholesome morning breeze could enter. The windows from having been shuttered were less opaquely coated with dust than those below, and she saw what lay outside.

'Hugh, look at the garden,' she called. 'It's a perfect jungle: paths, lawn, flower-beds all covered with the wild.'

He peered out.

'There's a job in front of us then,' he said. 'But we'll take that after we've been through the house. It's a queer room, this, Vi.'

The chamber next door was as queer: this was the bedroom, said the charwoman, which Mr Robert had occupied when the two brothers were living together in the house. At Mr Henry's disappearance he had moved on to the ground floor into the room which he used until the day of his death. The upper room had been locked up since then:

she had not seen it since the day when Mr Robert had slept downstairs. His bed had been moved down, his wardrobe and his washingstand: a couple of crazy chairs alone now stood there, and as in the room next door, the shutters were closed when they entered. Mr Robert, she told them, had forbidden her to go upstairs any more when Mr Henry left them. Three more bedrooms, all absolutely empty of furniture, and a bathroom with brown stains down the side of the bath below the taps, completed this floor: the bedrooms had never been furnished at all, as far as she knew, and yet, for all the emptiness of this story of the house, it seemed to Violet as if something followed them as they went downstairs again.

There remained for exploration the two rooms on the ground floor which looked out on to the garden, and which for the last year had always been kept locked: these were scarcely more fit for human habitation than the rest. The dust lay thick everywhere, the carpet was in rags, the windows bleared with dirt. One must have been Robert Lister's dining room, for there were pieces of crockery and cutlery on the table, a glass, and a half-empty bottle of whisky, a jug of water and a salt-cellar, and a few tattered books were scattered on the floor beside it. One window looked out on to the street, and on the wall at right angles to that a glass-paned door led out into the garden. This was bolted at top and bottom; evidently it had been long in disuse for entrance and egress, and it was with difficulty that Hugh managed to push the bolts back into their rusty grooves. When that was done, he wrenched the door open, and it was good to let a breath of the sweet untainted air of outside penetrate into that sick and deadened atmosphere.

'My uncle never went out into the town, you tell me,' he said to Mr Hodgkin, 'and we can see that he never went into the garden. He must have lived indoors altogether, and indoors he never set foot upstairs. Good God! it's ghastly: just these three rooms with no presence there except his own. Enough to drive a man mad. And yet he chose to do it... What's that?'

He turned round as he spoke, wheeling quickly, and went out into the hall outside. But there was nothing there; a stair perhaps had creaked, or perhaps it was the yellow underwing moth that flapped against the pane that made him think that there was something astir.

The garden into which they now stepped was, as Violet had said, a mere jungle of wild and riotous growth, but it was easy to see how delectable a plot it must have been, and to feel what overgrown charms still lingered there. It was spacious for an enclosed space like this, with streets and houses all round it, a liberal acre in extent, and defended by its high brick walls from any intrusive eye. From no quarter could it be overlooked, so tall was its mellowed fencing, and only the peaks of house-roofs and their chimneys and the vane of the church-tower peered above the copings. A broad strip of flower-bed had once sunned itself along the house-front, bordered by box-hedging; a paved walk led by it, and beyond had been a stretch of lawn up to the farther wall. To the left the plot had once been divided by a trellis that now leaned tipsily askew this way and that, with great gaps in it, through which could be seen fruit-trees, now in flower, on this spring afternoon: there no doubt had been the kitchen-garden. But now rank weeds and grasses had triumphed over everything on lawn and border; the paved walk was plumed with them and thickly overlaid with mosses; creepers that must once have been trained up the walls sprawled fallen across the ground-growths, and tendrils of degenerated rose-trees threaded their thorns through the shrubby clumps of the box-edgings.

The two men pushed across the lawn through briers and thick grasses and entanglements, but Violet said she had had enough and sat down on the edge of the paved walk. The charm of the place struggled with the melancholy disorder of it, and she could imagine it cultivated and cared for, with its beds glowing again with ordered jewels, its lawn smooth-napped, its paved walks free of the tangle of growth, but there was something more than this tangle of weeds that had to be cleared away before peace could return to it. Something beyond mere neglect was amiss with it; something dead but horribly alive was watching her, even as in the shuttered room at the head of the stairs...

The stone seat faced the sun, and a little dazzled by its brightness, though delighting in the genial warmth of it after the airless seclusion of the house, Violet closed her eyes, wondering what it could be that wrought this strange perturbation within her. Hugh and Mr Hodgkin had vanished now behind the crazy trellis; their voices no longer came to her, and she felt extraordinarily sundered from the touch of human intercourse. And yet she was not alone: there was some presence, not theirs, moving up closer to her and watching her. Once she opened her eyes to reassure herself that it was only her imagination thus play-ing tricks with her, but of course there was nothing there, and again she closed them. An odd drowsiness invaded her, and she saw a shadow come across the red field of her closed eyelids. She thought to herself that the two men were approaching her, and that it was they who had come between her and the sun, and she waited for the sound of their voices or their steps. Perhaps Hugh thought she was alseep, and meant to give her forty winks or so: if that was in his mind, she wished he would stand aside, for with him cutting off the sunlight from her, the air had become very cold. She gave a little shiver, and opened her eyes. There was no one there.

It was startling: she had felt quite sure there had been someone standing close in front of her, but it certainly was not Hugh, nor indeed was there any sign of a living presence. But there he was, stepping over the fallen trellis, and coming quickly toward her.

'Violet, dear,' he said, 'isn't the place utterly enchanting? I'm going to have all the rags and rubbish turned out of the house at once, and get it washed and cleaned and renewed. I shall furnish it, too, and put a caretaker in, and then we'll bring the garden into order again. Then when it's all habitable we can settle what we shall do with it, let it, or sell it, or keep it. What extraordinary odd fellows they must have been, living in squalor and discomfort and letting everything go to ruin! But I shall restore it all with the money they saved over it. And frankly, I've fallen in love with the place: I want to keep it terribly.'

Hugh set to work with his usual volcanic energy to put the place in order again: he and Violet took rooms at the inn near, and spent hot and labourious days in turning out the dirty raffle that filled the house, reserving for later examination any papers that might possibly be of interest. All the upholstery was perished; carpets, curtains and rugs were only fit for the fire: there were cupboards, and presses full of threadbare stuffs, moth-eaten blankets and moldy linen, and a clean sweep had to be made of all these before the cleaning and redecoration of the house could begin. Day after day a bonfire in the kitchen-garden smouldered and burst into flames and smouldered again, for little even of the solider furniture was serviceable: rickety tables and broken-seated chairs seemed to have been sufficient for the uncles. After that the walls must be stripped of their torn and flapping papers, and scraped of their discoloured paint, the roof must be repaired, ceilings and fittings of doors and windows renovated. To Violet all this holo-caust of moldy raffles signified something more than the mere material cleaning-up, even as the opening of windows long-closed and the admission into the house of the air and the sun and the wholesome winds did more than refresh the staleness of its actual atmosphere: both were symbolical outward signs of some interior purging. And yet, even when all was clean and empty, ready for its new furnishing, the very essence of what they had been turning out still lingered. All was not well with the house: in some strange manner the shadow that had come between her closed eyes and the sun as she sat on the garden-bench had entered, and was establishing itself more firmly day by day.

She knew how fantastic such a notion was, and so, though it persisted, she could not bring herself to speak to Hugh about it. It haunted the rooms and the passages, and though she got no direct vision of its presence it was there, like some shy creature wary in hiding itself, but yet wishing to make itself manifest: sometimes it seemed malignant, sometimes sad and pitiful. Most of all it was perceptible in that pleasant square room at the top of the stairs which they had found shuttered, where the bedclothes were turned back as if he who had slept there had just quitted it, and where the apparatus of a man's toilet still lay on the dressing-table: the room, so the charwoman had told them, occupied by Henry Lister. Had this presence something to do with him, she wondered? She felt it also in the room downstairs occupied after his disappearance by Robert: there she felt it as something fierce or revengeful. Finally she began to wonder whether Hugh was conscious that there was something queer in that room at the head of the stairs, for at first he had intended to make his private den there, but he had abandoned that, and though the furnishing of the house was proceeding apace he had left it empty.

It was early in May that the house was ready to be occupied in a tentative picnicking fashion: vans had been unloading all day, a couple of servants had come down, and tonight Hugh and Violet were to sleep here, for to be on the premises, said Hugh, was the surest way of speeding such tasks as picture-hanging and carpet-laying. The dusk of the evening was warm, and he and Violet were sitting on the stone bench in the garden with a box of papers between them which must be looked through before they could be consigned to the bonfire. The garden was rapidly being tamed, the lawn had been scythed in preparation for the mowing-machine, the paved walk had been cleared of moss, and weeding was going on in the beds.

'But the soil is wretched and sour,' said Hugh, as he untied a bundle of papers. 'That bed by the house must be dug over deep and a cartload of rich stuff put in before it's fit for planting. Hullo, a photograph . . . Why, it's of the two uncles, and was taken here in the garden.

They're sitting on the stone bench where we are now. Before they became hermits, I suppose.'

Violet looked over his shoulder.

'Which is Uncle Robert?' she said.

'That one on the left, the older of the two, the bald one.'

'And the other the one who disappeared?' asked Violet.

'Yes,'

He looked up quickly as he spoke, and Violet, following his eye, thought she saw for a moment in the dust, some figure standing on the paved walk twenty yards away. But it resolved itself into a pale stain on the wall and a bush immediately below, and she took another glance at the faded photograph. There was a strong family resemblance between them; she would have guessed that the two faces, rather long-nosed, with eyes very wide apart, were those of brothers, but they were quite distinguishable.

Presently Hugh came to the end of the packet, and he took the bulk of it to toss on to the smouldering bonfire. The evening was now beginning to get chilly, and when he had gone she rose and took a turn down the paved walk. The light from the west glowed dusky-red on the brick front of the house, and glancing idly up at the window of the room at the head of the stairs, she saw a man standing there within, looking down on her. The glimpse she got of his face was but brief, for almost immediately he turned away, but she had seen enough to know that it was the face of the younger of the two brothers at whose photograph she had just been looking.

For one moment sheer terror clutched at her: the next, as if by some subtle recognition her mind told her that here was the visible manifestation of the presence of which she had for days been conscious. It was he who had shadowed her closed eyelids, it was he who, as yet unseen, had haunted the house, and in especial the room at the window of which she now beheld him. Though the flesh of her still quaked at the thought that she had looked on one who had passed beyond the dread dim gate, it was terribly interesting, and she continued looking up, half dreading, half hoping that she would see him again. Then she heard Hugh's step returning from his errand.

'What's the matter, Violet?' he said. 'You're white: your hands are trembling.'

She pulled herself together

'It's nothing,' she said. 'Something startled me just now.'

Looking at him, she guessed with a sense of certainty what was in his mind when he asked her what was the matter.

'Hughie, have you seen something too that—that comes from beyond?' she asked.

He shook his head.

'No, but I know it's there,' he said, 'and it's chiefly in that room at the top of the stairs. That's why I've done nothing with it. Have you seen it? Was it that which startled you just now? What was it?'

She pointed to the window.

'There,' she said. 'A man looked out on me from the window. It was Henry Lister. His room, you know.'

They were both looking up now and even as she spoke the figure appeared there again. Once more it turned away, and vanished.

For a long moment they met each other's eyes.

'Violet, are you frightened?' he said.

'I'm not going to be,' she said. 'Whatever it is, whatever it's here for, it can't hurt us. I think it wants us to do something for it . . . But, Hughie, why did Robert scream out "Have mercy"? Why did he run from the house?'

Hugh had no answer for this.

'I shall go in,' he said at length, 'and open the door of that room, and see what is there. I left it locked, I know. Don't come with me, Violet.'

'But I wish to,' she said; 'I want to know all that there is to be known. What we have seen means something.'

They went upstairs together, and paused for a second outside the door. The key was in the lock, and Hugh turned it and threw the door wide.

The room was lit by the fading evening light, but clearly visible. It was completely furnished as on the day when they had first looked into it. On the bed there lay the figure of a man faintly twitching. His face was turned away, but with a final movement his head fell back on the pillows, and they saw who it was. The mouth drooped open, the cheeks and forehead were of a mottled purple in colour, and round the neck was tied a cord . . . And then they saw a perfectly empty room, unfurnished, but newly papered and painted.

The deep digging-over of the flower-bed along the house front began next morning, and an hour later the gardener came in to tell Hugh what he had found. The digging was resumed under the supervision of the police inspector, and the body when disinterred was removed to the mortuary. The identity was established at the inquest; it was established that death had been due to strangulation, for a piece of rope was still tied round the neck. Though there could be no absolute certainty as to the history of the murder, only one reconstruction of it would fit the facts which were known; namely, that Henry Lister had been strangled by his brother during the night preceding his disappearance, and buried in the garden. Very early next morning Robert Lister, who in height and general appearance strongly resembled his brother, must have gone down to the river bank (having been seen on his way there by the labourer from the town) and left his cap on the earth, and thrown the stick into the river. He must also with a diabolical cunning have arranged his brother's room to look as if he had got up and dressed himself as usual. He then returned, and an hour or two later went to Mr Hodgkin's house, saying that he had found the front door open, and that his brother was missing. No search was made in the house or garden, for the evidence all pointed to his having dressed and gone out and met his death in the river. Why Robert Lister in that seizure of panic which gripped him just before he died called on his brother to have mercy on him was no affair for police investigation, but it seems likely that he saw, or thought he saw, some very terrible thing, some strange spectre such as was certainly seen by Hugh and Violet in the room at the top of the stairs. But that is conjecture only.

The two brothers now lie side by side in the cemetery on the hill outside Trenthorpe: it may be added that in all England there is none more wholesome or tranquil house than that which was once the scene of so tragic a history and of so grim and ghostly a manifestation.

SELECT
BIBLIOGRAPHY

ALL but three of the fifteen stories in this collection have never appeared in book form. The three that have—'The Ape', 'Through', and 'The Return of Frank Hampden'—were originally collected in *The Countess of Lowndes Square,* which was published in 1920, was never reprinted, and is thus something of a scarce book. I doubt that many people can have read it. As for the rest, most have been stumbled across whilst wading through the bound volumes of old periodicals held by that most civilized of repositories, the Bodleian Library, Oxford.

The stories originally appeared as follows:

The Storyteller

August 1912: 'The Friend in the Garden'
June 1913: 'Dummy on a Dahabeah'
May 1917: 'The Ape'
August 1917: 'Through'

Pearson's Magazine

December 1914: 'The Red House'
May 1915: 'The Chippendale Mirror'
December 1915: 'The Return of Frank Hampden'
December 1916: 'The China Bowl'
March 1917: 'The Passenger'

Eve

23 November 1921: 'The Light in the Garden'

Woman

December 1927: 'Sir Roger de Coverley'

Hutchinson's Magazine

March 1928: 'The Box at the Bank'
December 1929: 'The Flint-Knife'

Woman's Journal

December 1928: 'The Witch-Ball'

The original publication of 'The Shuttered Room' is so far untraced. It appeared in the famous American horror magazine *Weird Tales* in December 1929, but was almost certainly published in a British periodical earlier.

Two books have been published about the extraordinary Benson family—Betty Askwith's *Two Victorian Families* (1971) and David Williams's *Genesis and Exodus* (1979). The latter seems to me to be the superior study in almost every particular. For Arthur Benson (and Fred, *passim*), see *On the Edge of Paradise* (1980) by David Newsome—a marvellous biographical portrait based on ACB's voluminous diaries housed at Magdalene College, Cambridge.

The Tale of an Empty House and Other Ghost Stories, edited by Cynthia Reavell (Black Swan, 1986), is a handy selection of EFB's ghost stories drawn from his four collections.

ACKNOWLEDGEMENTS

GRATEFUL thanks are due to Richard Dalby (who generously added to the fruits of my own trawls through old magazines), Rosemary Pardoe, and David Rowlands, for general enthusiasm; Bob Price, Will Murray, and Bob Weinberg of America; the staff of the Bodleian Library and especially A.J. Flavell, Assistant Librarian, whose assistance is invariably courteous and friendly; the indefatigible Bill Lofts; and John Eggeling (who at the very last moment handed me on a plate a ripe and priceless fact about Fred Benson, which helped enormously). On behalf of myself and the publishers, I also wish to thank A.P. Watt Ltd, acting for the Estate of K.S.P. McDowell, for permission to reprint the stories.

EQUATION CHILLERS

A major new series of rare or previously unpublished stories by classic writers of weird and supernatural fiction, providing all fans of the genre with a feast of new pleasures. Each volume is selected and introduced by a leading editor in the field.

Published and in preparation:

THE FLINT KNIFE
Further Spook Stories by E.F. Benson
Selected by Jack Adrian

IN THE DARK
Tales of Terror by E. Nesbit
Selected by Hugh Lamb

WARNING WHISPERS
Weird Tales by A.M. Burrage
Selected by Jack Adrian

FEAR WALKS THE NIGHT
Tales of Terror by Frederick Cowles
Selected by Richard Dalby

THE MAGIC MIRROR
Lost Supernatural Stories of Algernon Blackwood
Selected by Michael Ashley

IN THE DARK

Tales of Terror by E. Nesbit

Selected and introduced by Hugh Lamb

Edith Nesbit (1858-1924) is best known for her classic children's books, in particular *The Railway Children*, and was the subject of a recent highly acclaimed biography by Julia Briggs. But she was also an accomplished writer of supernatural fiction, as this new collection amply demonstrates.

While her children's books have been reprinted steadily over the past eighty years, Edith Nesbit's tales of terror have fallen into unwarranted neglect. This new anthology makes amends for this by bringing together fourteen excellent stories, from the well-known 'Man-Size in Marble' and 'John Charrington's Wedding' to such forgotten gems as 'From the Dead', 'The Head', 'The Ebony Frame', and 'Hurst of Hurstcote'.

Hugh Lamb is a prolific and experienced anthologist of supernatural fiction specializing in Victorian ghost stories. His anthologies include *Victorian Tales of Terror*, *Gaslit Nightmares*, and a collection of stories by the French authors Erckmann-Chatrian.

WARNING WHISPERS

Weird Tales by A.M. Burrage

Selected and introduced by Jack Adrian

A.M. Burrage wrote superlative ghost stories. His two published collections — *Some Ghost Stories* (1927) and *Someone in the Room* (1931, under the pseudonym 'Ex-Private X') — place him squarely amongst the handful of front-rank writers of short weird fiction.

In spite of this, and the critical praise lavished on him by such experts as M.R. James, H. Russell Wakefield, and Sir Arthur Conan Doyle, as well as the fact that he wrote two of the most anthologized ghost stories of the past half-century, 'The Sweeper' and 'Smee', Burrage's name is now virtually forgotten, even amongst habitual readers of supernatural fiction.

Jack Adrian's collection aims to put Burrage back where he belongs, at the forefront of the classic English ghost-story tradition. He presents eighteen new tales, all of them previously unpublished in book-form, spanning the period 1912 to 1930, making this a major publishing event for all ghost fiction enthusiasts.

Of further interest ...

THE ILLUSTRATED
J.S. LE FANU

Ghost Stories and Mysteries by a Master Victorian Storyteller

Selected and introduced by Michael Cox

'Sheridan Le Fanu', wrote S.M. Ellis in 1916, 'retains his own special place and fame as *the* Master of Horror and the Mysterious.'

Today, Le Fanu's reputation is as high as ever amongst connoisseurs of supernatural and mystery fiction and well deserves the enthusiastic praise accorded to him by some of the most distinguished ghost fiction writers of the twentieth century — including E.F. Benson and M.R. James.

Born in 1814, the son of an Anglo-Irish Protestant clergyman, Le Fanu single-handedly created a new kind of fictional ghost story. Gone are the sheeted spooks rattling rusty chains and the peripatetic headless ladies that infest Gothic fiction. In their place Le Fanu created formidably real supernatural presences that emerge from within, as well as invade from without.

This selection presents the very best of Le Fanu's supernatural and mystery fiction, complemented by evocative illustrations by such artists as 'Phiz', Brinsley le Fanu, and Edward Ardizzone, as well as by contemporary photographs.

Michael Cox has published several books relating to supernatural fiction in English. In addition to a highly praised biography of M.R. James he has edited two collections of James's stories and is co-editor of *The Oxford Book of English Ghost Stories*.

GHOSTS AND SCHOLARS

Ghost Stories in the Tradition of M.R. James

Selected and introduced by Richard Dalby and Rosemary Pardoe

Country-house libraries...forlorn churches...quiet college quad-
rangles and damp cathedral crypts...a world where lurking supernatural evil is ever ready to pounce on the innocent, the guilty, or the
merely curious...where gentlemen scholars and studious clerics pay
the price of their fascination with the past...

25 chilling and salutary tales written in the tradition of M.R. James,
acknowledged master of the antiquarian ghost story, with stories by:

★ Sabine Baring Gould
★ A.C. Benson
★ R.H. Benson
★ Cecil Binney
★ Sir Andrew Caldecott
★ Ramsey Campbell
★ Patrick Carleton
★ John Dickson Carr
★ Frederick Cowles
★ Arthur Gray
★ Sheila Hodgson

★ A.F. Kidd
★ Shane Leslie
★ R.H. Malden
★ L.T.C. Rolt
★ David Rowlands
★ Eleanor Scott
★ Arnold Smith
★ Dermot Chesson Spence
★ Lewis Spence
★ Montague Summers
★ E.G. Swain

'Revives well-wrought tales by many forgotten writers.'
— *The Financial Times*

'Deliciously civilized.'
— *The Mail on Sunday*

DRACULA'S BROOD

Neglected Vampire Classics by Friends and
Contemporaries of Bram Stoker

Selected and introduced by Richard Dalby

The most famous vampire of them all is Bram Stoker's Dracula, published in 1897. But it was not the first piece of fiction to describe the
doings of the undead, and it was by no means the last.

This unique anthology gathers together twenty-three rare vampire
stories written by friends and contemporaries of Bram Stoker
between 1867 and 1940.

Richard Dalby has deliberately avoided stories that have been regu-
larly reprinted and has concentrated instead on reviving neglected
examples of the vampire genre — ranging from Frederick Cowles'
beautiful but deadly Princess Bessenyei to tales of vampiric trees and
fishes. A similarly wide range of authors is represented, including Sir
Arthur Conan Doyle, Algernon Blackwood, Julian Hawthorne (son
of Nathaniel), Vernon Lee, William Gilbert (father of W.S. Gilbert),
Eliza Lynn Linton, and M.R. James.

Dracula's Brood provides a veritable feast of pleasure for all lovers of
supernatural and fantasy fiction. It also throws new light on a small
but fertile corner of Victorian and early twentieth-century literature.